Under the Marble Sky

A Novel

Stefanie K. Steck

Enjoy your time in Marble!

Stefanie Steck

Copyright © 2022 Stefanie K. Steck

All right reserved

The characters and events portrayed in this book are fictitious. Any similarity to real persons, living or dead, is coincidental and not intended by the author.

No part of this book may be reproduced, or stored in a retrieval system, or transmitted in any form or by any means, electronic, mechanical, photocopying, recording, or otherwise, without express written permission of the author, except as use of brief quotation in a book review.

ISBN: 979-8-9866169-0-2 (Paperback)

Cover design and illustrations by Elle Maxwell

Edited by Cindy Ray Hale

This novel is for a few people.

First, to Nichole and Kyle. Thank you for dragging me to Marble and for being my forever friends. Little did you know a novel would come of it. Well, Nikki knew.

Second, to Rosalie Mirabelli. One of my absolute favorite people I have ever met. Thank you for your constant support and smile.

I love all of you more than you know.

One

- Sunday -

Why was this a good idea again? After driving through massive amounts of possible mud slide signs and having Maps send her in the complete wrong direction, Brooke was ready to give up and consider this a waste of money. Her Chevy Equinox had all-wheel-drive, sure—but the bumps were not sitting well with her, or the suspension. She hit the gas as the vehicle forced a roar and made its way up the steep hill to where the GPS was taking her. All she could see was the clear blue sky as the SUV made it up the hill. Then, out of nowhere, a small cabin appeared in front of her.

Brooke gasped in terror. The engine was full throttle, her foot firm on the gas pedal. She swiftly changed her footing and slammed on the brake. The Equinox stopped before she hit the cabin in front of her. Her seat belt locked, jerking her forward. She placed her palm on her chest, exhaling—unaware she was holding her breath. She shifted into park, putting on the emergency brake before doing anything else. According to the thermostat on the dash, it was sixty-five degrees outside. Thankfully, she'd brought a jacket.

Brooke reached behind her for her coat and turned the car off, grabbing her keys and her cell phone, which showed no service, and left the vehicle. To her left was a mountainside, and to her right was another slightly larger lodge. She walked around the car, looking down the road she had just come up. It was steep, and she almost couldn't see the bottom of the hill. The incredibly small town that was off the path was barely visible from the road. She turned her head back in front of her.

She gasped.

The view was hidden by the trees on the drive in, but it alone was enough to stop anyone in their tracks. The two cabins on either side of her fit into the backdrop perfectly, as all the fall colors cascaded down the mountain that stood in front of her. The small lake sat peacefully, undisturbed as trucks and other cars drove up the dirt road by it. The sun had settled in the west, making the mountain colors look brighter than she had ever seen. She looked down toward the town. Some paved roads sat between the trees, and smoke from the local barbeque rose in the air. She closed her eyes and breathed it in, catching the crisp mountain air as it hit her lungs, clearing her mind.

This was definitely a good idea.

A year prior, Brooke had pursued her dream of becoming a full-time author. She'd been able to quit her nine-to-five job to focus solely on her writing. Living in the city made it difficult, so when she heard of this retreat, she wanted to be a part of it. She saved for months and booked her trip—leaving Salt Lake City and driving seven hours to the small town of Marble, Colorado. The drive made her question the decision a few times but seeing the mountains and the lodge where she would soon be stuck with other authors made it all make sense. This was the perfect idea.

She drank in the scenery so she wouldn't forget any of it. She raised her phone to open the camera. A phone with no service was good for one thing—pictures. She positioned the camera up, capturing the mountain in front of her, and readied her aim.

"Welcome," an older male voice said behind her, making her jump, pulling the camera from the frame and blurring the entire image. She groaned. Oh, well. She had an entire week to take pictures.

Brooke turned to see a gray-haired gentleman walk out from the small cabin. A woman with a matty lap dog settled in her arms followed him. They both had smiles on their faces. Brooke smiled back at them. Where was their car? The only car parked there was hers.

"You must be here for the retreat," the man said, coming up closer to Brooke.

She nodded. "Yes. Hi, I'm Brooke Easten." She raised her hand to shake his.

He took it firmly and shook it up and down, jostling her entire arm. "You're the first to arrive, Ms. Easten. We're waiting for a few more, but welcome!" He opened his arms in exclamation. "What do you think of the lodge?"

She turned toward the lodge behind her. The deck was welcoming, and a few chairs and tables were set up with stairs that led to a larger deck below. She could make out a fire pit and entry into the house. Looking back at the main door, she couldn't see any of the inside or the sides of the building, but at least the outside was nice. "It looks comfortable," she responded. "Did you say I'm the first one here?"

The man nodded, and his hair bobbed with him. He was a fitter older man, with shoulder length gray hair that sat behind his ears, showing them off before trailing to a well-kept beard. The woman behind him wasn't as old as him, though her dark hair was graying.

"The others won't arrive until later." She smiled. "My name is Melinda, and this is Frank. We are the hosts for the week!" Melinda held out her hand to shake Brooke's. Brooke took it, thankful it was a calmer handshake. The matty dog, who looked older than any dog Brooke had ever seen, whined in Melinda's grip.

"When will they get here?" Brooke asked, not so sure she wanted to be the only one at the lodge.

"Oh, sometime soon, but I can promise you they will all be here for the bonfire tonight." Frank smiled. "Come on, let us show you the lodge and where you will be staying."

Frank didn't hesitate as he placed his hand on Brooke's shoulders, leading her into the lodge. Brooke tensed up as she was pushed forward. Melinda opened the door to the lodge as Frank kept his hands on her back. The main room was quiet but packed with furniture that Brooke instantly wanted to rearrange. The decor that caught her attention was the deer heads on the walls.

"Here is the land line with a number and wi-fi password. The wi-fi gets kind of weak after so many people are on, so we are suggesting to the writers they use a Word document and not the cloud." Melinda did the best Vana White pose as she showed off a small front desk against the wall, complete with a cordless phone, lamp, and visitor's guest book. The dog let out another groan, and Melinda moved. Brooke could swear that it had glared at her, a tooth sticking out from its bottom lip. Brooke furrowed her brow, thinking about how her cat at home would *not* approve of this dog.

"I have a mobile hotspot if that works best..." Brooke mentioned, turning away from the dog. She knew she was here to write, so she planned ahead, even if she wasn't sure about what she was working on next. "The website did mention the weak signal."

"Perfect!" Frank exclaimed. "This is the main gathering room. It has comfortable seating areas, and the lighting is perfect for evening conversation. Through here is the dining room and kitchen." He pushed her forward some more. Melinda was still talking about the wi-fi, and she heard something about a Jeep tour. Brooke was having a hard time combining the two as they spoke in unison. Even in her mind, which was constantly moving, she had difficulty keeping up with Frank and Melinda.

She began to walk faster than Frank, forcing him to remove his hand from her back. She walked to the left and into a skinny dining room with a long table that could seat up to twenty people. The view from the room was phenomenal. She walked to the windows to take a better look, seeing the deck below and a small glimpse of the town.

"The view is amazing," she piped in.

They both stopped talking, turned, and smiled.

"Isn't it?" Melinda asked, appearing out of another door. She motioned for Brooke to follow her into the kitchen. Brooke took one last peek at the mountains before following. "The kitchen has everything you need to make all your meals. We did mention that you would provide your own food?"

Brooke nodded. "I stopped in Carbondale and picked up a week's worth of food for myself, but the website said there would be one dinner provided?"

Melinda nodded back at her. "From the barbeque down the road. It's delicious. Just you wait. Here, let me show you your room. You're on the main floor."

Melinda led Brooke out of the kitchen and down a small hall, where she saw her name printed out neatly on the door. The sign above her name said *Galileo*. She opened the door to see her room for the next seven days. It was quaint and decorated as if she loved ducks, with a random jackalope on the wall above the bed. Brooke walked around and looked at the room, taking in all its charm. The attached bathroom was perfect just for her.

"This is great." She smiled.

"Brides and grooms normally stay the night here." Melinda smiled.

Brooke smiled back and then looked at the bed with curiosity.

"Oh, honey," Melinda added. "I made sure they cleaned everything."

Brooke smiled. "No, really. It's great. Thank you." Brooke slapped her legs. "Can I bring my things in and unpack, or should I wait for the others?"

Frank came up behind Melinda. "No, no, make yourself at home. You are free with your time until the welcome bonfire tonight at six sharp."

Brooke looked at her watch. "Great, I have a few hours. There's no rule regarding writing early, is there?"

They laughed. "Of course not!" Melinda said, her teeth showing. "All we ask is that you're at the bonfire at six so we can introduce everyone."

"That I can do. Thank you so much for showing me the house. Should I show everyone else around or..."

"Oh, no. We're the hosts. We will meet everyone as they come. We will see you at six. Alright, Ms. Easten?" Frank put his arm around Melinda and led her and the dog from the room.

"See you at six." Brooke waved to them.

The two hosts left the lodge, leaving Brooke alone in the empty cabin. She left the room to take a look around without two people talking in her ear. She grabbed the wi-fi password and looked at the giant buffalo that hung above the fireplace. She squinted at it. Then she noticed the arrow that hung under the buffalo. A simple arrow, with no bow, that wasn't centered. She shook her head and went to explore the rest of the lodge, taking in all its charm.

Two

While Brooke toured the cabin by herself, nestled in the town was a small white building with a worn wooden sign that read *Marble Touring Company*. Inside, Caleb Turner was concentrating on the finance books and blank reservation schedule, purposefully ignoring the world around him.

"Caleb," Ethan shouted for the third time, trying to get his friend's attention. "Caleb, you gotta pay attention, man."

Caleb was purposefully ignoring his friend. He didn't look up from the finance books. "I hear you, Ethan," he mumbled. He scooted the finances away and pulled the schedule log towards him, just as blank as it was before.

"You hear me, but you're not paying attention to me."

Caleb looked at Ethan through his eyelashes, not lifting his chin.

"When was our last booking?" Ethan began.

That made Caleb uncomfortable. His tours hadn't been doing as well for the past few months, but that didn't mean he was ready to give up on it. Ethan being blunt just hit him the wrong way.

"Yeah, I know," Caleb mumbled, returning to the finances.

Ethan was silent for a moment before pulling the book away from him. Caleb groaned and glared up at his friend.

"It's been four weeks, Caleb. I haven't taken a Jeep to Crystal in four weeks, and you haven't taken one out in longer. Are you even going to make rent this month?" Ethan placed his palms on the counter in front of him, getting as close to Caleb as he could.

"It's not rent. It's a mortgage and..." He took a breath. "I hope so," Caleb admitted.

Three years prior, Caleb came to Marble, Colorado to fish and never left. He began to work for the Marble Jeep tours, enjoying being in the environment and befriending Ethan. When the owner died and left the company in his name, he was excited to start a new phase in his life. He just never planned on a pandemic hitting the world, bringing his business down. Once restrictions were lifted, he began to see more business, but altogether, things weren't going so well.

"Maybe we need to advertise better? I see hikers all the time down at the lake. Why hike for hours on end when you can sit in a Jeep?" Ethan suggested, putting on his best salesman voice.

Caleb looked at him, lowering his brow. "Advertising costs money."

"Everything costs money, Caleb, but we need to spend money in order to make money."

"We don't have the money," he murmured. Caleb rubbed his forehead. "Maybe I should sell?"

"Lettie would turn over in her grave if you did. She trusted you, giving you this place."

"She left it to you, and you declined." Caleb glared at him.

Ethan shrugged. "I didn't have the mind and heart to run this place. You've been going strong for almost two years. We just gotta get back on our feet again. Now that the lodges are opening back up, we can put more flyers in there; maybe make a trip up and give them a special?"

The lodges were opening up again. That was an idea. "I know the Marble Lodge is holding some kind of retreat, and Beaver...I'm not sure about them." He looked over at Ethan, who had an expression on his face as if he were waiting for commands from a king. "Okay, I have some funds to print up more flyers. The file is on the computer. Why don't you take it to Carbondale and make some copies? Maybe leave a few there while you're at it."

Ethan nodded. "Yes, sir." He saluted and then went behind the counter to the computer. "What are you going to do this evening if this is my task?"

Caleb looked out the window and noticed the sun setting. "I'm going fishing."

"Typical." Ethan chuckled. "Have fun."

The lake was the reason Caleb stayed in Marble. It was small, serene, and full of fish. Caleb walked to his favorite casting spot, passing a few residences along the way, and settled in for some catch and release.

He baited his hook and cast off, seeing the fly hit the water with a small plop. Most days, Caleb would stay in the same spot for hours, watching the small bubbles appear. Everyone in Marble knew Caleb. They knew his story and why he redirected his life to be here. There was nowhere else Caleb wanted to be.

His line jerked and bumped. Caleb reeled the fish in. He pulled it up and looked at the small rainbow trout.

"Well, hi there," he said to the fish, unhooking it from the line. "Good to see you again, Bob." He placed the fish back in the water and gave it a small rub. He watched Bob the Fish as he swam away. When he turned to get the new bait, he was stunned to see a woman watching him.

She stood with her hands in her coat pockets, her blonde hair coming out of a beanie, and the eyes behind her glasses were fixed on the fish that was still swimming out of sight.

"I'm sorry, did you just talk to the fish?" she asked, still watching the water, her eyebrows pulled together.

Caleb looked at her with a confused look. He had lived in Marble for three years. He knew everyone in town, but this girl was definitely not from town. This girl was different. This girl captured his attention.

"It's the law in Marble," he replied with a sarcastic tone. "If you catch and release, you need to say hello, name them, and set them free again." He squatted back down to his bait.

"That can't be true." She turned to look at him. Her glasses sat on top of her nose, and if possible, made her blue eyes look brighter. Caleb took a deep breath and told himself not to look.

"You must not be from around here," he muttered instead, turning back to his tactile box to bait his hook.

She shook her head and watched as Caleb hooked the bait on the line. "No, I'm visiting for a week and decided the lake was too beautiful to pass up. I had just never seen someone talk to a fish before."

"Again"—he swung the pole back and cast into the lake—"it's the law."

She scoffed. "If you say so." She fidgeted her hands in her pockets and moved her feet back and forth, kicking at the gravel path.

"Have you ever fished before?" he asked.

The woman shook her head. "Not much. A few times with my dad, but I may need to again someday soon. Just so I can name a fish." She smiled, catching Caleb's attention; he didn't even notice his line tug. "I think you caught another one." She pointed at the line.

He spun his head quickly and reeled the line back in, only to bring up a massive amount of weed.

"Make sure you name it." The woman flashed her smile once more—almost dropping Caleb to his knees—before checking her watch. "If you see Bob again, tell him I said so long." She stuck her hand back in her coat and walked past Caleb.

Caleb watched her as she turned up the road, most likely heading to a lodge. He looked up the hill to the Marble Lodge and noticed a few others, a fire starting in the pit up on their deck. She must be staying there with a group for the week. He raised his eyebrows and laughed at himself before grabbing another bait for his line.

It wasn't every day a beautiful woman talked to you while fishing.

Three

Meeting the random fisherman on the lake was not something Brooke would have done normally. She had seen him cast and then walked up just in time to see him talk to the fish. It was just too cute to pass up saying something. The fact that the fisherman was handsome had nothing to do with it. Brooke was here to write, not to fish. She headed back to the lodge through the woods. The small trail line was most likely meant for bikes, not a hike up the steep trail, but Brooke just wanted to get back to the lodge, her mind focused on the fisherman.

How could she describe him? Maybe Andrew Garfield mixed with Thomas Rhett. He had short, dark-brown hair that was long enough to run your fingers through. It trailed down to matching scruff, enough to show he didn't have a need to shave much. He was tall, but his many layers didn't reveal much of his build. Not that it mattered, with hazel eyes like that. She smiled. It was a small town. She might run into him again.

She went down the stairs to the large deck to see the campfire already lit, with Melinda, Frank, and four others sitting around it. Someone had set everything out to make s'mores and hot dogs over the fire. She hadn't had a s'mores in years. Suddenly, her inner child was coming out.

Making her way to the benches, she was greeted by Melinda calling out her name and waving her over. She gave a small smile and went to the railing. She leaned over to get a look at the lake, maybe catching a glimpse of the fisherman before starting the event. Sadly, no such luck. Too many trees were covering the lake.

She sighed and sat on the bench, facing the others. Next to Melinda, sat Frank, who poked at the logs burning the fire. The others looked just as nervous to be there as Brooke did. Well, all but two women, who sat facing the mountains. They looked as if they had done this a few times before. Brooke was having a hard time reading them.

"Alright," Melinda began, "Now that we are all here, welcome to our fifth annual writer's retreat. We are happy to see two familiar faces, along with some new ones. Tonight, we will get to know one another and talk about our projects. We are here to encourage and help one another. I'll start." Melinda placed a hand on her chest and took a deep breath.

"I'm Melinda, and this is my husband, Frank. We are both writers of some sort, with Frank more in the editing and publishing world." She placed her hand on Frank's shoulder. "We wanted to open up a retreat for writers. Writers supporting writers. We are happy to say it keeps getting better. I am currently not working on anything. I want to be here to support you, and Frank is here to help with editing issues as they arise." She smiled. "Let's start with our veterans." Melinda motioned to the two women sitting across the fire.

One, who looked to be in her late forties, straightened up and cleared her throat. "My name is Rhonda. This is my third retreat with Melinda and Frank, and I am excited to be working on my fortieth novel." she emphasized, "Mystery thrillers are my genre. I started it the other day, and I hope to have the first draft done by the end of the week." She looked at the others. Was she hoping to see a round of applause? When no one moved, she continued. "I'm from Austin, Texas, and I have some of my roots in the book."

"Will the book be set in Texas?" Brooke asked, taking a marshmallow and sticking it on a skewer. No one had begun to make a s'more. Brooke's twelve-year-old self took the lead.

"Of course, all my books are set in Texas. All *forty* of them." She drew out the word forty once again.

Brooke held in a chuckle and put her attention back on her marshmallow. The woman next to her wasn't as proud. She stated her name was Joyce and that she was working on her fourth novel, a historical fiction taking place during the Civil War. She was more open to telling the story, actually getting Brooke interested in the concept.

Melinda and Frank looked over to the others. Sitting next to Brooke was Greg, who was working on a sci-fi fantasy novel. When Brooke asked, he said he had been trying to get it out on paper for years, but he just could never do it. He hoped that coming here would help clear his mind and allow him to finally put pen to paper. Joyce assured him it would.

Helen was the next author to introduce herself. She wrote murder mysteries, with a bit of comedy thrown in.

"I'm having a hard time implementing the comedy into the mystery in this one. My others have been received pretty well," Helen admitted, pushing her s'more together in her hands.

"Those two don't really work together," Rhonda mentioned.

"Oh, Rhonda," Joyce said, "I'm sure she could figure something out." Joyce smiled at Helen. "It worked for *Clue,* didn't it?"

"That was a screenplay, not a novel." Rhonda sneered, shaking her head. "What about you?" She looked across the fire to Brooke.

Brooke dusted her hands on her jeans and cleared her throat. "My name is Brooke Easten. I'm from Salt Lake, and this is my second book. The first was self-published. When an agent stumbled upon it, she wanted to represent me, and it was picked up right away. But now they want another one. I came here to try to find my next story."

"You don't have an idea?" Frank asked.

Brooke turned to him. "Oh, I have a lot of ideas. It's just which one is good enough to actually turn into something."

"That totally makes sense." Helen nodded, agreeing with Brooke.

"My first book is fiction, and since it grabbed the attention of a publisher, I want to top it. I'm just not sure how."

"So you're blocked?" Greg asked, tilting his head to face Brooke while stabbing a hot dog on the skewer.

Was she really blocked, or was she avoiding writing? "I wish I knew how to answer that," she responded. "I've always had a story to write, but maybe I wasn't expecting my first novel to be picked up by a publisher. So I got...nervous? Is it possible for an author to get stage fright?" Everyone was nodding with her. Everyone except Rhonda.

"I never start a project unless I have a clear idea of the plot and the characters. You shouldn't have come here unless you know exactly what you are working on." She shifted her body on the bench.

Brooke furrowed her brow. "I have ideas," she reiterated defensively. "I just need to make sure it's the right one for my next novel." Rhonda was going to be a handful for the week.

"Now, Rhonda," Frank said softly. "Everyone came here for a different reason. Your goal is to finish the first draft of your next novel. Joyce is in the middle of her manuscript and wants to perfect and finish it here. Greg and Helen are still gathering their roots as new authors. And Brooke?" He turned his head to her. "She needs inspiration. Trust me, there is a lot of inspiration here at Marble." He smiled, causing Brooke to smile back at him.

∽

After the event ended, Brooke sat alone at the benches. She had her favorite hoodie on, the hood laying on top of her head. But since it was freezing, she was also wrapped in a blanket. The September Colorado weather mimicked Utah, but with the air being so open and not crowded with the hustle and bustle of the city, it felt colder. She shivered, pulling the blanket closer. She had her head resting on the back of the bench as she stared out in the stars. They were so clear here compared to the city. Frank had said there was a lot of inspiration in Marble, and if the stars had anything to say about it, there was.

She was supposed to be thinking about her new novel. Where should she start? Who were the characters? Where would it be set? She closed her eyes, trying to envision everything. She'd had multiple plots in her mind…but now, all she could think of was the fisherman.

She groaned out loud, not thinking about who, if anyone, was around to hear.

"You *must* be blocked." The voice caught her off guard. She jerked her head up and saw Helen walking toward her.

"I think you're right." Brooke groaned, laying her head back against the railing.

"Me too. I have been writing this book for months. I haven't been able to finish it. I was thinking coming here would help me, but my room is across the halls from Rhonda's and all I hear is her typewriter. A *typewriter*," she emphasized, holding her hands up to her eyes and sat on the bench next to her.

Brooke chuckled, turning her eyes to look at Helen. "She seemed like the one to use a typewriter. I prefer my laptop, thank you very much."

"I'm thinking about asking Greg to switch rooms. He was the last to book, so he has the smallest room. It's pretty much a closet." Helen met Brooke's gaze, "So what's keeping you blocked?" she asked softly.

"Stage fright…imposter syndrome…whatever you want to call it," she admitted. "My first novel was taken so quickly by my agent and bought so fast by the publisher it was surreal—but now..." Brooke shook her head. "My agent wants the first draft by the end of the month."

"What was your first book about? Maybe you can do a sequel," Helen suggested.

Brooke shook her head. "I ended it well. There's nothing left to tell."

"What's the book? Maybe I've read it." Helen leaned on her elbows.

"It's called *Winter's Edge*."

Brooke was completely taken off guard by Helen's loud gasp.

"I didn't put the name together! You're Brooke Easten! *The* Brooke Easten!! I heard talks of *Winter's Edge* being made into a movie!" Helen's jaw was almost on the floor. "Please tell me it's being made into a movie." Helen leaned forward and placed her hands on the blanket covering Brooke.

Brooke widened her eyes. It was true she had been approached by a studio to buy the rights to her book, but she hadn't been able to give it away just yet. Her first book was all she thought about for three years. She would be working her full-time job, thinking about her characters and how they would get out of the predicaments she was putting them in. *Winter's Edge* was so much more to her than a movie deal.

"Do you see why I'm having trouble?"

Helen nodded. "That's an amazing book. It's going to be hard to top that one."

"Gee"—she groaned—"thanks for the motivation."

"What I'm saying is, if you could write another *Winter's Edge,* you could be the next Nicholas Sparks."

"No one can top his romance novels." Brooke gave her the side eye. "I worked on it for so long. It seems impossible to write a first draft in a short time."

Helen sighed. "If you don't mind me asking, how long have you been on this deadline?"

Brooke clenched her teeth. "It's been a while, a few months. I've been procrastinating." Helen raised her eyebrows at her. "Okay, okay, enough about my issues. What about you? Mystery and comedy in one, huh?"

Helen laughed at herself. "It's so much fun to write. I have a few self-published under my pen name that have done really well, but just like you and Greg...I seem to be blocked."

Brooke looked at Helen. The feeling was mutual. "You said your others are well received?" she asked.

Talking to other authors was something Brooke enjoyed more than writing. She loved being able to connect with others going through the same process as she was. They were never against one another; they were supportive of each other. They all had stories to tell.

Helen nodded. "It's a series, so the voices of the characters were always the same. That series ended, so now, on to something new. I have the plot, but it's turning into more of a thriller."

"Why couldn't it be?" Brooke asked.

"Because comedy is what has defined me," Helen said, using her hands to gesture through the air. "I can't change my voice now."

"But you said you do a pen name, right? So do a thriller but use a different name," she suggested.

It was as if lightning had struck Helen. Her eyes widened, and she looked over at Brooke. "I don't know why I didn't think of that!"

Brooke chuckled at her. "See how scary you can make this one, how suspenseful." She wiggled her eyebrows up and down, and Helen's smile widened.

"You're a genius."

Brooke shrugged. "Apparently not enough to write my own book, but I'm glad I could give you motivation."

Helen moved her torso, bumping into Brooke. Brooke turned to look at her new friend and smiled. One more reason this trip was a good idea.

"You're Brooke Easten. You can write anything. Just gotta find the right...*edge*?"

"I see what you did there. Thanks, Helen."

Helen took a deep breath and then turned to the house. "We should probably head inside. I doubt Rhonda has stopped typing away, but now that I've talked to you, I think I need to continue my thriller!" Helen stood, and Brooke followed suit.

"I should probably brainstorm...or maybe sleep. That was a long drive." Brooke adjusted the blanket on her shoulders as she and Helen made their way up the deck's stairs. "Sleep helps brainstorming, right?"

"Oh, definitely." Helen chuckled, following Brooke into the warmth of the lodge.

Four

-Monday-

The sun had barely risen by the time Caleb made his way down to the lake. He parked his truck and grabbed all his gear, ready to ignore the world for an hour. He could see his breath, and the lake was "smoking." Small bubbles appeared all around the surface, telling him there were plenty of fish.

This was Caleb's happy place. The crunching of the gravel under his shoes made him beam as he made his way to his favorite spot. It was so early there may be one or two others at the lake, but that wouldn't bother him. Here he didn't have to think about the company or the fact that it may go under soon. All he had to focus on was his line and the fish in the water.

A new sound hit his ears as he rounded the bend to his spot...was that clicking? *Clicking?* He focused his eyes and saw a camp chair with what looked to be a blanket sitting in it with a computer poking out and fingers moving like fire. The blanket was settled right in his spot.

He could have easily gone to another spot to avoid the random person, but this was where the fish were. Just like always, this was his spot, and the fish seemed to be waiting for him.

"Excuse me," he said as he approached, "do you mind if I set up here to fish?"

The blanket looked up, revealing the same girl as the night before. Her fingers stopped moving, and she grinned lightly up at him. "Only if you let me name one."

"It's you," he said, stunned. The fact that he had thought about this random girl most of the night seemed to catch him off guard. He would be lying to himself if he said he wasn't hoping to see her again.

"I enjoyed the lake so much I thought I'd come out here and try to describe it. I hope you don't mind me staying here. I've become one with the blanket," she said, scooting closer into the chair, if that were even possible.

Caleb shook his head. "It's fine. The clacking of the keyboard won't bother me or the fish. You gotta tell me your name, though." He set his tackle box down close to her feet and smiled up at her.

"Brooke," she replied sweetly.

"I'm Caleb. Welcome to Marble."

A faint smile formed on her lips, and she let out a light hum before returning to the keyboard, typing more.

"What brings you here?" he asked, trying to spark a conversation.

Brooke stopped her fingers and looked at him. "I'm staying at the Marble Lodge for a writers' retreat."

"That explains the laptop and the urge to describe the lake." He chuckled, pulling out the bait and hook. "You are busy working on your *New York Time's* best-selling novel, I'm assuming."

She scoffed. "Trying to."

"You're distracted?"

Brooke shook her head. "Blocked."

Caleb hummed. "Writer's block?"

"It's real," she retorted, her eyes darting toward him.

"I can imagine." He stood, holding in a laugh, finishing hooking his line and preparing to cast. "Watch your head. I don't want to catch your blanket." He pulled the line and casted into the lake, listening for the small plop.

The typing had paused, and Caleb's mind instantly went to her. Was she watching him? *Just ignore it,* he thought, *concentrate on the fish.* Easier said than done. He rolled his eyes and slightly turned his head, hoping to catch a small glimpse of her. He caught her eyes on him for a second before she quickly went back to her computer, her cheeks blushing slightly. Caleb's lips tugged a grin, and he cleared his throat.

"What's your book about?" he asked.

"Not sure. I'm blocked, remember?" Brooke replied.

He turned to look at her over his shoulder. "Well, it's taking place at the lake, I gather."

"I don't know yet." She typed for a bit before shutting the computer and snuggling herself deeper into the blanket. "I didn't think it would be this cold out here."

"It's September. I'm surprised we don't have snow yet." Caleb chuckled, reeling his line in.

"Did you catch one?" Brooke asked, sitting up a little straighter.

Caleb shook his head. "No, casting again."

"Why?"

"There's no fish there."

"How can you tell?"

"The bubbles." Caleb turned his whole body. "Why don't you and your blanket come here and cast." He held out the pole.

Brooke shook her head. "I am a burrito, and I am not moving."

He smirked. "How long have you been out here?"

"Since maybe five a.m. I came out to see the sunrise. I live in the city, so I barely get this close to nature," Brooke answered, taking her gaze from Caleb to look off toward the mountains. "Once the sun came up, I started typing."

"I barely got here after the rise, so you couldn't have been typing that long."

"Not long, a couple thousand words."

"A couple thousand words?!"

Brooke looked up. "That's not a lot."

"Seems like a lot," Caleb muttered under his breath. He casted his line and settled into the rhythm of fishing again. From the corner of his eye, he saw Brooke wrapped in her blanket. She scooted deeper into the camper chair she was sitting in, if that was even possible. Her laptop was tucked to her side, and only her face was visible. She looked cozy. Caleb tried to focus his attention on the line, but the woman in the blanket was not helping his fishing tactic.

Cast, let it float, reel it in, let it float, reel it in and let it float. He would have caught a fish by now if it weren't for Brooke. He wasn't doing it on purpose, but the mere fact that he was trying to impress her threw him off his game. She took a deep sigh behind him, and when he looked over his shoulder, she was standing. The blanket was still wrapped around her, but it dragged on the ground. She came up to his side and watched his line. They were both silent, watching the small red lure bob in the water.

"Is this all you do?" Brooke softly asked.

Caleb looked at her from the corner of his eye. "It's all you do." Caleb spun the reel twice. "You wait until..." As if the fish knew he was talking about them, the line jerked. "One bites."

Caleb pulled the line in and gently raised a trout from the lake. It was small and flopped around. Caleb reached out and grabbed it, leaning back down to the lake and trying to remove the hook from its mouth.

He looked up at her. "Do you want to name it?" he asked as he removed the hook.

"Hi, Kevin." She smiled.

Caleb laughed as he crouched to place the fish back in the water, rubbing it back to life under the small waves. "Thanks for the first catch of the day, Kevin. Say hi to Bob for me." He stood and pointed as Kevin swam away.

Brooke stood still, facing the lake. "That wasn't as exciting as I'd hoped it would be," she said, motioning her entire body toward him. Pieces of her blonde hair fell from the makeshift hood the blanket had made. Caleb raised his eyebrows and inhaled.

"It's fishing."

"Hmm." Brooke turned and went back to the camp chair. She plopped and looked back at Caleb. "It's freezing out here, but you come to take a fish from its warm home, name it, and then put it back. That doesn't sound fun at all."

"Typing a thousand words all before sunrise doesn't sound very exciting to me."

"Oh, trust me, it wasn't," Brooke complained. "At least with fishing, you know the outcomes. You're either going to catch a fish, or you aren't. With writer's block, you can be stuck for days, weeks, even months or years on end with no outcome. So all you can do is sit and write a description of a landscape with the hope that it sets your setting. With fishing, you cast toward the bubbles and reel in a fish."

Caleb cast his line one more time. "Sounds to me like you've never had this issue before."

"No, I haven't, and my first book…phenomenal. So phenomenal, in fact, that a studio wants to pick it up and make it a movie, but my agent wants another book. She wants to make money too. But I can't think of a single thing that could top my first book." Brooke gazed toward Caleb's line. "I have ideas. I have *plenty* of ideas but are any of them worth it?" she grumbled.

Caleb stuck a hand in his coat pocket and looked over at Brooke, keeping his other hand holding the pole steady. "You good?" Even though he didn't need to ask, he could tell by her tone and her fast talking that she was stressed.

Brooke shook her head, the frustration coming out in her eyes as she glared at the lake in front of her. He laughed, turning his attention back to the lake.

"Don't laugh. It sucks."

"You need inspiration."

"Everyone keeps saying that." She groaned. "I was told there was a lot in Marble, but so far, all I've seen is a lake and a fish named Bob."

"Don't forget Kevin," he said over his shoulder.

From the corner of his eye, he could see Brooke glaring up at him. She narrowed her eyes and leaned forward, tilting her body closer to him. "What about you, Caleb? What do you do here in Marble? Fish all day?"

Caleb shook his head and motioned in the direction of his home. "I own the touring company up the road a bit."

"The Jeeps?" Brooke asked. "There's a pamphlet for that at the lodge."

Caleb spun his reel. "Probably an older one. I haven't been to Marble Lodge in a while. Did you happen to see prices? I can tell you how old it is."

"No, I didn't. To be honest, I didn't even look at it." Brooke hadn't even thought about the pamphlets until now. Melinda made mention of it in passing, but other than that, she hadn't bothered to see what else there was here. "Where do you take people? Just around the town?"

"Up the road about six miles there is the old Crystal Mill and the town of Crystal." He pointed to the small dirt road and through the mountains. "It's a ghost town now and hard to reach, but my Jeeps get there, no problem. If you want inspiration, you should go up there."

"'Hard to reach, but my Jeeps get there, no problem,'" she quoted him. "Are you offering to take me?"

"That's no way to run a business, but I'll get you a good deal." He smiled over his shoulder.

She smiled back, and her blue eyes narrowed, still allowing a sparkle through her glasses. She heaved a sigh and then grinned. "Okay, when do we leave?"

Caleb began to reel in his line quicker than usual. Was it the fact he had just gotten a sale, or was it the fact that the sale came from an adorable, quirky woman? "This afternoon, twelve. I'll come up to the lodge and get you."

Brooke nodded. "Sounds good. Now"—she struggled as she stood out of the chair and loosened her grip on the blanket—"I am freezing, and as much fun as I am having talking to you, I am going to defrost myself. I'll see you at noon." She folded up her chair and wrapped her blanket in her arms, grabbing her laptop as she made her way back to her car.

"See you soon." Caleb grinned, watching her every move.

Brooke stumbled on the gravel, trying to hold everything in her hands.

"Do you need help?" he called, setting his pole on the ground and jogging his way to her.

She turned, her hair hitting her in the face. "No, no...I got it." She fumbled, dropping the chair.

Caleb chuckled and bent down to pick the chair up. "I got this. Let's get you to the car before you fall."

Five

Brooke hugged her mug full of coffee as if it were her saving grace. The blanket had offered her some protection out on the lake, but she certainly hadn't been prepared for it to be that cold. Greg and Helen sat at the other end of the kitchen's island as Brooke told them about the tour she would be taking this afternoon. The way she saw it, she could either lock herself in her duck-decorated room or write in a ghost town. Caleb being there would be a bonus. Caleb would *definitely* be the bonus.

"Some random guy offered to pick you up and just whisk you away?" Helen asked. "It sounds like a kidnapping to me."

Greg nodded. "Besides, aren't we supposed to be writing?" He looked at her, his brows coming together to add to his stare.

"This is research," Brooke answered, furrowing her brow and lifting her mug to her lips.

"Research?" Greg questioned. "Tell me, how hot is this fisherman?"

Brooke's glare deepened on Greg. Her truthful answer was *extremely*, but instead, she replied with, "He's about average. It's Marble, Colorado; there probably isn't a lot to compare him to."

Greg shrugged. "I guess that's true." He pushed himself off the counter and grabbed his coffee mug, not losing his gaze on Brooke. "There aren't that many people who live here, but still, I feel like attractiveness plays a part in why you are going on this tour. Like I said, you're supposed to be here to write."

Brooke looked at him and then back at Helen. "And I will write, but maybe I need to see the mill to properly describe it in my new book." With the look Greg gave her, one eyebrow raised slightly higher than the other, it was obvious he knew she was making excuses. He shook his head and turned back to the counter to the coffeepot.

"Maybe instead of a new book, you could continue *Winter's Edge*." Helen smiled, even though she knew the answer from last night was a no. "Maybe the mill could give you inspiration for the next storyline there."

Greg spun around. "*Winter's Edge?*" He had a shock in his voice.

Helen and Brooke both turned their attention to him.

"Yes, that's my book," Brooke said nonchalantly.

"My girlfriend is obsessed with that book." He pulled his cell phone from his pocket. "I need to tell her you're here." His face dropped when he saw his phone screen. "Ah, right, no service. She can wait until I get home." He shoved his phone back into his pocket. "You wouldn't happen to have a copy you could sign for her, would you?"

Brooke shook her head and shrugged her shoulders. "I don't carry them around with me, but as we are leaving, if we want to stop in Carbondale, I'd be happy to sign a copy for her."

Brooke was still having trouble with the fact that people wanted signed copies. To her, it was still a story in her mind that had helped her through a tough breakup and still had room for improvement, but to the rest of the world, it was a phenomenon.

Greg smiled. "That would be great! Now, tell me more about the fisherman and your lack of writing."

"How about"—Brooke looked at Greg, deflecting his comment—"you tell me about your writer's block." As much as she wanted to think about Caleb, she also wanted to get back on the discussion of writing. Greg was right, after all. She had paid money to come and write, and so far, she had only failed to describe a lake and try to set the setting.

Greg groaned. "Well, let me ask you this, how long did it take you to write *Winter's Edge*?"

"From start to publishing? Maybe three years."

Greg dropped his head. "I've had this idea in my head for years. When I say years, I mean *years*. I'm twenty-four, and I've been toying with it since I was thirteen. My girlfriend was actually the one to suggest I come to this retreat. She said it would help me."

"I can totally agree with that." Joyce entered the room, her sweet grandma voice filling the kitchen. "You can get a lot done here."

"If you stop talking and start writing." Rhonda appeared behind Joyce, her comment almost as deafening as Greg's. Brooke was almost shocked to see her out of her room. She hadn't seen Rhonda since the bonfire.

"Good morning, Rhonda." She smiled, trying to be polite. "How's your book going?"

Rhonda grabbed a mug from the cabinet and filled it with coffee. "I won't talk about it until it's done. Joyce, I'll see you at lunch." With that, Rhonda turned and left, going back up the stairs to her room where instantly Brooke could hear the typewriter.

Joyce looked back at the others sitting around the island, all with their eyes wide with Rhonda's lack of presence. "Don't let her get to you. She's really sweet and nice once you get to know her."

"Sure." Helen sneered. "I'm sure she is." Helen rolled her eyes, the sarcasm seeping from the action.

"Give her a few days to warm up to you." Joyce poured herself some coffee and then turned back to Brooke. "You left early this morning. I heard you went to the lake?"

"And she met a fisherman," Helen added, wiggling her eyebrows. "He said he was going to take her to the mill."

Joyce smiled. "The mill is beautiful. You'll love it." She completely skipped over the topic of Caleb.

"You've been?" Brooke asked, interested to know what it was going to be like.

She nodded. "I went on a tour last year. If it's the same company, the tour guide is wonderful. I felt very safe in his care." She sipped her coffee and then turned her back. "I better get back to my outline. Rhonda may be finishing her book, but I still need to figure out my conflict."

"Have fun, Joyce," Brooke said as she left.

Joyce vanished down the stairs. Greg looked at the two women in front of him.

"I should probably go to my laptop and attempt to write." he groaned.

"Let's go brainstorm together." Helen stood up. "I could use some help with suspense too." Helen turned back to Brooke and whispered, "Please don't get kidnapped."

Brooke let out a chuckle and shook her head as the two of them left, leaving Brooke alone in the kitchen. She rubbed her hands up and down on the ceramic mug, feeling the warmth the coffee offered. Caleb had mentioned he would be by to pick her up at noon. It was ten now. She had two hours to try to focus on anything but Caleb.

Taking her coffee with her, she went and settled into her room. Her laptop sat on the small desk that was provided, on and waiting for her. Setting her mug down on the coaster, she pulled the chair and rubbed her finger on the mouse pad. The computer sprung to life, showing her the cover of *Winter's Edge*. She quickly went to the Word document she had started at the lake and re-read the last few lines.

He flicked the rod with one swift motion, landing it smack dab in the middle of the lake. It had been months since he had last landed the bob in the water, and he remembered why he loved the feeling. The air was cold, and the lake was steaming—the perfect autumn morning to hook a fish.

She groaned, highlighting the entire page and hitting delete. She didn't need Caleb making an appearance in her book.

Winter's Edge was a love story between Daniel and Mira, and as much as they loved each other, their love wasn't accepted by either family. It was told during two timelines. One was from when they were younger, and the other was present day when Mira was dealing with her life after the death of Daniel. He left her pregnant and alone—until the end when the baby was born, a son she named after his father. It was tragic and broke Brooke to write, but it seemed to be very well received.

Many suggested she write a sequel, but this time, incorporating their son, having it be his love story. As much as she would make from that, she just didn't have the motivation to continue Daniel and Mira's story. She had killed a main character for a reason. She didn't want to return to them.

But now, all she saw as she tried to get the words on the page was Caleb casting his fishing pole.

As she stared at the blank document in front of her, a deadline looming overhead, she thought maybe, perhaps *maybe*, Caleb could make an appearance. Maybe he could be the heart of the new book.

She hit the small arrow, returning everything she had just deleted. The description of the lake, Caleb's walk up to her, and him casting the line all returned. Now that she had the base for her male, all she needed was the female, and the love story would follow. She rubbed the tips of her fingers against the keyboard and began to type away, creating a heroine.

∽

"Do you have the brochures I printed?" Ethan asked as Caleb was making the final adjustment to the Jeep for the tour.

"Yes. I have all the brochures." Caleb chuckled. Ethan had stuck a pile on the front seat, a pile on the back seat, and a pile in Caleb's back pocket.

"Good. Make sure you give some to both lodges up there. Maybe mention a discount."

"I told Brooke I'd cut her a deal, not the entire lodge." Caleb opened the door to the Jeep, tossing the final bag in the back seat. He always prepared, packing extra water and blankets, just in case. The tour would last a total of three hours. Many of the supplies he packed were unnecessary, but Lettie had taught him well. "If the others are interested, they can pay the full price."

"Introduce yourself when you get there. Tell them about the tours and how Crystal is beautiful this time of year." Ethan was rambling, spouting off anything he could to get Caleb to remember.

"I know, Ethan, I know." Caleb turned to his friend and laughed, adding an eye roll. "It's going to be great. I'll see you in three hours." Caleb climbed into the cab of the Jeep and started the engine. He waved to his friend and backed out of the driveway, leaving Ethan standing waving from the porch.

The drive from Caleb's house to the lodge was three minutes, tops. The Jeep handled the dirt roads like they were nothing, and the hill to the lodge was child's play compared to some of the other cars he saw make this road. He parked the Jeep in front of the main lodge and hopped out, hoping to see Brooke running toward the car. Why was he so excited to see her spending three hours in her company?

The few interactions he had with Brooke seemed to open something in him again, something he hadn't felt since he moved to Colorado. He had been so aloof, only making close friends with those he was around on a daily basis. The population of Marble was kind and welcoming to him, allowing him to break his shell when he saw fit. They were there for him, and he was always there for them. He was stable and grounded. Everyone knew that. Even though those facts were true, something shifted as he walked up toward the main lodge. Excitement, hope...*butterflies*.

"Hello, how can we help you?" An older man appeared from the smaller cabin, followed by a small dog, grabbing Caleb's attention.

"Hello, sir. I'm Caleb. I'm with Marble Touring."

"I can assure you. No one wants to go up to the mill. This is a writing retreat, and most of our guests are busy typing away." He smiled at him. His teeth were unusually white.

Furrowing his brow, Caleb nodded. "Right, I met Brooke by the lake this morning, and she mentioned needing inspiration. I offered to take her up to the mill and town."

The door to the main cabin opened and slammed shut, footsteps following. He turned, and Brooke headed down the steps, dressed warmly with her laptop in hand.

"It's okay, Frank." Brooke came up, flashing a smile. "Caleb told me how beautiful the mill was, and I'm having a bit of trouble setting the scene. No worries!" She held up her laptop. "I intend to write."

Caleb felt as if he was a teenager meeting a father before a first date. Frank sized him up and down, a parental look of concern on his face. Finally, after looking from Caleb to Brooke, Frank nodded. "Be safe, okay? I've taken that road, and it can be kind of tricky at times."

Caleb resisted the urge to salute. "Not a problem, sir. I take it all the time." He began to walk back to the Jeep. "It's about a three-hour trip, so we'd better head off." He climbed in, quickly moving the brochures that sat on the passenger seat so Brooke would have a clear space.

Brooke had a skip in her step as she went toward the Jeep. "See you soon, Frank." She waved before climbing into the Jeep. Caleb was already sitting in the front seat, waiting for Brooke, before turning the ignition. "Three hours? You failed to mention that part at the lake." He turned the wheel with ease, and the Jeep sailed over the gravel road, much smoother than Brooke's Chevy.

"It's about thirty or forty minutes there. We stop at the mill and spend some time there. Then we will go on to the town of Crystal. Twenty minutes at each location with forty minutes driving time each way. Three hours." Caleb turned over to her and flashed a smile.

Brooke blushed, returning his smile, and buckled up in her seat.

Six

The drive from the lodge to the mill was full of dirt, rocks, and breathtaking views around every bend. Brooke held onto her laptop with every bump, terrified she would lose it. The vehicle that Caleb had pulled up in was not your average Jeep. It was thinner, with no roof and the windshield was folded down, only adding to the experience. There was a bar you could stand and hold on to, but sitting in the front seat, Brooke held onto the door.

Caleb shifted the gears with ease, like he knew exactly what to do at every turn. He warned her at one point the road got narrow and it may feel like she would fall, but he assured her she was fine. Not that she didn't believe him, but she tightened her seat belt.

Despite the fact that there were giant mountains and rolling autumn colors surrounding her, Brooke had to force herself to focus on the scenery. She fought the desire to watch Caleb as he drove with care, taking every sharp corner and bump with clarity, even though it felt like she was going to fall from the seat. His fingers drummed the gear shift and steering wheel. He looked like he was concentrating, his gaze centered on the road in front of him. It was hard to focus on the mountains behind him with his captivating eyes distracting her.

Focused and intense, the hazel glistened through his eyelashes. Even though he was deep in focus and squinting from the sun, there was still softness in his eyes.

"We're almost there," Caleb said, breaking the silence. "Watch for the mill. We will stop there first."

Brooke nodded roughly as they hit a rock. She reached to place her laptop down, pressing it between her feet. Why had she even brought it? There were too many other things to keep track of besides protecting her laptop.

Oh, yeah. Inspiration.

"Why did you bring your laptop? You're supposed to be enjoying the view and taking in your vacation." Caleb broke the silence, his eyes still focused on the road in front of him.

"It's not a vacation, and what if inspiration hits?" She turned to look at him, lingering her eyes longer than she normally would have, stunned that he practically read her mind.

"Don't look at me." He smiled, catching her gaze with his. "Look at the view. The mill is right around this bend."

It took Brooke a few moments to shift her gaze from Caleb back to the sights in front of her. It seemed to come out of nowhere. A beautiful water mill rested on the side of a cliff into the river. Water flowed around it, crashing into the rocks on the sides of the cliff, the calming sound hitting her ears. Caleb slowed the Jeep and stopped, the jerk of the brakes making Brooke's entire body fall forward. Despite the stop, she didn't take her eyes from the mill.

"Told you." Caleb smirked as he shifted gears, pulling the parking brake to stop. He opened the door and jumped out. He walked to the passenger side and opened the car door for Brooke. She turned her gaze and watched him carefully. His movements were seamless, showing dedication to his job and his touring clients.

Brooke turned to leave the Jeep, stopping when she saw Caleb's hand extended in front of her. She moved her eyes from his hand, patiently waiting for hers, to his eyes. They were soft, welcoming, and inviting—they were captivating. She lightly touched her palm to his, and sparks ran up her arm. She caught her breath before stepping out of the Jeep, the crunch of rocks beneath her feet. Caleb's hand was warm in hers, strong and firm. Protective. She didn't want to let it go. Did he?

"It's gorgeous," she said softly, trying to keep her voice steady. She took a few steps, still holding Caleb's hands before woefully pulling her fingers from his. "How often do you get to come here?"

"Used to be every day." Caleb closed the Jeep door behind her, following her as she inched closer and closer to the edge.

"Used to be?" She turned, looking at him over her shoulder. He wasn't looking at the mill. He had his eyes locked on her.

He blinked and shrugged his shoulders, heaving a sigh before answering. "Yeah, well, things happen."

He sounded like he wasn't interested in continuing the conversation, and she wouldn't push him. She eyed him up and down before turning back to the mill. Curiosity tugged at her mind, but the details might come with time.

The old, worn-down mill was enveloped in the fall colors of the trees surrounding it. The wooden ladder that climbed the cliff was breaking down, and if anyone stepped foot in the building, it would most likely crumble into the river. But that helped captivate the beauty. The rustic look only amplified its surroundings. The river flowed down the cliff and past the mill, the rushing water sound overtaking the area, louder than Brooke had ever heard.

"What kind of mill was this?" Brooke asked, taking her gaze from the mill to Caleb, who still stood with his hands in his pockets, his gaze still concentrated on her. She fixed her posture, locking eyes with him.

Caleb took a deep breath. "Actually, it wasn't a mill at all. It was a powerhouse for the silver mine." He pulled a hand from his pockets and gestured toward the wooden frame. "It has three parts to it; the compressor, the gear stock, and the penstock. It's been out of commission since 1917."

"And it still stands here?" She flipped her head back to the scene, taking a few more steps toward the mill. She patted her coat pocket for her cell phone, but she'd left it in the Jeep.

He nodded. "It's become one of the most photographed areas in Colorado. It's been restored, of course, but everyone wants to keep it alive."

Brooke spun back to the Jeep. "Are pictures with cell phones allowed?" she joked.

Caleb chuckled, stepping out of her way as she bounded back to the passenger door. "Yeah." She opened the door to the Jeep, leaned in, and grabbed her phone, leaving her laptop on the passenger seat. "We're here for twenty minutes. If you want to take a look around, I can guide you, or you can just sit and..." He cleared his throat. "Write?"

Brooke hurried back to the edge of the cliff, her cell phone in hand. She opened her camera and readied her aim. "I would love to look around and take some pictures. You said there is a town?" She snapped a photo of the mill and turned back to Caleb.

This entire time she had been watching the mill, taking in the surrounding areas; she was trying not to notice Caleb. His unkempt brown hair was pushed back, and his beard was trimmed. Did he try to make himself look presentable for her? She smirked. Maybe she should have done the same. She narrowed her eyes, and their gazes locked for a millisecond before Caleb sighed and turned around.

"There is a town," Caleb said matter-of-factly. "We will go there once you've taken your fill of photos."

"We have twenty minutes?"

"Honestly"—Caleb looked at his watch—"we have all the time you want. I don't have another booking today."

Brooke snapped another picture of the trees around the mill, then looked at Caleb over her shoulder. "You don't? How many Jeeps do you have?"

"Three, but this one is the only one taking tours at the moment. Ethan is at the office, though, in case someone calls. If they do, he will contact me on the satellite phone in the Jeep." He tilted his head, motioning for Brooke to follow him. "Come on, let me show you around."

Brooke lowered her phone and stuck it in her back pocket, making sure not to trip over any rocks as she followed Caleb up the path. As he led her into the fall foliage, she tried to think of small talk. What did you talk about with a man you had just met and found extremely attractive? One thing she loved about being an author was how all it involved was her laptop and emails between her agent and editor. She didn't actually have to talk to people if she didn't want to. Which meant her social anxiety was climbing with every step they took. Did she talk about his business or her book? Or did she try to flirt?

"So," Brooke began, not really knowing where to take the conversation. "How long have you lived in Marble? Born and raised?" she asked, suddenly feeling sheepish. The town was too small to hold a hospital, obviously he wasn't born here.

Caleb shook his head slowly. "No, actually. I'm from Chicago. I've been here for three years now," he said over his shoulder, like he was making sure Brooke was still close behind.

"Chicago?" she asked, a little shocked. By his looks, he was a country boy through and through. The fishing trips, the scruffy, unkempt hair and beard, the flannel shirt under his Carhart jacket—it was hard to see Caleb living in the city. "I can't see you living in a big city. What brought you here?"

"Originally, the fishing, then I just kind of stayed." He chuckled, his voice hiding something.

"You had the ability to just uproot your life after a vacation?"

Caleb stopped and turned to look over at her. "Well, when life hands you lemons, you make lemonade, right?"

"Cliche, but true. What happened, if you don't mind me asking?" she pried, knowing full well a stranger wouldn't give another stranger the answers to his life story.

"My wife died," he said simply, with no break in the conversation.

"Oh." Brooke widened her eyes and bit her bottom lip. Thoughts went rushing through her mind. *He's a widower. His wife died. How long ago? Is he still mourning?* "I'm so sorry to hear that." She spoke softly, not knowing how to react in a situation like this. Did anyone really? All you could really do is give condolences and hope you didn't bring back bad memories.

Caleb shrugged. "Thank you," he said before turning his way back up the trail. "Where are you from, Ms. Brooke?"

"Utah," she muttered, pulling herself back to a positive mind after seeing Caleb move on from the topic of his wife so quickly. She cleared her throat. "Salt Lake."

"Ah." Caleb raised his chin. "Another big city. Are you enjoying your escape in Marble?"

"I mean it's different. Beautiful, but different." She stopped again, turning her back to look at the mountains behind her, pulling her phone to take another photo. "I'm not used to no cell service, that's for sure."

"That's one of the best parts," Caleb admitted.

"It didn't take you time to get used to it?" She looked over her shoulder at him. He had a smirk on his face, seeming to just enjoy her company.

He shrugged. "At first, yes, but once I made the decision to stay, it got easier. Landlines are still a thing, you know." He laughed at her.

Brooke shook her head. "Do you still have family in Chicago?"

He nodded. "Oh, yeah. They've been out to visit a few times. We keep in touch."

She smiled. "So Marble isn't completely cut off from the world."

Caleb smiled back at her, and instantly, knots formed in her stomach. "Not at all."

Seven

Caleb had lost his wife, Audrey, five months before he came to Marble. The cancer hit fast and hard. Seven months after they received her diagnosis, she was gone. They had been married for five years, and the majority of their marriage was talking about all the things they *wanted* to do, but they never actually did the things they talked about. Caleb worked for a law firm fresh out of college, hoping to boost his career in the legal world. Audrey had hoped to become a news anchor in Chicago. Their careers took over the things they wanted, and when they both recognized that, they knew that wasn't the life they had planned.

But life had other plans.

The timeline Audrey was given was vague. "Within the year," the doctors had told her. With treatment, maybe longer, but there was no guarantee. When Audrey denied all treatments, saying there was no point if the cancer was just going to overrule it anyway, Caleb got scared. He didn't want to lose his wife, the one person he considered his rock, but she was insistent that she live the remainder of her life as normal as possible.

It wasn't normal though. Caleb saw his wife get worse with each passing day, but Audrey ignored the ever-growing symptoms and changes. She wanted it to be *normal*. Caleb, though, was growing more and more afraid. The one thing in his life that was a constant, the one person who, no matter what, was always there, was fading quickly.

Together, they decided a vacation was in order. After researching and finding the perfect remote spot to just enjoy each other, they stumbled upon Marble. In an instant, they booked the trip and left for a week.

It was the trip back to Chicago where Caleb started to notice the change in her health. It was a rapid change, one that hit them both like a rock. Every day, something new happened. Weight loss, fatigue, nausea, and then the hospital trips, and then as quickly as the symptoms appeared, Audrey was gone.

Caleb handled everything on his own. It was his way of passing through the grief. After the funeral, he tried to focus back on his work, but it wasn't as fulfilling as it used to be. He no longer cared about the law office or any of his potential clients. He was tired of hearing the many condolences, bringing up the pain he was trying to push down day after day. He needed to grieve in his own way. He wanted to *feel* her again, and a way to do that, he thought, was back in Marble.

He traveled back, planning to only stay for a total of four days; but those four days turned into three years. He met Ethan, who helped him get a job at the touring company, and Lettie, who took him in and treated him like family. He rented the space above the touring company's office and started to build his new life and routine. Fish in the morning, work during the day, campfires at night. In Marble, he wasn't constantly reminded of losing Audrey. No one asked how he was doing, or if he needed anything. He was simply Caleb, the new guy in town. And as much as he missed Audrey, he welcomed the change.

When Lettie passed and left the company to him, he gladly accepted and promised to keep its integrity alive. And now here he was, close to letting Lettie and Ethan down. Not that it was his fault the business had lost clients since the pandemic, but as the owner, he was expected to bring it back to life—yet he had no idea where to even start. It was as if all the business classes he took in college made no sense and didn't apply to his life today.

After many cell phone pictures and a small hike around the mill, Caleb and Brooke climbed the road to make the rest of the journey to the town of Crystal. Brooke never went back for her laptop. She had seemed more interested in the area than figuring out how to put it on a Word document, which if he were being honest, was refreshing.

Caleb couldn't help but notice her. He hadn't been taken by a woman since Audrey, and Brooke had definitely found a way into his attention span. He hadn't mentioned Audrey in months. The people of Marble knew the story and decided not to dwell on it, but Brooke was new. She didn't know how he ended up here. To her, he was just a flannel clad fisherman who named the fishes he caught. For all he knew, Brooke wanted to stop the tour and go back to the lodge to frantically type everything on her computer. Caleb, however, didn't want that to be the case.

He cleared his throat. "The town is just up the road to the right." He broke the silence as they hiked up the trail. He pointed to the upcoming turn. "Crystal City is a ghost town now. It has a few seasonal residences, but during the winter, it's hard to reach. After the mill closed, the town shut down too."

"Do you know how long the town was active? And the mill?" Brooke asked.

"The town was founded in 1880 but boomed in 81. It even had a post office at one point, but by 1915, there were eight full-time residents, and then it became a ghost town once the mines closed."

"Oh wow, so it's heyday was short lived." Brooke folded her arms. "I'll need to look up the history when I get back to the lodge, it may make a good setting," she muttered to herself.

Caleb sighed. "Besides writing, what do you do, Brooke?" he asked, edging the question a little further.

Brooke glanced back up at him. "That's it, really. I write, I edit, I write some more. I used to work as an assistant to a publishing agent, but once my book hit big, I was able to quit to focus on writing. I honestly don't get out much," Brooke admitted. "Normally, it's me and my laptop hanging out in the studio apartment."

"In the city," he added.

She nodded. "In the city," she repeated.

"Have you always lived in Salt Lake?"

Before Brooke could answer Caleb's question, she gasped as the first buildings came into view. "Is this it?" she asked.

Caleb nodded. "Yup, welcome to the ghost town of Crystal, Colorado."

There were only a handful of buildings still standing, maybe ten total. They all had the same worn-down look that the mill had. Some windows were broken, and likely hadn't been entered in years. In the September weather, there was no one walking the road but Caleb and Brooke.

"This has been a ghost town since 1915?" Brooke asked, turning to Caleb.

He nodded. "More or less, that building over there"—he pointed to the largest building on the road—"used to be a saloon, and the post office was across the street. There used to be more to it, but a lot of the buildings were torn down after everyone left. It was just too hard to access and maintain during the winter months. In the late 1800s, the population reached 500."

Brooke looked at him over her shoulder and smiled. "You seem to know a lot about this place."

"I have to." He grinned back. "I *am* the tour guide."

Brooke chuckled. "That's true. You'll have to write down all you know…"

"For your novel?" Caleb finished her sentence.

She nodded and took more steps away from him. "You're right. It's absolutely beautiful up here. It would be fun to do a period piece."

"Your first book"—Caleb walked closer to her as she wandered farther into the town—"you said it took off really fast. I wonder if I've heard of it?"

Brooke groaned. "It's a drama romance called *Winter's Edge*."

"Oh yeah, no…" Caleb chuckled. "I haven't heard of it. This may come as a surprise, but I'm not much of a reader. My wife probably would have loved it. She was reading a different book every week."

Brooke turned at the mention of his wife. "What was her name?" she asked quietly.

"Audrey," he muttered. "And before you ask, it was cancer."

Brooke pursed her lips, looking as if she was placed in an awkward situation. Her eyes darted to the ground, seemingly unaware of what to say.

She cleared her throat. "How long ago did she pass?"

"About three and a half years ago," he responded simply. Caleb was short in his answer, telling Brooke he didn't want to talk about it.

She heaved a sigh and turned her head to look at the landscape, every now and then looking down on the ground, kicking the rocks between steps.

"So," he began again, filling the silence. "Have you always lived in Salt Lake?"

Not stopping from walking around the dirt path looking at all the buildings, Brooke answered, "Unfortunately, yes. Salt Lake is home." She sighed. "I haven't left on a vacation in years, so this is a nice change."

"Even without cell phone service?" Caleb asked, with a smile.

Brooke turned to him and mirrored his grin. "Yeah, even without cell phone service." Their gazes met. "My agent may have sent me a million emails and texts though. I'll hook back up to the wi-fi when I get back to the lodge."

"You're welcome to come to the touring company. We have a strong satellite signal, and only Ethan and I connect. It's all yours if you want to use it." Caleb watched her, hoping for a decent reaction. Even though the forty minutes of the tour was nearing an end, he was hoping he would get to see and talk to her again.

He missed this feeling. He didn't want it to end just yet.

She smiled. "I may take you up on that." She took one last glance at him before turning her back to adventure in the ghost town some more, taking out her phone to take as many pictures as possible.

Eight

Caleb took the road back to the lodge with as much ease as he did on the journey there. The bumps didn't come as much of a surprise to Brooke as she held onto the door handle. The mill was stunning, and the ghost town was the icing on the cake. She had enough pictures and visual references to change the description. She had a setting now. The town, the mill—they had made their way into her new novel, the setting coming together. She could keep her fisherman but change it to a period piece. Joyce was working on a civil war novel. Maybe she could pick her brain.

Caleb stopped the Jeep in front of the lodge and opened his car door in sync with Brooke. She climbed out, grabbing her laptop case and slamming the door shut. Caleb walked around to meet Brooke on the passenger side of the car.

"I hope you liked the trip," he asked, a smile tugging on his lips.

Brooke nodded with excitement and glanced at him, his expression showing more than a simple goodbye. "I really did. It was so beautiful. Thank you for the ride. How much do I owe you? If you wait just a moment, I can go grab my wallet..."

Caleb gestured his hand, waving her off. "No need. It was a pleasure. I did say I'd offer you a deal." He smiled back at her.

Brooke's eyes grew wide. "Wait...what?" she stammered, completely taken aback. He had said that they weren't doing any tours—yet he wasn't letting her pay? "Are you sure?"

"Extremely." He waved her off again. There was a hint of uncertainty in his voice.

"I...I..." Brooke stared at him. "Thank you. I'll find a way to make it up to you." Her smile grew, her eyes beaming.

Caleb reached forward, holding out his hand for her to shake. "Come by the office as much as you like. I can guarantee my wi-fi is stronger than in there." he nodded towards the lodge.

She glanced at him up and down then slowly shook his hand, her eyes settled on his, taking all of him in. "I will. Thank you again."

Caleb nodded once to her, dropping his head and hunching his back, awkwardly stepping back to the Jeep. Brooke held back a chuckle. It was like he didn't want to leave but got the feeling he thought he should. But did she really want him to leave? She enjoyed the trip, and it was more than just the town.

Brooke's dating life had ended abruptly a few years prior, leaving her to only focus on her work. The knots in her stomach weren't exactly a new experience, but here—with *these* knots—it was Caleb. She cleared her throat.

"Maybe I'll see you at the lake tonight?" she said, louder to catch his attention before he was on the driver's side of the Jeep.

He perked up, straightening his back, and his smile reappeared on his face. "I'll be there." He waved goodbye and climbed into the driver's seat, putting it in gear and turning the vehicle around, giving one last wave before he headed down the steep road.

As the dust cleared, he turned left and headed back to the office. She tucked her hair behind her ear. Caleb wasn't something she was looking for, but there he was. During their small hike to the town, she couldn't help but notice all his features. His strong jawline and muscles in his neck every time he turned back to look at her. If only he wasn't wearing a heavy coat, and she could see more of him. His eyes had lit up as he'd talked about the history of the town, and when he'd mentioned his late wife, there'd been love and passion in his voice. Just the thought of him waiting at the lake for her later sent a thrill up her spine.

She shook her head and walked up the steps to the lodge's door. She would see Caleb tonight for sure, but for now, she had to write. She had research to do now and an outline to build. A whole new story to imagine.

Walking inside the main room, she saw her new friends, each with a laptop settled on their laps. Joyce, Helen, and Greg all sat with their gazes locked on her.

"Hi." Brooke smiled, coming into the living room to sit next to Joyce. In the distance, typewriter keys clacked, followed by the *ca-king* of a new line beginning. "Rhonda's hard at work, isn't she?"

"We all are," Greg muttered, annoyance clear in his voice. He shot a glare at her. "Well, *most* of us. That's what we are here for, right?"

Brooke bit her lip and narrowed her eyes at him. Why was he annoyed that she took a trip with Caleb? He knew she was looking for the right thing for her novel, and she might have found it. Was he angry that she may have found the way to her novel, and he hadn't?

"How was the tour, honey?" Joyce asked, stopping her typing to focus on Brooke.

"It was beautiful. It made me think of something." Brooke turned on the couch, lifting her leg up and facing Joyce. "I want to do a period piece."

Joyce looked over at her and smiled. "Really?" She had enthusiasm in her voice.

"Set where?" Helen asked, looking up from the laptop.

"The town of Crystal. Caleb took me, and it's absolutely beautiful. Apparently, it had everything, but according to Caleb, it was only used for a handful years."

"That is a beautiful place, and the guides do know a lot about the area. It would make a good setting. Romance is your genre, right?" Joyce asked.

Brooke nodded. "Romance was the side story in *Winter's Edge*. I want to focus more on the characters and the town, but, Joyce"—Brooke leaned her arm on the back of the couch and placed her fingers gently on Joyce's shoulder—"I was wondering if we could talk. Can I pick your brain for period pieces?"

Joyce smiled. "Oh, I'd love that. Let me finish up these chapters, and then we can sit and talk. Get a notebook and pen! Research is involved!"

Joyce's enthusiasm got Brooke excited even more. "That's perfect. I can go and set something up before we dive in. Is that okay?"

Joyce nodded. "Perfect."

"And the fisherman?" Greg asked. "We all saw him. How's the fisherman?"

Brooke felt her cheek blush. "Caleb. His name is Caleb."

∽

Caleb pulled into the lot in front of the office and slowly took his time gathering everything before making his way into the building. He was giddy and shocked. He hadn't felt this way in a long time, and he didn't know what to make of it. Nothing had really happened, just the time spent with Brooke and the conversations they had. There was no one like her in Marble, and she was so different than any woman he had known. With a smile on his face and a skip in his step, he climbed the front stairs and opened the squeaky door into the office.

Ethan was behind the counter, looking as if he was waiting patiently for Caleb to come back.

"How was it?" he asked right away, not skipping a beat.

Caleb smiled. "It was great." He walked up to the counter, the smile still on his face, the thoughts of Brooke still lingering.

Ethan had one eyebrow raised and hummed an "uh-huh" sound. "How much did you charge?"

Caleb raised his eyebrows, locking gazes with Ethan. He took a deep breath and set the emergency bag on the floor. "About that…"

"You didn't." Ethan groaned. "Did you at least hand out the brochures?"

Caleb was silent. He had forgotten all about them. "*Yees*."

Ethan lowered his eyebrows. "Oh, well. It's okay. They are still in the Jeep. I can take them up."

"Feel free, but they are all there for a retreat. That Frank guy seemed to be annoyed that I took Brooke up. She even brought her laptop to write if *inspiration* hit.'"

"And did *inspiration* hit?" Ethan raised an eyebrow.

Caleb walked behind the counter to stand next to Ethan. "I think so, but she didn't use her laptop. She left it in the cab the entire time. She may come by to use our internet. It's not the best service at the lodge, and she wants to do some research."

"*Research*?" Ethan repeated. "On the town, on the mill? On what?"

"The town," Caleb quickly replied. "She said she may want to do a period piece now." Caleb wiggled the mouse and watched the computer come alive in front of him.

He typed in the password and quickly opened a web browser. He typed *Winter's Edge* in the search bar, bringing up an Amazon page for Brooke's novel. He scrolled down to the author's info, raising his eyebrows when he saw the photo of her standing in a winter setting, surrounded by trees covered in heavy snow. Her smile radiated even through the computer. He found her bio and read silently.

Brooke Easten grew up in South Salt Lake City, Utah, where she always loved to tell stories. From a young age, she would make up fairy tales, even giving roles to friends to act out. Her greatest accomplishment in school was writing the spring play, having it be performed by her classmates. After high school, Brooke attended the University of Utah, graduating with a B.A. in Communications with a A.S. in English. Besides writing, Brooke loves to hike the trails in Salt Lake and go to the movie theater to watch anything that's playing. Brooke's goals include writing a best-selling novel, to have it someday be brought to life on screen, traveling to London, and being able to write full time. Brooke currently works as a publishing assistant in Salt Lake where she lives with her cat, Margie.

"She's cute," Ethan said behind him, making Caleb jump back to reality.

Caleb turned back to the computer, scrolling up to the cover of Brooke's book. "This is her first novel."

"Salt Lake, huh?" Ethan elbowed his arm. "That's only a six-hour drive, but that's without stops."

Caleb looked over at him. "I've never been. Trying to stay out of big cities." Caleb clicked the screen closed, returning to the normal backdrop of the computer screen.

"You're from Chicago. Salt Lake is a lot different than Chicago. Why are you looking her up?" Ethan asked, returning to his notebook in front of him.

"Just curious," Caleb answered.

"Mm-Hmm." Ethan hummed, raising his eyebrows again, keeping his eyes locked on the paperwork.

Caleb snapped his gaze to Ethan. "What?" he asked.

"Oh, nothing." Ethan sighed. "Nothing at all."

Nine

Once Brooke decided on the setting, the rest seemed to flow from her easily. After she had met with Joyce to get the basics of writing historical fiction, she had gone to her room to set her characters. Before she knew it, the sun was setting, and the air was getting colder. She glanced at the small clock on her computer screen. Was Caleb at the lake yet?

She closed her computer after making sure her document was saved and stretched her arms up, leaning her back over her chair, letting out a loud audible groan, and she felt her spine move. Sitting in front of a computer was going to be the death of her posture. She stood and stretched once more before opening the door to the hall, letting in the cold air from the kitchen and main area.

Leaving her room, she could see the faint light from the main room, Greg sitting on the couch with his computer on his lap. His fingers were moving just as fast as hers would, and when she approached, grabbing her coat and slipping on her shoes, he stopped.

"Are you going somewhere?" he asked, glancing up at her from his laptop.

"I'm just going down for a walk around the lake," she muttered.

"Have you written anything?"

"As a matter of fact, yes. Joyce has helped me a lot with bringing a period piece to life. I have my setting and characters." Brooke glared at him. His reaction to her leaving was *really* starting to get on her nerves.

He nodded. "All that's left is a plot."

"Why does it bother you so much?" she asked, more fire in her voice than intended.

Greg looked at her through his glasses. He didn't respond.

She narrowed her eyes down at him. "Have you left the cabin at all?"

Greg shook his head.

"Come down to the lake with me. It's beautiful down there, and you could meet Caleb." Brooke leaned on the couch, trying to coax Greg out of the spot he had settled. She doubted he would move, but she could at least offer the escape from the lodge. He was so hell-bent on the writing that Brooke was worried that would become more stressful than anything else. She could see his mind working, dabbling with the idea that maybe leaving the lodge was a good idea before he closed his eyes and shook his head.

Greg groaned. "Not tonight. I may have hit a breakthrough," he mumbled. His fingers returned to rapid fire on his keyboard, the clicking filling the silence in the room.

Brooke sighed and reached for the screen door, sliding her beanie over her blonde hair. "Okay, well, if you change your mind, you can come down."

"Have fun with your fisherman," Greg muttered under his breath.

Brooke rolled her eyes as she left the lodge.

As she hoped, Caleb was in his normal fishing spot when she arrived. He had a small lantern lighting up the area and a second fishing pole. Brooke approached slowly, her hands in her coat pocket, watching him as he cast his fishing line. He hadn't seen her yet, so she took the extra moment to watch. He had perfect posture as he swung his arm back, his eyes never leaving the lake in front of him. It was like he knew that spot on the lake like the back of his hand, and he didn't have to worry about what was behind him while casting. His arm swung forward, and his body moved with the motion seamlessly. She couldn't tell where his movements were more exact—here with the fishing pole or in the Jeep with the gear shift. She heard the clicking of the reel as the line flew through the air. Off in the distance, the bobber went *plop*.

"Nice one," she said softly, approaching him.

Caleb turned, his smile widening after he noticed her. "I was beginning to think you weren't coming."

"I hit a stride. Once I started writing, it was hard to stop." She came up to stand beside him. "The tour really helped, thank you."

"Period piece?" he asked, tilting his back to glance at her.

She nodded. "Joyce, one of the writers at the retreat, is doing a civil war novel, so she gave me a few pointers on how to start a historical fiction. I have a lot of research ahead of me."

"Did you get anything done?"

Brooke nodded. "Oh, yeah. I have a male lead and a setting. I'm just thinking of the plot now."

Caleb began to reel in his line and turned to look at her. "Well…here," he said, handing the fishing pole to her. "Consider this more research."

"What?" she asked, taking the pole with caution. "I've been fishing before…"

"When you were younger, right, so…" He bent and grabbed the second fishing pole that was there. "I'm going to teach you to fish." He wiggled his eyebrows at her.

Brooke held onto the pole with wide eyes. "Um, okay. It can't be that hard, can it?"

Caleb smirked. "It's not hard at all. You just gotta have patience and follow a few rules."

"Naming fish?" Brooke asked.

"Naming all the fish." Caleb smiled back. "Now"—he bent down to his tackle box and pulled a small white Styrofoam box from the bin—"let's bait your line."

Brooke widened her eyes. "Like...with a worm?"

Caleb laughed. "Well, this is a cricket."

"A cricket?" she repeated.

Caleb grabbed the end of her fishing pole, holding a dead...hopefully dead...cricket and stabbing it with the small hook.

"Is it dead?"

"Now it is," Caleb pointed out sarcastically, securing the cricket to the hook. "It's a cricket," he said, smiling up at her. "And if it makes you feel better, it's most likely still alive. I don't think I got its heart."

"It's heart?" she repeated.

"Look"—he held up the line—"it's legs are still moving."

Brooke winced and shook her head. "Isn't there like...fake...bait we can use?"

Caleb glared up at her. "Do you want to catch a fish?"

Brooke shrugged. "In all honesty, I just wanted to come spend some more time with you. I'd figured you would fish, and I would name them all."

Caleb shook his head, narrowing his eyes. "No way. I planned and brought a second pole to teach you. I promise, you will enjoy it."

Brooke looked at the cricket on the end of her line. Its little feet were wiggling, and it looked like it was trying to get free. Caleb was baiting his line the same way he had baited hers. Even in the dark, she could see his hair blowing in the light breeze. Caleb stood next to her and held his pole up.

"Okay so," he began, playing with his reel. "There's this button here—"

Brooke smirked and looked at him through the light of the lantern. Did she tell him she remembered what her dad had taught her about fishing many years ago, or did she let him explain it as simply as he could? She felt herself blush, even in the cold. Caleb was being too sweet and too helpful for her to stop him now. As he was explaining, her mind drifted away from what he was saying and just focused on him. His movements were flawless as he held the line, gentle, yet with purpose. As he told her about the different features of the pole, his eyebrows would raise and furrow at different points as he concentrated on his teaching. His fingers glided against the metal and the wood, spinning the reel, creating a small clicking sound, gently making their way back up to the tip of the line. Brooke was intrigued, and she wasn't interested in the fishing.

Brooke blinked. Maybe she should listen to what he was saying.

Caleb's voice became louder. "And when you're ready to cast"—he motioned his arm back, ready to throw—"you let go." He flipped his arm forward. The clicking sound from the rod hit the mountains and then came back at them. It was so quiet, yet the clicking echoed.

"Easy breezy." Brooke sighed.

"Lemon squeezy," Caleb finished the common saying. "Cast." Caleb gestured his head toward the pole.

Brooke followed his motions from earlier, trying to remember his steps versus her dad's so many years ago. She hit the lock and pulled her arm back, flinging it forward with as much gusto as she could. The line whished through the air, landing with a *plop* near Caleb's.

"Very nice!" he exclaimed.

She shrugged. "Beginner's luck." She glanced over at Caleb, who was watching her and not the lake. "Now what?"

"We wait. Remember this morning?"

"My blanket burrito. Yes, I remember it very well." Brooke tilted her head, suddenly wishing she had her blanket with her.

"Fishing is meant to be relaxing, calming," he said very, very calmly, lowering his voice as the sentence drew out.

"How do you know when you catch a fish? I've never caught one with my dad," Brooke said honestly.

Caleb turned his reel a few times. "You will feel the pressure. Kind of like a jerk in the line. What kind of fishing did your dad take you on?" Caleb asked, turning to look in her direction.

"Mainly in a boat, and it was mainly, 'this is what you need to do with your life.'" Brooke lowered her tone to mock her father. It wasn't that her father wasn't a supportive parent, he just thought she needed to do what *he* wanted her to do. "He would bait the lines with these bright orange rubber things, and then we would sit and wait for the pole to move. He didn't do any of the things you do." Brooke gestured to Caleb's tackle box. "Should I reel it in like you did?"

"Spin the reel three times. Get that cricket moving." Caleb smiled.

Brooke did as he told her. The line felt light, as if there was nothing there. From the corner of her eye, Caleb's pole jerked, and he began to spin his reel faster.

"You caught one?" she asked. How had he already caught one? He had just cast his line. Brooke looked at her pole and bobbed it up and down, hoping that would get the attention of a fish. *Come on, fish.*

"Most likely." As the line got closer and closer, the water splashed and finally a dark, thin blobbing fish flopped all over the surface. "Gonna name him?" Caleb leaned over to unhook the fish. Brooke stayed still, reeling in her line three more times.

"Let's see, we have Bob and Kevin—what are some other names you would use?" she asked as he rubbed the fish in the water.

"There are maybe twenty Bobs in this lake." Caleb groaned.

Brooke chuckled. "Well then, hello, *Robert*."

Caleb nodded and pulled his hand from the lake, shaking the water off. "So long, Robert."

As Caleb turned back to his tackle box, Brooke turned her attention back to the lake. She couldn't see her line, but she reeled it in once more. Then, ever so lightly, there was a tug.

"Caleb," she said, with a shock in her voice. "Caleb," she said louder. "There was a tug!" She wanted to jump. She was pretty certain there was a fish on the end of her line. "What do I do?"

Caleb stood and came up behind her, reaching his arm over so his hand was next to her on the reel handle.

"Yep, I can feel it. Okay, reel it in." He took one step back, letting Brooke take control.

She spun the wheel, feeling the weight of the fish pull back. She wasn't sure if she should tug on the pole or let the line do the job, but thankfully, with Caleb behind her holding onto the handle, he helped guide her in, pulling up, holding some force against the massively strong fish.

"What did you catch?" he asked. "This guy is heavy!"

The water started to splash, louder than Caleb's fish had, and when the fish appeared on the surface, Brooke jumped with glee.

"I caught a fish!" she exclaimed.

Caleb bent down and began to unhook the fish. "This is a keeper, one to eat." He held the fish in his hands. "Here, come close to the light. Do you have your phone?"

"Always," Brooke responded. She reached in her back pocket with her free hand and pulled her phone out, opening the camera and handing it over to Caleb.

"Kneel down, let's take a picture of this." He took the phone and handed Brooke her fish.

She reluctantly took it and made a face. "It's slimy." She grimaced.

He pointed the phone at her, kneeling down next to the small lantern, aiming the camera at her with the giant fish in her hands. She smiled and waited for him to take the picture. After a few camera sounds were made, Caleb looked at the photo and then held it out for Brooke, who still held onto the fish. She looked from the phone to the fish, trying to figure out how she could successfully take her phone without getting fish slime all over it. Finally, Caleb chuckled and shoved it in her coat pocket for her.

"You gonna name it?" he asked, pushing her phone down one last shove.

"It is dead? Are we gonna eat it?" she asked. "Because if we are going to eat it, I'm not going to name it."

Caleb laughed. "I'll take it home and see if it's worth eating." He took the fish from her, which wasn't floppy anymore and was most likely dead. "It liked your cricket."

Brooke smiled, looking at the dead fish in Caleb's hand, then glanced back up at him. "I caught a fish."

"That you did. Congrats." Caleb set the fish on the ground next to his tackle box, dusted his hands off on his pants, and then picked his pole up. "Bait up again. Let's catch some more!" He smiled.

Brooke smiled and bent down to bait up her line from his tackle box, letting Caleb touch the cricket to stab to the hook. She wasn't expecting to fish, yet here she was, not wanting the time to end.

After Brooke had caught and named four fish, proud to admit it was two more than Caleb, she laid in her bed in the lodge, thumbing through the many pictures she had taken that day with Caleb. It was hard to believe that the tour and her fishing adventure were the same day. Her gallery went from the beautiful mountains, the mill, and the town, to the dark lantern-lit photos from the lake. She had snapped a few of Caleb as he casted his line or stood, waiting patiently for a tug. Her face holding her lifeless first catch was pure joy. Her smile was wide, and the lantern's shadow hit her in the right place.

If only she had a connection, she could post it to her Instagram. *Maybe tomorrow*, she thought, *at the touring company. With Caleb...*

Ten

-Tuesday-

The sun crept through the windows of the office, hitting Caleb with blinding light. His nightly fishing trip with Brooke had made it so he missed chances at the lake this morning, but after the day he experienced, ignoring everything to do with the company, he decided to spend his morning looking at the finances—trying to find a way to make the mortgage.

The numbers were starting to scare him. He didn't know if there was a way out…a way to save everything.

"Okay," he muttered under his breath, "if I put a Jeep up for sale…" He turned to the computer, figuring out how much he could sell a Jeep for. After seeing the number, he groaned. "I wouldn't be able to book as many trips and still lose money." He rubbed his forehead, trying to make a dollar amount appear magically.

It wasn't that the company was hard to run. It didn't cost that much in reality. Gas for the Jeeps, his mortgage of the property, and supplies. Twice a year, he sent the Jeeps in for maintenance and oil changes, keeping them safe and running smoothly, but other than that, it wasn't hard to turn a profit. The business started to go downhill once the tourists stopped coming. Once the pandemic shut down the entire world, they took a hit, and now that it wasn't labeled a pandemic anymore, he was having a hard time bouncing back. There was only so much that brochures and pamphlets could do for a business. He needed to do something else. He just didn't know what.

Ethan had moved to Carbondale a few months prior but continued to commute into Marble every morning, normally arriving after Caleb returned from the lake. He was just as committed to saving the place as Caleb was but had zero input to put forth. They were both fresh out of ideas.

Caleb heard the front door unlock and looked up just in time to see Ethan saunter in as if on cue. "Good morning!" he exclaimed. "How was the lake last night?"

Caleb heaved a sigh, half wishing he could return to the lake with Brooke instead of trying to make money magically appear. "It was great. I have some fish in the kitchen we need to clean up and see if we can filet. Brooke caught them."

"*Brooke caught them*," Ethan repeated.

"Yep, Brooke caught them." He turned to Ethan, who was staring at him with one eyebrow raised. He didn't respond. He rolled his eyes and turned back to the computer.

"Any bookings today?" Ethan asked, even though he knew the answer.

Caleb groaned. "What do you think?" he answered bluntly. When Ethan didn't respond, Caleb continued. "I was looking at selling a Jeep."

Ethan snapped his head in Caleb's direction. "We can't sell a Jeep. We need the three."

"There's only two of us."

"But we need the three if one is being serviced, and we should probably look into getting them serviced soon because they have been sitting for weeks." Ethan gestured his entire arm toward the window, making Caleb turn to look at the Jeeps, sitting silently by the side of the house.

Caleb shook his head and closed his eyes, trying to force the stress out. "I'm worried I won't make the mortgage next month," Caleb finally muttered.

There was a light knock on the glass of the front door, catching both Caleb and Ethan's attention. Brooke stood at the door, her laptop case in hand. She smiled at Caleb and waved. Caleb gave her a light smile and then gestured for her to come in. She opened the door and slowly closed it behind her, trying to avoid the loud, classic rattle of the metal door frame.

"Good morning," she spoke softly.

"Morning, Brooke." Caleb smiled at her, placing his hand on Ethan's shoulder. "This is Ethan. He works with me."

"Hello." Brooke waved. "I'm Brooke."

"Oh, I know." Ethan smiled. "Good morning."

Brooke lowered her brow and then turned to Ethan. "I was hoping to use the wi-fi? I want to post some photos from last night, and maybe check my email."

Caleb's smile grew. "Yeah, of course. Let me get you the name and password." He rummaged through the drawer under the computer screen, grabbing the scrap piece of paper with the information Brooke would need. He walked over to her and handed her the paper. His fingers lightly brushed against hers as she took it from him. Caleb took a deep breath, trying to ignore the touch. "Make yourself comfortable."

Brooke set her laptop down on the small table that sat in front of the window, photos of the Crystal mill and town surrounding her. Caleb left her and walked back to Ethan. They had to finish their conversation, but he wasn't sure if he could with Brooke there. He made mention in passing that he hadn't taken a tour in a while, but since Brooke hasn't mentioned it again, he figured she hadn't heard.

He looked at Ethan and inhaled. Ethan's eyes went from Brooke back to Caleb.

"Anyway," he said, trying to get Caleb's attention back to him, "can we talk about the mortgage..."

Caleb lightly shook his head.

"I know you don't want to talk about it with her here," Ethan whispered, leaning toward Caleb over the counter. "But this is something that will not only impact you and me, but the town. So we need to figure out what to do."

Caleb glanced behind Ethan at Brooke, who had already connected to the internet and was looking at an email. Once her fingers began to type quickly, he looked back to the books.

"Okay, well, I'm not worried about this month, but since we have had absolutely no income this month whatsoever, I'm nervous for October. I may have to dip into savings, but that means you wouldn't get a paycheck." He looked back to Ethan. "Not even half a paycheck like you got this month. I won't be able to pay you a cent."

Ethan shrugged. "I have emergency savings. I can survive a month."

"And what happens if we don't have any reservation next month, and the month after that? If I sell a Jeep, we can lighten the load, but we will have cash for a few months for supplies, payroll, and mortgage." Caleb groaned, turning the finance book toward Ethan. He looked at it and turned a few pages.

Brooke's typing stopped. Caleb was all too aware of the silence. He desperately wanted to pause the conversation.

"We can print more—" Ethan began.

Caleb shook his head, stopping Ethan before his thought rambled on more. "Pamphlets only get you so far. You saw what happened yesterday. I left them in the car."

Brooke took a deep breath, typed a few keys, then grew silent again. Just having her in the room was distracting to Caleb. He glanced up at her, then back to Ethan.

Ethan was locked on the finance books, a spreadsheet they had both looked at numerous times before. He flipped a few pages, then sighed. "Maybe…" He sighed. "We sell a Jeep," he finally said, his tone broken, full of defeat.

Caleb looked over at Brooke, who seemed to be focused on her computer and not their conversation.

"Maybe." Caleb groaned. "I really don't want to, but we are going to have to figure out something before it gets too late." Caleb rubbed his eyes, the tension headache hitting like a rock. He needed something to get his mind off this, but at the same time, he needed to keep his mind *on* it. He dropped his hands and heaved a sighed, locking eyes with Ethan.

Ethan shrugged. "I'm going to go look at the Jeeps, figure out which one we can let go of. I think Ole' Red needs an oil change anyway. Maybe I'll take her into Carbondale…"

"We have maintenance fees this month. That's fine," Caleb interrupted, keeping his voice low.

Ethan nodded and took a deep breath. "Okay." He turned to the pegboard wall and grabbed the key with the red keychain. Walking out to the front door, he passed Brooke, who was still typing furiously on her laptop. "Nice to meet you, Brooke. I hope to see you again."

Brooke stopped and looked up at Ethan. "Nice to meet you too." She smiled, seemingly completely unaware of the awkwardness that filled the room moments before.

Caleb watched as Ethan made his way over to the Jeeps. Closing the finance books, he went to join Brooke at the small table.

"Do you want some coffee?" he asked, leaning on the second chair. "I can make a fresh pot if you'd like?"

Brooke smiled up at him. "I'd love some." Her voice was soft and kind. The sparkle in her eye was just as inviting. "I already had maybe seven cups at the lodge, but what's one more?" Brooke laughed.

Caleb shook his head. "I hope you like dark roast. I might have some creamer..."

"That sounds great."

"You got it." He turned and left the main office, going into the kitchen to prep the coffee pot.

He grabbed the carafe and dumped the coffee from the morning down the drain, filling it with fresh water. Checking the fridge, he smirked when he saw the creamer on the shelf.

"Thank you, Ethan," he mumbled, knowing it was Ethan who'd placed it there. Caleb liked his coffee bitter. Ethan had a different taste, thanks to his wife.

He placed the creamer on the counter and looked out the window above the sink, where Ethan could be seen clearly. He was hunched over, his torso in the Jeep, his arms pulling all the blankets and water bottles from the back.

Caleb watched him for a moment, trying to think of ways he could make the mortgage and not sell anything that belonged to the company. Either way, he would lose. He would lose his job, his home, and his friend. Losing Ethan would be the worst part of it all. Ethan was there when he first came to Marble, getting him to the job in the first place. He knew Ethan and his wife, Meredith, were talking about starting a family, and if the company went under, Ethan would lose the opportunity to become a father. If it wasn't for Ethan, he wouldn't have any of this, and there he was, emptying out a Jeep, thinking about selling it.

If it came to selling more than a Jeep, Caleb might move to Carbondale, work as a tour guide for a company there—or maybe return to Chicago. He scoffed at the thought. That was *not* an option. Colorado had become Caleb's home in the three years he had lived here, and he wasn't about to return to the city.

Filling the filter with grounds, he pressed *brew* and leaned against the counter, folding his arms. What the hell was he going to do?

Drip...drip...drip.

The bubbling sounds from the coffee maker caught his attention, pulling him from the company to Brooke in the lobby. She had certainly been a breath of fresh air, reminding him that other women lived in the world, and that he was still attracted to them. He tried to guess how she would like her coffee. Would she prefer a small dainty cup, or would she rather a large cup o' joe? He leaned toward the latter and grabbed two large porcelain mugs with the company's logo on them.

"Pitch black coffee," he exclaimed, coming from the kitchen with the two mugs in hand, the creamer tucked under his arm. "I do have cream and sugar if I made it too dark for your taste." He set his mug down in front of Brooke, who was staring intently at her computer screen. "Something interesting happen in the ten minutes I was away?" he asked, watching her expression carefully, setting the creamer next to her mug.

Brooke sighed. "My agent is getting a little restless. My deadline is coming up."

"And still no story." Caleb sipped his coffee.

Brooke gripped her mug and pulled it to her lips. Sipping gently, she shook her head. "No, I have a story now. I just have to email her the premise behind it." Her faced winced and she reached for the creamer, adding a small amount to her mug.

"Do you need someone to try your idea on?" Caleb wiggled his eyebrows up and down and he took another sip.

Brooke looked at him with narrow eyes. "Promise you won't get mad?"

"Why would I get mad?" he asked, now even more curious to know what the woman he just met could have done to make him mad.

She ran her palms through her hair, pulling it tight to her head before resting her hands behind her head. "Well, because you're kind of in it."

He widened his eyes. "Me? I'm in your book?"

Eleven

Brooke pursed her lips and nodded. She wasn't sure if she wanted to tell Caleb the fact that he would make an appearance in her new novel, but before she knew it, she was word vomiting and now she had to find a way to explain herself. She had tried to keep herself distracted while Ethan and Caleb talked about the company and possible selling of a Jeep, but eavesdropping was inevitable, until she received the email from her agent.

She read it over a few times while Caleb was making the coffee, and she could hear her agent's high-pitched tone, getting rather annoyed that there was no manuscript for *Winter's Edge 2* currently sitting on her desk. She tried to start the email of the new idea by focusing on the town of Crystal, but she wasn't sure how to even begin. Her first novel was already written when she was picked up by a publishing agency, but this was new ground.

Maybe getting it all out with Caleb could be a way to help her do a quick outline, at least get a base line down before she presented it to her agent. But then the idea of getting it all out in the open seemed to close her off. Caleb's open jaw and wide eyes made her want to push back and forget she said anything.

She looked at Caleb's expression, pursing her lips; she nodded. *Just...talk...Brooke.* "Please don't be mad. Just watching you fish gave me an idea to have a fisherman, and then, it just kind of happened. Then you took me to Crystal yesterday and I got this idea, and the fisherman is the main character and he's based on you. Please don't be mad," Brooke rambled. She was filling the silence, and Caleb just stared at her, his eyes wider. "Please say something," she ended, out of breath.

He raised his eyebrows and gave her a crooked grin. "Okay," he said. "Well, I'm glad I could be your inspiration." His smile grew. "How did you describe me?" He leaned his elbow on the table, his fingers close to hers.

"I haven't yet, all I have is a fisherman at the lake in the morning."

"You wrote that yesterday, didn't you?" Caleb asked. "You weren't describing the lake." He narrowed his eyes, his smile turning into a smirk.

She shook her head. "No, I was describing the lake. The fisherman came before the tour."

He leaned back in his chair and folded his arms, the same snarky grin on his face. Brooke wished she knew him better. Did he like this idea, or was he irritated by the fact that she had used him for her own gain? She wished she could read him, but alas, she hadn't even known him a total of forty-eight hours yet.

"You're mad, aren't you? I can change it—" she began quickly, turning to her computer to open the document.

"No, no, keep it. In fact, I insist I be in your book. But now"—he raised a finger at her—"I would like to know what you're thinking."

She licked her lips and moved in her chair, closing her computer, thinking of the right way to pitch her novel to a non-reader. "Okay," she began, inhaling as much air as she could, "I want it to be set in the late 1800's, possibly when Crystal was at its peak. The fisherman who still doesn't have a name—"

"Caleb is a popular name," he interrupted, slight sarcasm in his voice, bringing his mug to his lips.

Brooke tilted her head and squinted at him. His light tone and demeanor actually helped. "He has no name yet…" she reiterated. "He's my main character. I'm thinking he can live in Crystal and work at the mine or mill. One day, he meets a woman who is in trouble, hiding from something. He is willing to hide her and protect her from whatever it is, and they fall in love." She sat back in the chair, raising her hands up to signal the end of her pitch, before clapping them together and laying them on her lap.

Caleb stared at her with an expression she again couldn't read. He had one eyebrow raised, his arms still folded and lips tight. Brooke furrowed her brow and waited, very impatiently.

"You gotta say something," she begged, leaning forward.

Caleb shrugged. "I mean, it sounds like a love story." He leaned forward, reaching for his coffee mug. "I'm sure women will eat it up." He took a drink.

Brooke shrugged. "It sounds stupid, doesn't it?"

He shrugged again. "I'm honestly not one to judge. I don't read much."

Brooke's hands hit the table. "Well, you're no help." She groaned. "This is why I prefer email," she mumbled.

Caleb looked over the rim of his cup and out the window. What was going on in his head? Why did he have to be so damn mysterious?

He set his now empty mug down on the counter. "What time is it?"

She looked at the clock behind Caleb. "It's 10:15."

He stood. "Alright, come with me. I have the perfect person who can help you." He moved quickly, going behind the counter to grab a Jeep key. "Come on, let's go." He motioned to her again.

Brooke swiftly put her laptop in its case and followed him. Caleb held the door open for her and then jogged over to the same

Jeep they adventured in yesterday. Ethan poked his head out from the hatch and watched as Caleb jumped in the driver's seat.

"Where are you two headed?" Ethan asked as Brooke went around to the passenger side door.

"I'm taking Brooke to the general store. Do you need anything?" Caleb asked.

Ethan shook his head. "Nah, thanks though. I'm taking Ole' Red to Carbondale." He waved at them, holding a rag in his hands.

Caleb waved back as Brooke buckled up. She watched as he shifted the Jeep and left the parking lot.

"The general store?" she repeated. "We left in such a rush to go to the general store?"

"Rosie is only there in the mornings, then Sean takes over."

"And why are we going to see Rosie?" Brooke asked.

"Because she's a reader and one of the sweetest ladies I know, so she can help you."

Brooke widened her eyes and forced back a cough. "Caleb, I don't know if you got this feeling, but I don't really talk about my books to...people."

"But you need advice, right?"

Brooke nodded, keeping her voice silent.

"And I guarantee you Rosie can help with that or at least tell you if it's something she will read." Caleb turned the wheel, heading down the dirt path, and before she knew it, they were parked in front of a small log building. Caleb jumped out and came around to the passenger door, opening it and holding his hand out for Brooke. "Come on, it's going to be fine."

Brooked looked at his hand and then at the small wood building in front of them. Hiding her fears, she took his hand and followed him up the steps to the store's entrance.

Brooke felt as if she stepped through time. There were a few tables set up with books and small art pieces. Shelves surrounded the walls and created aisles, filled with goods from toilet paper to Ritz crackers. A counter stretched out in front of the back wall, in front of more shelves that held all kinds of medicines. A shorter, dark-haired woman sat behind the counter, a book laid out in front of her.

"Good morning, Rosie," Caleb exclaimed.

Rosie looked up, and a smile grew on her face, one that radiated and would brighten up any room. "Caleb, sweetie. We don't have an order for you." She kept her smile as she closed her book and pushed it to the side.

Brooke slowed her stride behind Caleb, taking in the store. She looked at all the books on the table, ranging from the history of Marble to a few fiction titles. The art pieces were done by locals in town, mostly all landscapes, but one oil painting of the mill caught Brooke's attention. That one may be going home with her.

"Nope, no order. I have someone I need you to talk to," Caleb said in the background. Brooke snapped her attention back to him and slowly walked over the counter, putting on a smile. "This is Brooke Easten. She's an author from Utah, and she's here on a retreat. She needed input and has told me I am no help."

"Well." Rosie sighed, clasping her hands together and placing them on the counter in front of her. "That's because in the three years I've known you Caleb, I've never seen you pick up a book." She smirked at him. Brooke could see they clearly saw each other as close friends, maybe a grandmother figure? She grinned at the interaction between them.

Caleb shook his head and chuckled. "It takes up too much time, anyway." He turned to Brooke, placing his hand on her back and gently pushing her forward. "Brooke has an idea for her new novel, and before she sends it off to her *very* demanding agent, she needs someone to bounce the idea off of. Would you mind talking to her?"

Brooke's body language suddenly became very tense. She stood up straight and gently placed her hands together in front of her. She hadn't been this nervous since meeting with her agent for the first time, and this was just a woman who lived in a remote mountain town. Why did the thought of talking to Rosie make her so nervous? She glanced at Caleb, who was looking down at her, his eyebrows raised and his eyes beaming.

"I would be happy too!" Rosie exclaimed. "I am the most avid reader in town. I've read so many books…" she trailed off. "I could turn this place into a library if I wanted to with my collection. I'd be so honored to help an author." Rosie turned towards Brooke, wide eyes and excitement sprawling all over her face.

Brooke beamed back. "Thank you. It would really help. As Caleb said, my agent has been really demanding." She breathed in, calming her nerves. "It's only a rough idea of what could be."

"Well let's hear it." Rosie waved her hands forward in a "give it to me" motion.

Brooke's smile widened, and suddenly, all her nerves were gone. She was able to blurb out details to Rosie that she didn't have when she was talking to Caleb just fifteen minutes ago. She spoke about the town and lake, her fisherman, and the woman in need. She reiterated several times it was a work in progress and details needed to be shaved through, but the expression on Rosie's face turned into excitement as Brooke's vision came to life. More and more of her missing plot was emerging as she spoke, bringing it all together. She only hoped she could remember it all once she got back to the lodge. Also, she tried to make a mental note to ask Rosie for her phone number so she could bounce ideas off her all the time.

After Brooke thought her vision was translated correctly, she took a deep breath and placed her hands on the counter in front of Rosie. She sighed and watched both Caleb and Rosie for their reactions.

"This isn't a simple romance novel you're thinking about writing." Rosie smiled. "I will tell you this, if this book truly is your next project and it does sell, I will carry it here. I must. It will hold a story of the town's past."

Brooke smiled. "Do you really think so? It doesn't sound overdone?" She looked at Caleb. His eyes were wide, and his eyebrows were raised.

"There's more history and love in that little blurb than I've heard in a long time. It would definitely be meaningful to not only you, but to Colorado. This book needs to be written." Rosie widened her eyes and locked gazes with Brooke, telling Brooke she was serious and truthful in her words. Brooke began to get more excited, suddenly very thankful that Caleb brought her here.

"You didn't explain it like that twenty minutes ago." He murmured. "I may even read this book."

"You're just saying that to make me feel good about it." Brooke groaned.

Caleb smirked. "Maybe, but I fully support this idea. It has movie potential."

Brooke side-eyed him, a small tug in her lips, before turning back to Rosie.

"Honey," Rosie said gently, "I think you could make this something amazing. I've never read your work but just the love and passion you had, bringing out little details. Now, give the fisherman a name, and give that woman a tragic story, one that the fisherman can mend."

Brooke felt her cheeks grow red. Smiling, she looked back up at Caleb. "Thank you, Rosie. That means a lot. It really does."

Rosie winked at her. "Anytime, dear. In fact…" She pushed herself off the counter and opened a drawer under an old register. Pulling out a worn-out business card, she handed it to Brooke. *Marble General Store, Rosie and Sean…* Down below, the phone number. "You can call the store anytime and just ask for me. I'd be happy to hear from you and talk about your books."

Brooke held the business card to her chest, as if it would disappear if she let it go. "Thank you, so much."

Rosie wiggled her eyebrows. "Anytime. Now"—her tone changed as she turned back to Caleb—"why don't you have an order this week?"

Brooke tuned them out, full of the adrenaline that was writing for her. Coming up with a new idea and having it come to fruition.

She held back tears of joy…or maybe tears of relief. She could email her agent with an idea.

Twelve

They returned to the touring company, Brooke's legs shaking up and down as Caleb drove the three minutes back. He watched from the corner of his eye as she looked out the window at the scenery, taking in deep breaths. He suddenly wished he knew her well enough to read her mind. He could always tell what was happening in Audrey's mind. Her facial expressions and body language gave everything away. One look at Audrey, and Caleb would have her figured out with a snap of his fingers. Brooke wasn't as clear.

Brooke would shift in her seat, purse her lips, and then form a soft, sweet smile. She would look from her feet to the window, every now and then glancing at Caleb. He couldn't tell if she was still nervous, or if a weight had been lifted from her shoulders.

"Did that help?" he asked as they climbed out of the Jeep.

"More than you know," Brooke exclaimed, rubbing her palms on her thighs. "Can I use the wi-fi one more time to send a quick email? Then I will be out of your hair, I promise."

Caleb opened the door for her, taking her hand once again helping her step from the Jeep. "You don't have to rush out. You're welcome to stay as long as you'd like." He held onto her hand, lingering in the spark.

Brooke smiled at him, like she felt the same spark, and his cheeks warmed. He shook his head. He didn't blush. He never blushed. Not since Audrey.

"I really appreciate it, but I probably should go back to the lodge. I haven't spent hardly any time there." She pulled her laptop from the case and sat at the table. "Frank and Melinda are probably never going to invite me to another one, and Greg has been on my case constantly."

"You were invited?" Caleb asked, sitting down next to her. Maybe if he kept the conversation going, she would stay a little longer. He watched as she turned the laptop on and ran her fingers against the silver keyboard. He wanted her to stay. He wanted her to talk with him. He wanted her. "And who's Greg?"

Brooke shook her head, looking up at him, locking eyes. "Oh, no. I paid a pretty penny to be here. We all did. Greg is another writer who has been pestering me about *not* writing. I haven't even seen him leave the lodge." She paused as her computer booted up. "Do Frank and Melinda live here?"

Caleb leaned forward, breaking eye contact with her. "No, they rent out the lodge, and you pay them, I'm assuming. And Greg— why is it bothering you that he's 'pestering' you?"

Brooke tilted her head. "Because I paid my own way to come, so did he. We're adults. It's not like we are being babysat and graded on our screen time."

"Greg has no say in what you do, so stop letting his comments bother you so much."

Brooke narrowed her eyebrows and shot Caleb a look. "Easier said than done," she grumbled. "Okay." She readied her fingers and fidgeted in her chair. "Wish me luck with this email."

"You don't need luck. You got it." Caleb stood. "Rosie even said so." He turned, leaving Brooke at the table to complete her task.

The office phone ringing caught Caleb's attention, pulling him away from the table. The phone had been quiet for so long he had forgotten what it had sounded like. He turned back to Brooke, who was already busy clicking away on her computer. He had thought the answering machine could grab it, then decided it would be best to answer it. Leaving Brooke at the table, he answered the phone, anticipation suddenly weighing on him as he remembered he needed tours. Funny how Brooke made him forget the *small* fact that his business was failing.

"Hello, Marble Touring Company," Caleb answered, reaching for his appointment book, being hopeful.

"Yes, hello," the man on the other line said. "We were interested in hiking to the mill, but someone told us about your touring company. We thought we'd check to see if you have any openings today?"

Caleb's heart lit up. "Yes, yes." *Okay, Caleb. Don't sound too desperate.* "I do have one left actually, at two pm. Would that work for you? It's a three-hour tour and takes you to the Crystal Mill and the town." He grabbed a pencil, circling the two pm line in his agenda.

He heard faint talking on the other line—a woman and a child. Three people. That was three hundred dollars toward the mortgage.

"That could work. Could we give you a call back once we have finalized our plan? We're staying at a KOA, so we should be able to get back to you before one pm."

"Yes of course. We book up pretty quickly, so let me know as soon as you are able." He ruffled through some papers, trying to make it sound like he was quickly trying to find something for his potential client. "The next booking we have isn't until next week," he lied. But that was business, right? He so badly wanted to take this trip.

"Ooh, yeah. Okay, let me talk to the wife and figure out what we can do. If we do, it's two adults and two kids under ten. Do your Jeeps accommodate that?"

Caleb did a celebratory dance in his head. It wasn't three hundred toward the mortgage, but four hundred. "Indeed, they do. And I can throw the family discount on for you, giving you a total of three hundred fifty."

He heard the phone go faint as the price was said amongst the people on the line. When the man finally returned, he said, "Okay, thank you. We will discuss it and give you a call back."

"Perfect, I look forward to hearing from you." Caleb said goodbye and set the phone down. He tried not to get too excited. This, after all, wasn't a sure deal. He glanced up at the clock. It was just past eleven am. He had plenty of time to source up the Jeep and add all the necessary supplies to it.

He looked back to Brooke, who was stretching her neck, her fingers not moving as fast as they once were. She ran her fingers over the mouse pad and tapped on it. Sitting back into her seat, she took a deep sigh.

"Email sent." She took another deep breath, relieving the sigh. "Just in time too. Sounds like you have a tour to give." She shut her computer and slid it in her case. She gave him a sweet smile.

He raised a corner of his lips. "Hopefully. They said they will call back."

"Well, if they need a nudge just give them my number. I can talk them into it." She smiled, standing. Then she shook her head. "Oh yeah, no cell phones here." She waved off her mistake. "Thank you, Caleb, for everything. Maybe I'll see you at the lake tonight."

"I'll be there for sure—more around seven, once it starts to cool down."

Brooke's blonde hair fell over her shoulders as she stood up straight, clutching the computer case to her body. She hesitated. She knew she had to go to the lodge; but she didn't want to leave.

She glanced at the small table once again. She could be productive here. She looked back up at Caleb. "See you tonight then." She turned her back to him, taking one small step toward the front door.

Caleb watched her push the front door, his mind yelling at him to get her to stay, then he decided to go for it. He didn't just want to go to the lake. Maybe Brooke would be up to something else?

"Um, hey," he stammered.

Brooke stopped and turned back, looking at him with wide eyes.

"Are Frank and Melinda feeding you there?"

Brooke chuckled. "No. They are providing food for a farewell BBQ, but other than that, I have PB and J and SpaghettiOs." She slouched.

"Well, would you like to have dinner with me tonight at the Slow Groovin' BBQ? They are the best, and you can't complete your stay in Marble without eating there." The second he asked, he wanted to slap himself. When he first met Audrey, it took him months to ask her out on their first date. And now, here he was asking a girl he had known less than forty-eight hours to dinner. Maybe she wouldn't consider it a date, but then again, maybe she would.

Her smile grew. "I'd love to, actually." She bit her bottom lip. "But I really need to get some work done, and you have a tour to give. What time?"

Caleb mirrored her smile. "I'll pick you up at seven?"

Brooke nodded, her cheeks blushing. "Sounds perfect. See you then." She stumbled out the door and to her car. Caleb watched as she climbed in and looked around, most likely trying to remember her way back to the lodge.

He smiled inside. A possible booking and a possible date in less than fifteen minutes. Even without fishing, today was a good day.

∽

"Guess what!" Caleb exclaimed as Ethan drove back up the driveway. Even though the Jeeps were loud, and the dirt path was crunching underneath the massive tires, Caleb made sure his voice would carry over.

Not long after Brooke had left, the phone call came, confirming a tour group for the mill. Caleb could barely contain his excitement.

"What?" Ethan slammed on the breaks, trying not to run Caleb over. He looked at Caleb through the Jeep's door, brows furrowed.

"We got a tour!" Caleb's smile grew. "Two pm!"

Ethan leapt out of the Jeep. "You're joking."

"Nope."

"Do we really have a booking? How many people?"

"Four. Two adults and two kids. I told them a family discount for three fifty."

Ethan pumped his fist in front of him, "Yes! That's amazing."

"I know, right? Little wins. One booking today means more to come! They were staying at the KOA. They said someone told them about us, word of mouth. We need to take some pamphlets there." Caleb and Ethan went into the building, both buzzed off the news.

"Please tell me I can take them," Ethan begged. "I haven't been to Crystal in a month, and you took that chick yesterday."

"Brooke," Caleb corrected him, irritation quickly covering the glee he felt. He shook his head, pushing aside the new emotion. "and I was thinking you could go. That way you'd actually get to tell your wife you did something besides argue with me all day."

Ethan laughed. "Sounds great. I can get the silver Jeep ready. She's got a full tank of gas, right?"

Caleb nodded. "I filled her after taking Brooke up yesterday. How did Ole' Red's check-up go?"

"She's doing great. She got an oil change and her tires rotated. Mr. Spencer from the dealership made me an offer." He seemed to slip that last little but in nonchalantly, possibly hoping Caleb wouldn't hear it. Caleb definitely heard it.

"Jack made you an offer on the Jeep?" he asked, turning back to Ethan as he approached the counter.

Ethan nodded. "Yeah, we got to talking about how we mentioned possibly selling a Jeep, and he offered me fifteen thousand for Ole' Red. *Cash.*" Ethan raised his eyebrows and stared Caleb down. "I told him it wasn't my decision since Lettie left everything in your name, but that I would talk to you about it."

Caleb looked out the window at the oldest Jeep in the parking lot. "I'll have to think about it. Fifteen K is a lot of money and could possibly get us through the winter months when we have even fewer bookings."

"Less than zero?" Ethan implied.

Caleb shrugged. "I'll have to think about it, but for now..." He rubbed his hands together and looked at the clock. It was one-thirty—only half an hour until the first tour in four weeks. "Let's get that silver Jeep ready."

"You got it, boss."

Forty minutes later, Caleb waved from the porch as Ethan drove off with the family to take them to Crystal. The high of actually getting a reservation was a wonderful feeling, one that Caleb hadn't felt in weeks. He had forgotten the look on the visitors face as they climbed in the Jeeps, ready to go see something incredible. That was the reason he stayed so long and why he agreed to take the business from Lettie.

He turned and looked at the small white building he called work and home. He took a deep breath, taking in the September chill air. This was all he had, all Ethan had, and he didn't want to let it fail. He couldn't let it fail.

Thirteen

Stretching her back and raising her arms over her head, Brooke looked at her computer screen. 5,472 words down in three hours. That was an accomplishment. Once she found her story, she had no trouble getting it all on the page.

Once she got back to the lodge, she found all her fellow writers deep in their computers (or typewriter). She made herself a quick, small sandwich and went to hide in her room. With the lingering knowledge that Caleb was going to take her to dinner later, she ate light, saving room for the BBQ she had been promised was fantastic. With her hydro flask full of water and snacks next to her computer, she typed. And typed. And typed. For three hours.

She checked the small *autosave* in the corner, making sure it had set to "saved," then she shut her computer and stood. Her legs were aching to move. After a few lunges in her room, she was ready to face the others. She grabbed her dishes and opened her door, certain everyone was doing just as great as she was.

She was only half right.

Helen was in the kitchen, a plate in front of her with a half-eaten salad. Greg sat on the corner, his head resting on his arms, his eyes closed. Joyce was at the stove, making herself a small dinner. Rhonda was nowhere to be found.

Brooke stopped and stared at them, trying to read their body language. Who should she dare approach?

"Did everyone have a good day?" She decided to address the crowd, hoping to get some reaction from them.

"Yes," Joyce's soft voice carried through the silent room, "I hit a goal today." She smiled.

"That's awesome." Brooke walked around the abnormally large island and set her dishes in the porcelain sink. "Helen? Greg?"

Helen nodded. "I was able to outline the first few chapters. Greg, on the other hand…" Helen glanced over at Greg, who Brooke couldn't decide if he was sleeping or just resting.

He groaned. "I'm done. I'm not meant to be a writer." He pulled his head up, showing how much exhaustion was on his face. His eyes were surrounded in dark circles, and his normally well-kept hair was ragged and unbrushed. A five o'clock shadow rested on his cheeks and chin. Greg. Looked. Tired.

"It's been twelve years…*twelve years*…and I can't get these damn ideas on the page. How do you do it?" He glanced at all the women in the room with raised eyebrows. "Are men just not allowed to be writers?!" he asked, looking up at the ceiling and raising his fists in frustration.

Helen turned to him and pulled his arms down. "Apparently, you haven't heard of Stephen King, or Tolkien, or Shakespeare, or…"

"Okay, I get it." Greg glared at her. "Those men had talent."

"And so do you," Joyce said, gently setting her plate full of food on the counter and taking her seat next to him. "You just need to find your voice."

Greg's glare was directed toward her. "And how do I do that?" he mumbled.

Brooke looked at her fellow writer. The one who had been so adamant that they were there to write and only write. She had seen him work hard on his computer, never really knowing what he was working on, but writing, nonetheless. When no one answered him, she spoke. "You write."

"I've been writing," he mumbled, dropping his head back on the table. "That's all I've been doing."

"Have you left the lodge at all?" Brooke asked. "Have you even stepped outside? Have you tried to clear your head at all?"

Greg shook his head from side to side, heaving a sigh. He lowered his head and mumbled. "No."

"Even Rhonda has gone out for some fresh air," Helen muttered, and she reached up and patted his back. "Some sunshine will do you good."

"Here's my suggestion." Brooke walked around the island, coming up to Greg's side and wrapping her arm around his shoulders. "Start a fire-pit tonight and make some s'mores and then tomorrow morning, take a walk around the lake. Get out of the lodge."

Greg sat up and turned his gaze to her. "Have you gotten anything done? You've barely been in your room."

Brooke grinned, thinking of her morning with Caleb. The email for her agent and time talking to Rosie. It was the first day she felt like she'd actually gotten work done. "Not that it really matters to you, Greg, but I have, actually. I wouldn't say I'm blocked anymore. I have a storyline, my main characters, and a love story." Her smile widened. "I emailed my agent today, and she wants the first seven-thousand words of a first draft by the end of the week. Fifty-four hundred down."

"You wrote over five-thousand words since you've been back? It's only been three hours." Helen widened her eyes and looked at Brooke.

"Well, yeah." Brooke shrugged. "When you're being pressured by a publisher, you don't stop."

"I wish I was being pressured by a publisher," Greg mumbled. "Maybe I would be able to write if I was."

Brooke hummed. "Trust me, it doesn't help."

"It really doesn't," Joyce reiterated. "It makes it worse,"

"So much worse." Brooke shook her head. "But seriously, take my advice and get out of the lodge. The lake is beautiful. Maybe we can see if Caleb can take us up to the mill again," she thought out loud. Not only would she love to see the inspiration for her novel again, but she wanted to see Caleb more.

"Ah, the fisherman!" Helen sat up straight and gleamed. "You went to his place this morning, didn't you?"

"Well, not his place, his office. I used his wi-fi," she said, brushing off the fact that she went to see Caleb and the wi-fi was just part of the deal.

Greg squinted his eyes. "Gonna see him again?"

Brooke pursed her lips. "Yes, actually," she said softly, releasing her arm from Greg's shoulder and walking back to the sink. "He's picking me up at seven to take me to dinner."

"Like a date?" Helen asked.

Brooke looked up and out the window. She hadn't thought of it like that, but maybe that was the intention. "I doubt it," she brushed it off. "It's just to that barbeque in town."

Helen and Greg raised their eyebrows at the same time. Brooke looked over to Joyce, who calmly ate her food and stayed out of the conversation.

"It's not a date." She raised her tone. "I've known the man for two days."

"Love stories have happened faster," Helen said softly.

"It's not a date," Brooke repeated. She glanced at the clock, noticing it was close to six. "Now, if you'll excuse me, I'm going to go write some more." She turned to leave the kitchen, with every intention of showering and getting ready for dinner. "Leave the lodge, Greg!" she shouted from the hallway, hearing the three of them chuckle as she entered her room, shutting the door loudly behind her.

Brooke's laptop stayed shut the entire time she was getting ready. She showered and curled her blonde hair, applying a thin layer of mascara (just in case it was a date) and, thankfully, she'd packed comfortable but cute clothes for her week. Jeans and a loose cream sweater would do great. Paired with her boots and coat, she would look like she was just hanging out with a friend. Not on a date.

Not a date.

At seven sharp, the red Jeep came barreling up the hill and halted to a stop. She left the room and bounced to the door. Caleb was climbing out of the Jeep as she shut the front screen door behind her. He was dressed in the same outfit as this morning, carpenter jeans and a blue flannel shirt. He at least combed his hair, but his beard was the same scruffy as it was this morning.

"Hey." He smiled. "I was going to knock."

Brooke waved her hand. "No need. My luck, Greg would answer the door and tell you I was too busy writing to go on a *date.*" She uttered the last word a little too casually. Maybe he didn't notice. She climbed in the passenger side and waited for him to get in. "I did get a lot of work done today, so thank you for that." She smiled at him.

"You're welcome. I don't know why you're thanking me, but you're welcome."

"Five thousand words deserves a thank you."

Caleb shifted the Jeep and turned the wheel down the hill, mouthing the words *five thousand.* "You really wrote that much since you left my place?"

Brooke nodded. "Well, yeah…I'm a writer. It's kinda my job."

Caleb shook his head, a small chuckle filling the air. "Then I'm very glad you got things done, breaking through the writer's block you had literally yesterday."

"Once again, thanks to you and the mill and the town. Oh, and Rosie."

Slow Groovin' BBQ appeared out of nowhere once they crossed the small bridge. The lights were lit, not too much to ruin the night sky of Marble, but enough that people who were brave enough to eat outside could see their food. She could smell the meats from the smokers that sat in the grass outside the building. The smoke filled the air, and so did the scents. Turkey, pork, and beef could be taken in from miles away if you focused for long enough.

"It smells good already," Brooke said, leaning forward to look at the restaurant.

"I hope you're not a vegetarian because you would be eating bread, and that's it," Caleb joked.

Brooke shook her head. "Oh no, not a vegetarian. One of my good friends is. She would hate this place."

Caleb laughed. "I guarantee you will love it."

They parked and walked inside. Brooke took in the building while Caleb waved and said hello to everyone in the place. Once Brooke had a menu in her hand, she was wide-eyed.

"Any suggestions?" she asked, leaning over the table to Caleb.

"We will have to start with the mac and cheese, maybe a salad too; and we are definitely getting a barbeque platter."

Brooke raised her eyebrows. "That all sounds great." She put her menu down, trusting him.

"What do you want to drink? They have a decent tap selection."

"No." Brooke shook her head. "I don't drink. I'll just have Dr. Pepper, if they have it." She smiled.

Caleb wiggled his eyebrows. "They do."

Not long after they sat, a server came to take their order. Caleb already had his drink in hand and gave the server their order before handing back the menus.

"What do you think?" Caleb asked as Brooke looked around the building. The ambiance was perfect, with dim lighting and country music playing in the background. It was small, but enough to gain the attention Caleb said it so deserved.

"It's cute." Brooke smiled.

"*Cute,*" Caleb repeated. "Just wait till you try the food. It won't be *cute* anymore."

Brooke's Dr. Pepper was placed in front of her. She reached for it and took a sip through the straw. Even the Dr. Pepper tasted better than normal. She hummed. "Well, they did the soda right."

Caleb chuckled. "And the beer." He held up his glass before taking a drink.

Brooke quickly looked down, so as not to be caught staring. She licked her lips and took another drink of her Dr. Pepper.

This is going to be an interesting night.

Fourteen

Once the appetizers arrived, Caleb watched for Brooke's reaction. Slow Groovin' BBQ was possibly his favorite place in the state of Colorado to eat, and not just because it was the only place in Marble to eat. When he first moved, he frequented Slow Groovin' at least once a week, but it had dwindled down to once a month during their busy seasons. Ethan would come down for lunch some days, and bring Caleb back food left from his platter, but coming to enjoy the restaurant and the employees was a different experience. Sometimes takeout just didn't cut it.

Watching Brooke as she bit into her mac and cheese was the icing on top of the already amazing day he'd had. He could see the euphoria on her face as her eyes closed and hummed.

"Okay," she mumbled, "this is amazing." She pointed her fork at the bowl while glancing at Caleb through her eyelashes.

Caleb took a bite. "Told you."

She tilted her head and gave him a side eye. Caleb lifted his mug and took a drink, watching her intently. What did he do in this situation? His first date with Audrey had been years ago, and he had pretty much forgotten how to act. Besides, was this even a date? He thought it was, but did she? Caleb poked at his salad, trying to figure out what to say, if anything, next. His light mood suddenly turned into anxiety. He had no reason to be nervous, yet here he was, his palms starting to get sweaty and his breath picking up. He pursed his lips and set down his fork. Brooke ate in the silence, enjoying her meal, seemingly unaware of his mild anxiety attack happening right before her.

He heaved a long, shaky sigh. "I'm sorry," he muttered.

Brooke looked from side to side. "For what?" she asked, confusion sweeping over her.

"I don't do this often, so I'm sorry for wasting your time." He leaned back in his chair, almost as if he were trying to get away from her.

Her eyebrows furrowed and the look of confusion that swept across her face only deepened.

"Don't do what often? Eat?" Brooke asked jokingly, trying to lighten the now tense mood, stabbing more noodles with her fork.

"Ask beautiful women out on dates," Caleb muttered.

She coughed, trying not to choke on her mac and cheese, and looked at Caleb. "I wasn't sure that's what this was."

Caleb shrugged. "I meant it to be, well; I hoped it would be. I've been enjoying spending time with you, and I wanted to...I don't know what I wanted."

"I've been enjoying the time with you too, Caleb. I wouldn't have agreed to come here if I didn't. But it wasn't really clear what this was." She set her fork down. "So it's a date?" She placed her hands on her lap, seeming impatient as she waited for his answer.

Caleb looked up at her, his nerves beginning to fall away as he locked her gaze. "Do you want it to be a date?"

Brooke picked her fork back up. "I would love it to be a date."

Caleb smiled. "Then it's a date." Every muscle in his body relaxed. He was on his first date in *years*. He sighed, leaning forward on the table with his elbows, grabbing his fork and stabbing his salad. *Now don't mess it up,* he thought to himself. He shook his head and chuckled. "I still don't know what to do." He laughed.

Brooke smiled. "Well, we talk. We get to know each other. When was your last date?"

"Audrey," he said simply. "When was yours?" Then it hit him. For all he knew she had a boyfriend back in Salt Lake City. He froze and waited for her response.

"Maybe six months ago. Obviously, it didn't work out." Brooke groaned.

The server came back and placed a large wooden platter in front of them, carrying the three different smoked meats they had chosen to share. Brooke took it in with wide eyes. Caleb smiled, once again waiting for her reaction.

"Oh. My. Food!" she exclaimed, pulling her side plate toward her, grabbing her fork and picking out a few slices of meat. Caleb mimicked, trying to pull his focus to what meats he was placing on his plate, failing miserably as he gleefully watched Brooke.

"So no boyfriend in Salt Lake. You live alone with a cat…"

"I never told you I had a cat." Brooke looked at him with a smirk on her face.

Caleb took a sharp breath and said sheepishly, "I may have looked up your bio on Amazon." He moved his dinner around on the plate.

Brooke's smirk grew, and she giggled. "Yes, my cat. Her name is Margie, and she's a brat." Brooke took a bite and smiled. "My turn to ask you a question."

"I didn't really have a question…" Caleb began.

Brooke hummed and pointed her fork at him. "My turn."

He shook his head. "Ask away."

"You're from Chicago. What did you do before you became an expert fisherman?"

"I was in law school. I worked at a firm, and I wanted to be made a partner."

"Chicago and a lawyer? You are like a secret agent, living double lives," Brooke exclaimed.

Caleb grabbed his mug and took a long drink. "How do you figure that?"

"I honestly can't see you as anything but a flannel-wearing, scruffy-looking fisherman."

"Flannel-wearing?" He looked down at his blue flannel shirt. "Scruffy-looking?" He touched his beard, which he had trimmed specifically for tonight. "I won't deny the fisherman part, but I didn't suddenly become an expert. I fished in Chicago. When people think of Chicago, they think of the big city. I was from the suburbs. My life used to be a lot different before I moved here."

"What made you want to go to law school?"

"Actually," he said, leaning back into the chair, wondering if it would be acceptable to pick meat from his teeth with a toothpick on a date. "I wanted to go into politics."

Brooke scrunched her nose.

"I know, I know. Yet again, a secret agent. I much prefer my life here in Marble."

"I can believe that. It's beautiful here." She beamed. "There isn't really any politics here."

"Oh, there is, but it hides. Now it's my turn for a question." He squinted his eyes at her.

"I wasn't done with my question." Brooke widened her eyes and smirked at him.

"Too late." He smiled back. "What made you want to be an author?"

"I just like telling stories. In high school, I submitted a few poems to the school newspaper, and it became a weekly thing. Soon, it evolved into a short story, and then before I knew it, it became *Winter's Edge*." Brooke took a bite of the chicken that had been calling out to her. She moaned in delight. "Oh, that's so good."

Caleb laughed at her reaction, raising his eyebrows at her moan. "I'm glad you like it." He grabbed a piece of pork from the platter and a roll, setting them on his side plate. "That's your famous almost-made-into-a-movie book, huh?"

She nodded, licking the sauce from her fingers. "Yeah, but I'm not too sure on that yet. It's my thing, you know? Those characters mean so much to me. I don't want to murder them by having someone change the entire premise of the story."

"Your Amazon bio said that was your goal, to see you work on the screen."

Brooke glared up at him. "It's different now that it's happening."

Caleb chewed on the tender pork, trying to chew as fast as possible to respond. "Okay, okay...makes sense. Your turn," he mumbled, nodding his chin toward her.

Brooke thought. "Okay, what kind of movies do you like?"

"Movies?" Caleb thought. "I don't really watch movies, but if I had to choose a favorite..." He narrowed his eyes trying to think about the last movie he saw. It had been years since he watched a movie.

"If you say *The Godfather*..."

"Not that. I've never actually seen that one."

"*Die Hard?*"

He shook his head, still thinking of a movie he'd enjoyed. "Oh"—he snapped his fingers and pointed—"*Hitchhiker's Guide to the Galaxy*."

Brooke gasped. "I love that movie!" she screamed. "Not many people like that movie."

Caleb widened his eyes. "Seriously?"

She nodded quickly. "It's one of the best movies. Please tell me you own it, and we can watch it before I leave. I haven't seen that in years!"

"I think I do. My entertainment setup isn't all that amazing though..."

"As long as you have a couch and a TV, I'm game!"

He smiled. Another possible date with Brooke. "Okay, it's a date."

Brooke smiled and locked his gaze. *Another date.* "Your turn."

Caleb thought. "Um…" How hard could it be to come up with questions to get to know her? "Would you want to live in Salt Lake forever?"

Brooke shook her head. "No, but I don't really have anywhere else to go. I just bought my studio, and Margie is…like I said, a brat." Brooke pulled the bone out of a chicken leg. "I've lived there my entire life. I'd like to try something different. Be brave like you were when you moved here."

"It wasn't an easy move, but a necessary one," Caleb admitted.

"How did you find Marble?" Brooke asked.

"Does that count as your question?"

Brooke nodded, taking a bite of the chicken.

Caleb took a deep breath. "Audrey, actually." He sighed. "When she got sick and decided not to do any kind of treatment, we came here for a small vacation. I fished, and she read and named every fish I caught. We actually hiked up to the mill. She died shortly after we got home." Caleb's tone softened.

Brooke held his gaze. He was ready for a "Oh, Caleb I'm so sorry," but instead, he heard, "That's why you name fish," she said with a smile. "What was she like?" she softly asked.

He chuckled. "Annoying as hell. We bickered a lot. She wanted to be a news anchor, so she was always on her phone. She worked for a small station in Chicago as an assistant and was told that she could possibly go on screen at any minute, so she was always prepared." He smiled, just thinking about her. "She was stubborn. She hated to clean or do any chores. She was terrible at finances…" He looked at Brooke, a soft smile was forming on her lips. "But even though she was all those things, she was perfect. She was my everything."

Brooke reached forward and grasped his hand. "She sounds amazing. Annoying quirks and all."

Caleb moved his fingers, lacing his fingers with hers. Her grasp felt comforting and warm in his hand, a feeling he hadn't had from anyone. He looked at their hands on the table and then at Brooke. Her face, her blue eyes shining behind her glasses, was just as comforting as her hand in his.

"She was, but it's been three years." He rubbed his thumb against the back of her hand. "I do miss her, every day...." Caleb sighed, not letting go of Brooke's hand. "My turn."

Brooke grinned. "Your turn."

"If you weren't an author, what would you be?"

"Caleb!" Both Brooke and Caleb jumped at the loud mention of his name. Ethan suddenly appeared at their table. Caleb had welcomed the tour group back, and once he told Ethan he had planned to take Brooke to dinner, Ethan agreed he'd close down and take any extra calls they may get. Caleb didn't expect to see him here.

"Hey, Ethan..." Caleb groaned. He had the thought he should let go of Brooke's hand, but since she made no movement in doing so, he held on to her grip. "Did something happen?"

Why else would Ethan be here? Caleb tried to keep his expression subtle, but the attempt at a "no death glare" wasn't going over very well. Ethan saw his expression and gave a nervous smile.

Ethan shook his head. "Nope, just wanted to come and let you know we got another call of a possible reservation tomorrow. They weren't sure, but I took down their info and gave them a decent price."

Caleb pursed his lips and nodded. Cursing Ethan, this information could have been saved for the morning. "That's great news."

"More toward the mortgage, right?" Ethan slapped Caleb's back. He turned to Brooke and shrugged. "Sorry to ruin the night. I just had to tell Caleb the good news."

"Not a problem," Brooke replied.

"I'll see you in the morning." Ethan nodded toward Caleb and waved. "So long!"

"Bye...Ethan..." Caleb muttered. "Sorry about that." He turned to Brooke. "That could have waited until morning, but sometimes Ethan doesn't quite understand the timing." He sighed. "Okay, so...if you weren't an author—"

"Caleb, I don't mean to pry but," Brooke asked hesitantly, interrupting him, "is the touring company in trouble?"

Fifteen

Brooke wasn't going to bring up the company. She told herself she wasn't going to ask that when questions began to fly through the table. She was going to keep it light and have a good time with Caleb. She was going to continue to have a good time, and then Ethan had to come in and mention the mortgage.

She heard the conversation in the office this morning, even though she had tried her hardest to focus on her laptop, but they weren't exactly quiet. They had talked about selling a Jeep. Caleb had said he hadn't taken any tours in a while. Life was handing him lemons....

Caleb's expression was solemn. She could tell he didn't want to talk about it, but yet—he answered.

"The pandemic hit us harder than we thought. For a while, we were shut down. No one came to the KOAs or the lodges. It was just everyone in Marble, all two hundred of us. We had savings then. We had means to survive, but we haven't been able to bounce back after that. Even with the lodges opening back up and people venturing out in the world again, we've never made a full recovery."

Caleb paused, taking a deep breath, finally letting go of Brooke's hand, reaching behind his head to rub the nape of his neck. "We are at a loss now that we are running out of our savings. I didn't pay Ethan a full paycheck last month just so I could make the mortgage. He understood but told me he couldn't keep that up. They can't survive on his wives salary alone, as he put it, but then he says it's okay and that he has savings. He doesn't want to give up just yet either." He rolled his eyes. "We don't know what to do anymore."

"What's going to happen?" she asked, not really knowing where to take the conversation.

He shrugged. "I don't want to sell it. Hell, I live there. If I sell, I would need to move, probably away from Marble. And then there is the possibility that whoever is buying it turns it into something else, and there will be no more tours going to the town. The town of Crystal could become a distant memory if that happens." He dropped his hand to his lap, slapping his leg. He reached out for his half-empty glass of beer, trying to keep his hands busy. "I can't let that happen. We talked about selling a Jeep this morning, and we got an offer on one. He offered enough cash that I could at least make the mortgage until spring."

"Do you do tours in the winter?"

"The Jeeps are equipped for it, but it's a rough road. You can imagine no one plows it." He smiled, easing the tension in the air. "It's by special reservation. If we don't get reservations, then we close for the season. We have every year and we were always able to make it, but this year..." He rubbed his forehead, "I have no savings to make it through the season."

Brooke played with her fingers on the table, the half-eaten platter of food in front of her. Her brain began to spin.

"Anyway." Caleb took another deep breath and leaned forward. "It is what it is."

"I hate that saying," Brooke muttered. "It's not always 'it is what it is.'"

"Well, it's better than saying the alternative." Caleb chuckled.

"No, not even that. Situations are always allowed to change," Brooke said softly.

"If you have any ideas as to how I can change it, feel free to share. Ethan and I are at a total loss. We've handed out pamphlets and brochures. We've hung up flyers in Carbondale and Grand Junction. I even thought about getting a billboard up on 1-70, but there aren't many to choose from." He groaned. "Ethan's wife works in a hospital, and she keeps flyers and handouts there."

Brooke furrowed her brow. She sealed her lips tight, hearing the frustration in Caleb's voice. He didn't ask her to dinner to talk business. She needed to change the subject—quickly, before he possibly ended the date early.

Before she could say anything though, Caleb filled the silence. "I believe before we were so rudely interrupted, it was my turn to ask a question."

Brooke met his gaze. She grinned and nodded. "It was. What was your question again?"

∽

The lodge was quiet. It was only past nine, and both the lodges had their lights on. She heard Frank's yappy dog bark as they climbed out of the Jeep. Caleb stuck his hands in his coat pocket and quickly walked around to her, matching his stride with Brooke.

She veered off to the edge of the parking lot, taking in the night view of the lake and mountains. The moon's reflection hit the lake, making it sparkle. Leaning forward on the railing, she took a deep breath. The air was so clean and fresh. Nothing like she would breathe in Salt Lake.

"I love this place," Caleb said softly, walking up behind Brooke.

Brooke turned to look at him as he walked up behind her. "It's beautiful. I can see why you moved here."

Caleb turned to look at her, a grin on his lips. "Thinking about moving?"

Brooke shrugged. "If only I could just pack everything up like you did. Start over." She chuckled at herself. "I don't have anything to start over from. Let's face it, I'd come here to hide from my agent."

Caleb leaned on the railing, his hand out in front of him as his elbows rested on the wood. "Well, then come back to visit at least. When does the retreat end?"

"Sunday night. Check out is Monday morning. I think Frank said we have until ten or so to give the cleaners enough time to clean it up for the next wave of people."

Caleb looked up at Brooke. "So I have you until Sunday." He nodded. "More fishing trips and a movie night."

Brooke smiled down at him. "You fish, I'll write. How does that sound?"

Caleb's eyes locked on hers. "Sounds great and *Hitchhiker's Guide*..."

Brooke turned her body to face him, leaning her hip against the railing. "Definitely *Hitchhiker's Guide*." Her smile grew. "One night, come here, and we can make a fire and have s'mores."

"S'mores?" Caleb asked. "I haven't had a s'more in years, but I make the best one."

"No time like the present to dust off that recipe."

"Let's do it. Right now." Caleb pushed himself off the railing and faced Brooke, only inches apart from her. "Let's go make a fire." He pointed to the fire pit below.

Brooke laughed. "I think everyone in the lodge would kill us if we made it now. You don't know Rhonda."

Caleb tilted his head. "Another night then. We have until Sunday."

Sunday. It seemed so far away, yet so close. Brooke sighed. She came here to write and only write. Her plan had quickly gone down the drain the moment she saw Caleb name that fish.

"I had fun tonight," she said softly.

"Me too," Caleb replied. "Interruption and all, it was great just to spend time with you."

Brooke took a small step forward, closing the gap between them even more. "Are you going to go to the lake tomorrow morning?"

Caleb nodded. "I didn't today, so it's the law I have to tomorrow."

She shook her head. "There's another law that I didn't know about in Marble."

"If you live in Marble, you must fish every day and then name the fish. It's simply the law."

Brooke closed her eyes and shook her head, giving him a silent chuckle. "Well, then I'll see you tomorrow at the lake. I'll bring my laptop."

"I'll bring breakfast and coffee."

She licked her lips. "Sounds great." She stared at him. She took in his eyes and every feature on his face as the moon hit his skin just right. She could feel her heartbeat rising and her cheeks blushing. If he didn't make a move soon, she would.

Caleb reached his hand up and brushed her hair from her forehead, gently placing it behind her ear. "Brooke..." he began.

She silenced him, placing her lips on his. She had never kissed a man with a beard before. She had expected it to be hard and prickly, but it was soft and gentle. His lips were warm and soft, the perfect complement to hers. His lips parted, allowing the kiss to grow deeper as his hand grasped the nape of her neck, his free hand sliding along her back, pulling her body closer to his. She breathed him in before breaking the kiss, shivers racing up her spine.

"I'll see you tomorrow?" she whispered, the tip of her nose gently touching his.

Caleb gently kissed her again. "I can't wait."

Brooke ran her hand up his chest to his neck, running her fingers through his hair. *Kiss him again*, she thought. Biting her bottom lip, she hesitated to make another move.

"You should probably go inside," Caleb muttered, nodding toward the lodge behind Brooke.

Brooke nodded. "Okay, yeah." She gently pushed herself away from Caleb, every inch of her telling her not to. Caleb ran his fingers down her arms and grasped her hand as she got closer and closer to the lodge. She let her fingers linger on his for a moment longer before she pulled her hand up to wave at him. "Tomorrow."

"Tomorrow," Caleb repeated, standing his ground, watching her awkwardly fumble up the stairs.

Brooke felt as light as a feather, shaky from a first kiss. Chills ran down her body as she turned to wave to Caleb one last time before opening the lodge door. Once inside, she leaned against the door and inhaled. The Jeep's engine rumbled to a start, and the tires crunched against the dirt. The lights flashed as she leaned her head against the door.

Oh, man...

"Hi." The sudden voice brought her back to life. She jerked her head up and looked to the living room.

Helen and Greg sat on the couches, watching her with the same smirks on their faces. If she was the teenager, they were the parents.

"What?" she asked, pushing herself off the door.

"How was the date?" Helen asked.

Greg shook his head and groaned.

"It...was..." she began, "good. We talked and ate some amazing food."

"And the kiss?" Helen's smirk grew.

Brooke stared at her wide eyed.

"She watched from the window," Greg answered.

Brooke pursed her lips and didn't respond. She didn't want to kiss and tell. That kiss was for her and Caleb.

"I think I'm going to go to my room," she muttered.

"Okay, but I want details tomorrow!" Helen's voice grew as Brooke approached her room.

Brooke rolled her eyes and shut her bedroom door. Flicking on the lamp, the room came to life. She took off her coat and tossed it on the bed. The shivers had subsided but lingered, the kiss and Caleb still fresh in her mind. Glancing at the clock, she counted the hours until she would meet him at the lake.

She changed into her pajamas, deciding she had time to get those last two thousand words down, so she opened her laptop and waited for it to boot. The little ding made her smile as she opened her Word document. She brushed her fingers over the keys, as if to set off her mind, but as she looked at the words on the page, she had no motivation to finish.

Instead, her mind went to Caleb and then to his company.

"I wonder..." she whispered.

She hooked up to the internet and began to type.

Sixteen

- Wednesday -

"Mornin', Caleb."

Caleb looked to his left, watching the wobbly, older man approach him, tackle box in hand. "Morning, Mr. Garrett. How are you doin' today?" Caleb asked, returning his attention to his line.

"Doin' just fine," the old man responded. "Looks like you're setting up a party this morning?"

Caleb looked down at his small set up. Two thermoses of coffee next to two small thermoses of warm oatmeal sat on a flannel blanket near his tackle box. He brought a chair for Brooke to sit on while she wrote and draped a blanket over it in case she wanted to be a burrito again.

Had it bothered him that Brooke hadn't shown up yet? Most definitely. He wouldn't admit it, even though inside he was screaming. Absolutely not. He reeled in his line, silently wishing that Mr. Garrett would move onto his fishing spot.

"I was supposed to meet a date here, but she didn't show. I must've scared her away." He looked down at the breakfast he had brought. "The oatmeal may be cold by now. If you want some, feel free."

Mr. Garret grumbled, looking down at the four thermoses. "I didn't know you were seeing anyone, Caleb." He began to shuffle away. "She'd be a fool to stand you up." The old man continued to grumble as he walked off to his normal spot.

Caleb chuckled at himself, casting his fishing pole. How could he be so stupid? How could he think that Brooke was actually interested enough to come to the lake again? Before sunrise? That kiss, though. If anything, that kiss was worth the rest of the time he had spent with her. He inhaled and exhaled, praying she would still show.

The sun had risen completely and glistened on the lake, the reflection looking like floating rows of gems on the water. He had watched the entire sunrise by himself, when he hoped he would watch it with the faint clicking of Brookes keyboard.

He sighed, reeled in his line for the final time and began to dismantle the fishing line. He had just clipped the line to the hook when he heard the faint call of his name. He turned to the small parking area and saw Brooke running toward him. Her hair was a mess, and he was pretty sure she was still wearing her pajama pants. As she got closer, he noticed she had forgotten her glasses.

Any anger he had that she may have stood him up faded. He just watched as she bounded toward him, chuckling. His breath was shaky, and his heart began to beat faster and faster. *She didn't forget.*

"You came," he said once she got closer, trying to calm his breath.

"I'm...sorry..." she said between breaths. "I slept in. I was up way too late. I woke up in time to brush my teeth and grab my coat..."

Caleb raised an eyebrow and gently bent to place his pole on the ground. Brooke was still talking, but he had tuned her out after she said she brushed her teeth. He stepped toward her, gently cupped her face in his palms, and kissed her.

Brooke melted into him, and he felt every muscle in her body relax. She lightly hummed as he pulled away. She opened her eyes, and her gaze locked on him, a sweet soft smile on her lips.

"You came," he repeated, his voice completely steady now that she was in his arms.

"I did," she whispered. "I'm sorry I missed the morning. I slept in."

Caleb brushed her bottom lip with his thumb before dropping his hands to grab his fishing pole. "You said that. I hope everything is okay."

Brooke sighed. "Everything is great. I was just looking up things last night and lost track of time." Brooke shivered. "But I want to talk to you and Ethan. I was hoping we could meet at your office?"

"To me?" Caleb asked. "And Ethan?"

She nodded. "Yeah, I...um..." She began to kick the rocks around beneath her feet. "I think I have an idea." Brooke smiled, looking down and seeing the setup Caleb had. "You brought coffee and breakfast, and I missed it."

Caleb chuckled. "The coffee is probably still warm, but I'm not sure about the oatmeal."

"Oatmeal?"

Caleb stopped. He didn't even know if she liked oatmeal. It was his go to breakfast, so he just assumed. "It's uh..." he stammered, "cinnamon raisin."

Brooke smiled and stepped closer to him. "I love oatmeal."

"This oatmeal is probably bad by now. How about I make you some more when we get back to the office?"

Brooke nodded. "Okay." Her eyes flickered, and she seemed to have snapped back to reality. "I'm still in my pajamas. So how about I go back to the lodge and shower? Then I'll go to the office."

Caleb bent over, grabbed her a thermos of coffee and handed it to her. "Sounds like a plan. Take this for your drive, and I'll see you soon."

Brooke took a sip of the coffee and turned to walk back to her car, looking behind her shoulder with every few steps. Caleb laughed as he watched her.

Damn, she's cute...

"Oh good." The grumbly voice of Mr. Garrett appeared behind him. "She didn't forget about you."

Caleb turned to look at him, a grin on his lips. "No, Mr. Garrett. She didn't."

～

"I don't mean to be a busybody," Brooke began, her laptop in front of her. She had returned to the office an hour later, dressed and ready for the day. She pulled her blonde hair back into a ponytail and had her glasses perched on her head. Caleb had told her she looked like she belonged in a bookstore, which got a good reaction out of Brooke. "But after Caleb told me what was going on with the company, I did some research on you guys..."

"Some research?" Ethan furrowed his brow and glared at Caleb. "On us?"

The three of them were sitting at the same round table Brooke had occupied the day before, coffee in front of them and finished bowls of oatmeal waiting to be taken to the kitchen.

Brooke nodded. "Yes, and I couldn't find anything."

"Good." Ethan sat up straighter and crossed his arms.

Brooke scrunched her nose. "Not really. Not if you're trying to run the business. Your website hasn't been updated since 2018."

"We don't really have a need for it," Caleb began. "Lettie created it to keep up with the times, but it hasn't done much for us."

"Obviously." She gestured around the office. "How do people make reservations?"

"They call," Ethan answered, his chin resting on his fist with absolutely no emotion on his face.

Caleb noticed the glare Brooke shot across the table. He pursed his lips and covered his mouth with his fingers. He held back a chuckle.

"How do they get your information to call? The number on the website says disconnected." Brooke pointed to her laptop screen, keeping her eyes on Ethan.

"What? You called it?" Ethan grumbled.

"Ethan"—Caleb looked at his friend—"I have a feeling she's trying to help us so...maybe we should listen."

Ethan sighed and then turned to Brooke. "Fine, I'm sorry," he said not so apologetically. "Go on." He gestured with a wave of his hand.

Brooke turned to Caleb and gave a soft smile. "Yes, I did call it, and it gave me that annoying beep and said it was no longer in service."

"The brochures and pamphlets have the current phone number. We had to change it when Lettie died," Caleb answered. He reached behind Ethan to the shelf against the wall, grabbing one of their current flyers. "We just had some new ones printed, actually."

Brooke slid the flier toward her and looked at it. "These are great but, a lot of people don't even pay attention to this kind of thing." She ran her fingers over the cream paper. "I have an idea, but you two need to be willing to work with me. It may help enough to make the mortgage and to last the season. But, please"—she turned toward Ethan and locked his gaze—"you need to be open-minded."

Ethan held her gaze for a second and then looked at Caleb. "What is she going to charge?" asking Caleb as if Brooke weren't sitting right across from him.

"Nothing," Brooke answered for Caleb. "I just want to help."

Caleb smiled and rubbed his palms on his thighs, leaning forward to try to see what was happening on Brooke's computer screen. "Okay," he said, "What do you think we need to do?"

Brooke's smile grew as she watched him. "Well, first, we are going to update this website. We need updated pictures and phone numbers. Maybe we can do a little bio on the both of you, and maybe even Lettie. We can dedicate everything to her."

Caleb's heart fluttered. He loved the idea of involving Lettie. She was the one who brought him in and accepted him. She gave him a place to call home and a future in Marble. He knew she would appreciate the gesture. "I like that," he mumbled.

"And I want to set up a blog for you. I think it would be great to update your followers on all the adventures you take. Post pictures of the road and the mill. Just write down the day-to-day life in Marble."

"Followers?" Ethan asked. "We don't have any *followers.*"

"But you will, because we are going to set up an Instagram and Facebook account for you. Maybe even a TikTok." Brooke began typing away on her computer, pulling up the Facebook website. "We can connect everything, so if you post on one, it will automatically post on the other. I have a blog, and I'll mention you in it and give some discount to my followers if they follow you." Her eyes never left the screen as she spoke. "But this will need to be a constant thing. One of you will have to manage it until you can hire someone to manage it for you."

"Hire someone?" Ethan repeated. Each time he repeated what Brooke said, his voice was filled with more disbelief.

"Eventually. I mean, do you two plan on running the entire thing by yourselves? How many tours do you have?"

"Well, we have the town and mill"—Caleb held up one finger—"then we have the mine"— two fingers—"and we have a photo tour which runs anywhere from four to six hours"—three fingers—"and then we have the Lead King Basin route..."—four fingers.

"So you have all these tours available and only two of you?" Brooke raised her eyebrows. "Let me ask, when Lettie ran the place, did she take tours, or did she stay here?"

Ethan shook his head. "It was me and her husband until he passed away. Then Caleb came along. She mainly stayed at the office for phone calls."

Brooke raised her eyebrows. "So what happens if you both are out on a tour?"

"They...leave...a...message?" Ethan said slowly, starting to catch her drift. Brooke leaned back in her chair, folding her arms across her chest. She knew he was starting to see it as she was, but she had a feeling he wasn't done putting up a fight. Still, a small smile formed in the corner of her lips.

Caleb looked over at him. "We may need to hire another person in the future." Caleb turned back to Brooke. "But for now, we need to focus on getting reservations. So maybe getting an updated web base is a good place to start."

Brooke smiled in satisfaction, sitting up straight again to turn back to her laptop to begin typing. "I can help with the blog and social media. I have a friend in Salt Lake who helped me build my website. I'm going to send him an email..."

"We can't afford to pay someone..." Ethan moaned.

Brooke stopped typing and slammed her laptop closed. She turned her head to Ethan. Caleb went wide eyed. He had only seen a soft, sweet Brooke. This was a new Brooke. One that was full of fire and passion. And he liked it. He smiled and watched as Brooke put Ethan in his place.

"Listen. I am setting up the blog and social media for free. My friend in Salt Lake will cut me a fantastic deal which I planned on paying for. Can you just please take the help to try to better your friend's company so you can...I don't know...get a paycheck." Brooke glared at him, pointing a finger in his face.

Ethan sat wide eyed as Brooke pointed him down. He slouched and took a deep breath. "Yes, okay. I'm sorry."

Brooke kept her eyes on Ethan and opened her laptop again. Caleb burst out in laughter, standing up and gathering all the dirty dishes from the table. "Oh, this is going to be great."

Seventeen

Brooke and Ethan were not going to get along. She could tell. She wanted so desperately to help Caleb, but Ethan being pessimistic the entire time, especially after seeing his excitement last night, was not helping her motivation. But he was Caleb's friend and employee...so she would try her hardest to make it work. Within the next few hours, she had set up an Instagram and Facebook page for them and emailed her friend for a website. She had completely skimmed over the email from her agent.

Ethan had retreated to behind the counter, thumbing through the computer for photos they could attach to their new feeds. Every now and then, Brooke would catch him glaring at her from across the room. She could just feel the tension. Caleb had left the office to go clean out a Jeep. He had remembered there was a possible reservation and wanted to make sure it was ready at any moment.

Brooke turned her gaze to watch him from the window every few minutes. Then when Ethan would clear his throat, she returned to the computer. This happened a few times before Brooke decided it was enough.

"Okay," she asked, gently placing her palms on the table. "May I ask what your problem is with me? I thought you would be excited to make changes."

"I'm all for making changes," Ethan said, not looking up from his computer screen. "The problem I'm having is you and Caleb."

Brooke narrowed her eyes. "Why does that bother you?"

"You don't know Caleb. You don't know what that man has been through."

"He told me a lot last night. We had a great talk."

"Just because you talked doesn't mean you know anything."

Brooke pursed her lips. There was obviously no getting through to Ethan. If she wanted to have Caleb in her life while she was here and possibly after, she would need to be civil with Ethan, strictly business.

"Well, hey." She sighed. "I'm only here until Sunday night and then I'll be back in Salt Lake, but I want to help Caleb with the company. I could just tell his heart was shattered as he told me about it last night. He doesn't deserve that, and honestly, you don't either."

Ethan shrugged and looked at her, locking his eyes with hers. He nodded. "You should have seen him yesterday when he told me we had a family book a tour. That guy can wear his heart on his sleeve. He was jumping for joy."

"I was here when he took the call. I could literally see his demeanor change." Brooke smiled. She looked back at her computer. "I think this could help. Setting up a social media presence and starting a blog...it could really work."

"What would we write about?" Ethan asked, leaning on the counter.

Brooke smiled and shifted her body in her chair, facing Ethan. *You shouldn't underestimate yourself,* she thought. *It seems you have broken through to him.* They were both here for Caleb. Caleb was their connection, and they would both make sure they succeeded for him.

"Anything, really. Anything that has to do with the business, that is." She stood and made her way over to the counter, carrying her computer in her arms. "When I started a blog, I had no idea where to begin. I just wanted to write novels, not newsletters." She chuckled at herself, but Ethan didn't return the giggle. "So I wrote about my life and what I was doing.

"My first novel was still in the editing phases when I picked up my blog. I needed an escape from editing and formatting, so I wrote about how frustrating it was and how stupid I thought I was for thinking I could write. It was almost like a diary." She typed her website into the search bar and spun the computer at Ethan. He looked at the screen and furrowed his brow.

Brooke's site was much like the cover of her first novel. Dark blue with mountains on the bottom and snow lightly falling around the menus and captions. Reviews on the novel interchanged with her readers' photos. On top there were the basic tabs, even an option to shop. Brooke's smiling face sat at the bottom, a small blurb about her with clickable options to her blog posts. It was very professionally kept and done, making Ethan look up at her, still trying to be as skeptical as he could.

"That's well and good for authors, but we are a touring company," Ethan said. "We can't really talk about the day-to-day lives of Caleb and Ethan."

"Why not? Give a personal touch to the company." She raised her shoulders. "I think a bio on you would be perfect. Caleb said you're married?"

"Twelve years going strong."

"See, that's amazing. Clients would like to know that." She gestured to Ethan. "You gotta have some interesting stories to tell, and those stories would do great on a blog. Hell"—she smiled—"I could even help write them for you while I'm here, and then you can post them as you go."

Ethan nodded. "Okay, I can see where you're going with this. I still don't like the social media detail, but..." He clenched his teeth. "You're right. I'll find a picture of me, and then maybe we can write something up."

"You and your wife. Let's make it *personal*." She hit Ethan's shoulder. He looked at his shoulder as if he had just been violated. She scrunched her nose.

"I don't like you that much yet." He groaned.

She backed up, her hands in surrender. "Gee, I'm sorry. Maybe one day, huh?"

Ethan shook his head. "We'll see."

Brooke rolled her eyes. "I don't give up so easily." She grabbed her computer, setting it gently back on the table. She brushed the keys with her fingertips, something she noticed was becoming a habit, and looked out the window. Caleb was fiddling with a rope in the Jeep, trying to undo a knot, looking very concentrated. She glanced over her shoulder at Ethan and left the building. She wanted to be close to Caleb.

She walked up to him, sticking her hands in her coat pocket, wishing she had her beanie. Caleb was sitting in the trunk of the silver Jeep, the same one they had taken on their few adventures. She approached slowly, but when she got close enough, he raised his head and smiled at her.

"Had enough of Ethan, have we?" he asked, looking back down at the rope in his hand.

"He doesn't like me." Brooke sighed, hoisting herself onto the Jeep next to Caleb.

"Give him time. He'll warm up to you," Caleb mumbled.

She looked at the rope in his hands and then back at the building. "You took to me really fast," she joked, bumping into his shoulder with hers. "Ethan doesn't like the fact that I really like you."

"Yeah, he'll get over that." He looked over at her. "I really like you too, so he can suffer."

"He won't suffer in silence. That's for sure."

Caleb laughed, still concentrating on the rope. The knot was tied pretty tightly. Brooke looked at it and raised her eyebrows. Not even an Eagle Scout could get that untied. As he fumbled with the knot, Brooke thought about Caleb. She watched his fingers move delicately on the rope, trying to pull the two pieces apart. She looked at the white building in front of her, a realization dawning. He lived here. This was more than just his place of work. It was his home. If the company went under, he would lose his home. A blog and social media were all she could think of to help jump start them, but was it enough?

"I don't want you to lose your company," she said softly, leaning into him, resting her head on his shoulder.

"I won't," he said quietly, leaning his head on top of her, still fumbling with the rope. "I really think your ideas will work, and if you help us get started, we should have no problem keeping them up once you go back home. But..." He raised his head, lowered the rope, and looked at her. Brooke caught his gaze. "I don't want this to be everything we do together. I still want to show you things and fish with you while you write and have a movie night. I want to get to know Brooke more, not just business Brooke."

She took a deep breath and nodded.

"I mean, the way you snapped at Ethan. That was pure gold, but...I want my Brooke back."

My Brooke.

"Your Brooke, huh?" She smiled.

Caleb wiggled his eyebrows. "I think it's safe to say that until Sunday, you're my Brooke."

She leaned in and gave him a small kiss on his cheek. "*My* Caleb."

"Ooh," Brooke awed as Ethan was flipping through photos of him and his wife. "I like that one."

In the time since she and Caleb had come inside, she had found out that the potential reservation had fallen through, and Ethan's wife, Meredith, was the cutest curvy girl Brooke had ever seen. Ethan told Brooke about how they met and that she worked as a nurse at the hospital in Carbondale. Working long shifts and always wearing scrubs, Meredith always loved the chance to get dolled up for photos. Ethan was blushing and smiling the entire time, looking at the pictures.

"Yeah, Meredith is beautiful, but I look funny." He groaned.

"You always look funny," Caleb called from the kitchen.

Brooke shook her head. "We just need a nice one you want to share, and make sure your wife is okay with it. Steven said he needs current photos for the website." Brooke's web designer friend had followed through and agreed to have a website up by the end of the week, complete with a clickable "book a tour now" button.

"Well, there's a problem." Caleb reemerged, glasses of water for him and Brooke in his hands. "I haven't had my picture taken in years. I think the last one was with Audrey."

"We can change that easily." Brooke smiled at him.

Caleb raised his eyebrows, almost like he was afraid of the thought of getting his photo taken.

Then, as if a light bulb appeared over Brooke's head, she had a brilliant idea.

"We should go have a photo shoot," she exclaimed.

Ethan and Caleb both stared at her.

"Please, no," Caleb finally said, breaking the silence. He glared at her.

"Imagine what the website would look like? The social media feeds!" Brooke was almost jumping with excitement. "We can go up to the mill and the town, take updated photos of you two and the town." Brooke's smile grew. "It will be great, trust me!"

The look on Caleb's face showed anything but excitement. Ethan's expression was just as daunting.

"You're going to make us wear nice clothes, aren't you?" he mumbled.

"Professional clothes, and yes. This will be a great idea. I can guarantee it." Brooke rubbed her palms together. "Steven will be over the moon."

Ethan mumbled. "I guess I need to go home to change." He looked down at his beige button-down shirt and torn jeans. Brooke gave him an agreeing nod.

"Wear flannel!" she screamed as he made his way to the door. "Oh! If your wife is home today, bring her! I bet you she would *love* to have a picture of the two of you!!"

Ethan let out a huge groan as he opened the door and fumbled with his keys in his pocket.

Caleb turned to Brooke. "You just got Ethan to agree to a photo shoot," he said, wide eyed. "I am, however, not convinced we still need to do one."

Brooke turned to him and gave him a small kiss on his scruffy beard. It was still as soft as she remembered.

"Trust me. People will want to see the face of the men driving them around for hours at a time."

He shrugged. "You're right." He chuckled. "Ethan lives in Carbondale. We got a good hour before he heads back up. All I own is flannel."

Brooke lifted her chin. "Perfect. Wait till Ethan gets back to pick your color. I'm not a photographer, but my Galaxy has a fantastic camera."

He raised his eyebrows. "Fine," he said, giving in. "I'm going to take a shower. Should I shave?"

"No," Brooke said quickly. "I mean..." She hesitated. "Maybe comb it?" She clenched her teeth as she cupped his cheek in her palm, brushing his beard with her thumb. "I'll go have lunch and return with my phone and enough space for a lot of pictures."

She started to back up. Caleb grabbed her wrist and pulled her toward him, wrapping his arms around her waist, pressing his lips on hers. Brooke breathed him in and let the kiss linger.

"See you soon," he whispered against her lips.

She sighed and nodded. "Really soon."

Eighteen

Brooke arrived back at the lodge to almost everyone sitting outside on the balcony. To her surprise, Melinda and Frank were there, as well as Rhonda. She approached with caution. Were they going to give her an intervention? In the back of her mind, she knew they had no control over how she spent her time. Yet seeing them there made her nervous. Yes—this was a writing retreat, but they couldn't force her to stay cooped up. As she locked her car, she could hear her parents' voices inside her head.

Now, Brooke—she could hear them now—*You are here to break through your writer's block, not spend time gallivanting around with a local you just met. We will lock you in your room and ration your food until your novel is complete. You may no longer see Caleb...*

"Afternoon, everyone. It's a beautiful day, isn't it?" She smiled.

"It really is," Frank said, leaning his head back and closing his eyes, taking in the sunlight. "It's supposed to be nice the remainder of the week. We all had to take a break and come enjoy the sun."

Brooke sighed, looking up at the crystal-clear blue sky. The few clouds that hung around didn't even come close to covering the sun. A perfect day to take some photos.

"Where have you been this morning?" Rhonda asked, lifting a glass of water to her lips.

"Now, Rhonda," Joyce whispered to her, obviously trying to stop something before it started.

"I went to the touring company's office to steal their wi-fi," Brooke told half a lie. She had used the wi-fi, even though it wasn't for writing purposes. "I had to email my agent. They sent about fifty emails in the three days we've been here."

"Any good news?" Melinda asked.

Brooke looked behind her at Helen, who wiggled her eyebrows up and down. It obviously wasn't in reference to her writing.

"Yes, actually." She smiled, pulling up one of the metal chairs and taking a seat next to Greg. "I sent them a proposal for a new idea, and they seem to like it. They want the first seven thousand words. I'm at fifty-four hundred."

Frank beamed. "That's great. Gotta get the rest of them. Are you going to be here the rest of the day?"

Brooke inhaled. "Actually, I'm going back up to Crystal with Caleb and his employee, Ethan. Since my book is set there, I want to take as many pictures as possible. Just for references when I get home."

Greg spun his head toward her. "Can I come?"

Brooke tilted her head at him, making sure she heard him right. "Sure, I don't see why not. It's beautiful out there. You're going to love it."

"You told me to leave the lodge, and I don't think you meant just the porch." he groaned.

"It's a start." Brooke smiled.

"How many people can they take? I'd like to see it too," Helen asked, leaning forward on the table.

"They have several Jeeps. I'm sure we can ask Caleb if we can tow some more." Brooke smiled. Maybe if Caleb could cut Helen and Greg a deal, they could use that toward their mortgage. But first, she would need to tell Greg and Helen the real reason for going up to the town. Sure, she was taking pictures, but of Ethan and Caleb, not necessarily the town.

"I think that's a fantastic idea." Melinda smiled. "Taking a break from your work."

"Well, I"—Rhonda stood, huffing—"will be getting back to my work." She went inside, the door almost slamming behind her.

Brooke blinked. "I'm sorry, but what is her deal?"

"She's old-fashioned." Frank stood. "But I half agree with her. Take the afternoon and get your inspiration, clear your head, and then come back to work on what really matters."

What really matters, Brooke thought.

~

With Helen and Greg piled in the car, Brooke drove the dirt roads to the company. She had no way of telling Caleb that she was going to have stowaways, but the two of them seemed rather excited.

"Okay, so..." Brooke sighed as she turned the road. "There is something I need to tell you."

"That you're in love with the fisherman?" Greg said, not taking his eyes from the window. "Yeah, we know."

"Well..." Brooke didn't need that topic to go any further. Besides, she could hardly call it love. She had only known the man three days. "The thing is..." she trailed off, unsure of why she was so nervous to tell them the truth. "I already got plenty of photos of the town when I went up there on Monday. This trip is for Caleb and his friend Ethan."

"What do you mean?" Helen asked, turning her head to look at Brooke.

Brooke told them the entire story, including the ideas she had to boost their business. Both Helen and Greg seemed to be in favor of what she was doing, even though Greg had said so many times they were there to write.

"Frank did say, do what *really* matters," Greg mumbled. "Does this matter to you?"

Brooke looked at him in the rear-view mirror. "It does."

Greg shrugged. "Alright, then let's get those men some head shots. And then"—he raised a finger to the mirror—"we will write."

There it is. Brooke laughed to herself as she pulled into the touring company. Ethan had just returned, wearing a red flannel shirt and a nicer pair of jeans. His brown boots still had mud covered all over them, but Brooke figured it would add character. Climbing out of the other side was the adorable curvy girl Brooke recognized from the photos. Ethan's wife, Meredith.

Brooke did a quick count. Six people. Jeeps held five. Either they were going to have to bend the rules and shove Greg's tiny body in the back or take two Jeeps. She pursed her lips. Maybe she could offer to pay for the gas.

The three writers left the vehicle and walked up the plank steps. Brooke carefully opened the door, noticing Ethan and Meredith, but no Caleb.

Ethan turned to her. "Caleb said he had to pick a complementing color to red." He gestured down his chest.

Brooke laughed, wondering when they were going to mention Helen and Greg, who were being abnormally silent.

"Brooke, this is my wife, Meredith. You were right. She's absolutely in awe with the idea of taking new photos." Ethan gestured to his wife.

"I'm in awe of anything that can help this place." Meredith stepped forward, her red hair gently resting on her shoulders. She had fair skin, which made her pink lips pop more, and her light blue dress complemented her every curve. Brooke shook her hand, happy to meet someone else connected to Caleb.

"Nice to meet you, Meredith." She smiled. "This is Helen and Greg, fellow writers from the retreat. They need a bit of inspiration as well, so I invited them along."

"Well, to be fair"—Helen stepped forward, placing her hand on Brooke's shoulder—"you invited Greg, I begged. Hi, I'm Helen." She held out her hand, which Meredith took.

"Lovely to meet you." Meredith smiled. Brooke already adored her.

While the three new friends talked, Brooke walked over to Ethan. "I hope it's okay that I brought them. They needed out of that lodge. I'll pay for gas since we have to use a second Jeep."

Ethan shrugged. "Nah, it's fine. I haven't taken Meredith on this drive in a long time. We will take one, and Caleb can be the tour guide."

"Where is Caleb?"

"Upstairs. He said he would be down soon." Ethan pointed to the ceiling. "He had on a red shirt too, but when I came in, he said he needed to change."

"I told him to wait." Brooke laughed.

"I'm not one to wait." She heard Caleb's voice. He came out from the kitchen wearing a white and black flannel shirt, beige cargo pants and the same muddy boots Ethan was wearing. "Hey, Mer..." He waved to Meredith, who waved back.

Brooke looked at him more intently, noticing the way he moved as he entered the office, that intense look in his eye and small grin upon his lips. He had trimmed a few random strays on his beard and combed it. His hair was wet and freshly brushed. He was finishing buttoning up his shirt as he walked around the counter to Brooke, making her inhale sharply as his body closed in on hers. Caleb locked her gaze and gave her a sly smirk, keeping it only a moment when his eyes noticed the two others. He glanced at Brooke and raised his eyes.

"I brought Helen and Greg. They are staying at the lodge and desperately need to get out," Brooke whispered to him. "I left the mean one at the lodge."

Caleb shook his head and smiled. He leaned in and whispered, "Will I still be able to sneak a few kisses?"

"Maybe. Just keep it to a minimum." Brooke felt the heat rise in her cheeks and quickly turned away. "Hey, Helen," she called, "this is Caleb."

Helen came rushing over as soon as she heard her name, and Greg followed. "Caleb!" She stuck out her hand, a large grin on her lips. "It's good to finally meet you. Brooke has talked about you nonstop."

Caleb raised his eyes and turned to look at Brooke.

"She really has," Greg agreed with Helen. Greg pushed Helen away, getting her to go to the map that hung on the wall.

Brooke grinned and looked at Caleb. "I haven't talked about you that much."

Caleb didn't respond, he just wiggled his eyebrows and mimicked her grin. Still keeping his gaze locked on her, Caleb suddenly clapped his hands, making Brooke jump out of her trance.

"Okay! Since there are more people here than I thought there would be, we are going to have to go over a few tour rules..."

Brooke stood back and watched as Caleb gave the intro to the tours. Mainly, the information was for Helen and Greg, but he addressed everyone, even Ethan. To her surprise, Helen and Greg listened intently and nodded along with safety precautions. He even noted that the Jeeps have no windows and no roof, so he was glad they had all dressed appropriately. Greg even made a snarky comment about how they were all aware the Colorado weather could change at any given moment, which warranted an elbow to the side from Helen.

Brooke rolled her eyes and watched as Caleb ignored the comment and continued to talk about the roads and safety. Once that was over with, all six of them went out to the Jeeps. Ethan and Meredith climbed into the red one, and Caleb led the others to the silver one.

"It's a bumpy ride, so make sure you buckle up and hold on to anything you don't want to fall out of the Jeep," Caleb said as he started the Jeep. Ethan and Meredith had already pulled out ahead of them.

"Oh, that's comforting," Greg mumbled.

"Didn't Brooke bring her laptop on Monday?" Helen asked, grasping onto the overhead rail as Caleb shifted the car and began to follow Ethan.

Brooke turned her body to look back at the two. "I never even opened it." She smiled. "Just wait until you see the mill. It's breathtaking."

Nineteen

Caleb hated having his picture taken. Even on his wedding day, when Audrey made him pose and do fake smiles. The pictures turned out beautiful, of course, and Audrey had hung them all over their house, but she knew he hated every second of it. He hated the awkwardness of everything a camera offered. The last photo that was taken of him that he could remember was for the law firm's website. And *that* was posed to perfection. He took a deep breath and narrowed his eyes as Brooke raised her phone at him and Ethan, regretting giving her permission to do this.

"You have to smile," she said, tilting her head slightly to look at them.

Caleb shook his head while Ethan gave the dorkiest grin Caleb had ever seen.

"Caleb, please," Brooke begged.

Ethan elbowed him. "I hate this too, man, but come on."

Caleb raised his head toward the sky and let out a loud groan.

Under the Marble Sky

Ethan and Caleb stood in the middle of the town of Crystal, some worn-down buildings on either side of them. Meredith was patiently waiting to have her photo taken with Ethan while Helen and Greg roamed the area, looking at everything, just as Brooke had the first time she was there.

Caleb took one deep breath, lowering his head with an exhale, and smiled. Brooke smiled back at him and began to tap her phone screen. Keeping the two boys where they were, she walked closer.

"These look great," she said once she was in ear shot. "I got some great ones of the two of you with a lot of the town and then some close up, but I need solo shots now before we drag Meredith into this."

"I can't wait!" Meredith screamed, making Brooke giggle.

Caleb walked over to her. "Can I see?" He walked up behind her and leaned over her shoulder, bringing his cheek close to hers.

Brooke blushed and began to flip through her gallery, showing off the photos she had just taken of the business partners. There were so many photos from just minutes of him standing there awkwardly. How she had managed to capture anything that made Caleb look natural and professional was beyond him. There were too many pictures, and they all looked the same.

"Why did you take five million pictures?" he asked, watching as she slid her finger, showing what looked to be the same picture over and over. "It's the same one?"

Brooke turned to look at him. "No, your face is different in every picture, and Ethan is blinking in a lot of them. I'm sure Steven will find one that is perfect for the website banner, but now I need solo photos of you for a bio."

"I don't need a bio."

"Yes, you do." Brooke closed her gallery app and lowered her phone. "If I'm making Ethan have one, you have to have one too." Brooke reached down and touched his hand, lacing her fingers with his. "I can take Meredith and Ethan's photos first if you like."

Caleb tightened his grip on her hand, loving the way their fingers fit together like the perfect puzzle piece. He lightly tapped his fingertips on her knuckles.

"Yes, please. I'd rather not have everyone looking at me as I pretend to smile at a phone."

"You know, you don't have to smile. You can just grin." Brooke took one large step and spun her body to face him, making him stop in his tracks. She had a large, goofy smile on her face. Caleb shook his head and grinned. "See, genuine. Like that one." She reached up and lightly brushed her thumb against his bottom lip.

Caleb stood up a bit straight and licked his lips. "You have to make goofy faces at me then in order to get a grin."

Brooke wiggled her eyebrows. "I can do that."

Caleb leaned in for a small kiss, but Brooke backed away before their lips could touch, blinking her eyes to return to the task at hand. She rubbed her thumb against the back of his hand and released her grip. All the warmth Caleb felt went with her.

"Meredith, Ethan..." Brooke turned and walked away. "Are you two ready to take some photos?"

"Hell, yeah!" Meredith grabbed Ethan's sleeve and pulled him to the middle of town.

Brooke chuckled at them and started to pose the married couple. Caleb stuck his hands in his pockets and watched, laughing at all the ways Meredith was making Ethan smile. After a few different shots, Brooke ran up to them and showed them all the photos on her phone. Seeing Meredith react and Ethan's smile grow made Caleb relax.

As much as he hated the experience of a photo shoot, he knew this would change things. This moment was going to mean so much more than he and Ethan first thought. Changing a website and setting up a presence on social media might turn the tables for them. Taking a few simple pictures with goofy grins and writing a little snip about who he was could change their business, or at least brand the business.

Brooke was talking with Ethan and Meredith as they leaned into her, looking at the small photos on her phone. Helen and Greg had settled by one of the many worn-down buildings and were seemingly enjoying the area. Dark clouds formed in the sky above them, taking away most of the natural light they had, but maybe that would make the pictures better?

All of this was happening very fast, but it had to. He had Brooke only until Sunday. It didn't feel like just a few days ago he first saw her on the lake. Caleb didn't want the week to come to an end, but he knew eventually she would return to the city and potentially forget all about him. He watched her, the smile on her face, the laughter as Meredith critiqued Ethan's funny faces. There was no one more beautiful than her.

Her hair flew around her cheeks from the wind, and she lightly lifted her hand to tuck it behind her ear. Her eyes, even though she was squinting from the sun that poked from the clouds, still shimmered bright blue even from a distance. Her smile and laugh were contagious. He could see that with every time Meredith would laugh along with her as they made fun of all the faces Ethan made. Just watching her, Caleb could feel the same spark when he first held her hand.

"Caleb." He heard his name, snapping him back to reality. He widened his eyes and looked at Brooke. "It's your turn for some solo shots. Come on."

He groaned. "Okay." He turned to Helen and Greg. "Are you guys doing okay?"

"Don't worry about them," Brooke joked. "They are just enjoying the show."

Helen laughed. "Really, though, we are."

Caleb furrowed his brow and went back to Brooke. She had him stand in the exact spot he and Ethan had stood, but this time, she stood closer to him. She raised her phone, tilted her head to look at him, and gave him a goofy grin. He raised an eyebrow and shook his head.

"You gotta give me something." She smiled.

Caleb let out a quick exhale and smiled. The smile Brooke returned made his smile grow, hopefully becoming more genuine like Brooke wanted. She tapped her phone a few times and backed up, getting a fuller view of the town. Caleb stuck his hands in his pockets, hoping he was giving off a casual and relaxed vibe.

"Way to be sexy, man," Ethan called, making Caleb jerk his head toward him.

"You know I hate this." Caleb groaned.

"But you do it so well," Meredith said.

"You really do," Helen called. "I can see what Brooke sees in you for sure."

Caleb looked at Helen and then toward Brooke, raising his eyebrows. She was blushing, her cheeks quickly turning bright pink.

"Just a few more, and then I think we have it," Brooke said, shyness in her tone.

Caleb caught her gaze. He half expected her to turn and hide, but she just tilted her head and pursed her lips, the corners raising slightly. She raised her phone once more, and Caleb gave her the same grin she had asked for earlier. In his mind, these pictures were just for them, and for some reason, that made it easier.

"Can I see?" he asked once she lowered the camera.

She shook her head. "No."

"They got to see their photos." He pointed to Ethan and Meredith, a smirk tugging at his lips.

Brooke shrugged and then walked over to Helen and Greg. "You can see once we get back to the office," she said over her shoulder. "I don't need your comments on how..." she paused, "...great you look. So you can see them when they are posted."

Caleb scoffed and walked over to the Jeeps where Ethan and Meredith were sitting. They were holding hands, sitting close together on the back of the Jeep. Their expressions were basically shouting at Caleb. Especially Meredith. Her eyes were yelling at him to go over to Brooke.

"She's cute." She smiled.

Caleb reached in the back behind them for a bottle of water, not responding to her comment.

"He took her on a date last night," Ethan added.

Meredith gasped. "At the barbeque?"

Caleb nodded. "She needed to try it before she left."

"When does she leave?" Meredith asked.

"Monday morning," he said, bringing the water bottle to his lips, not wanting to hear Meredith's next comment.

"That's soon." *That's the one.* He knew she would mention the time frame he had. "What are you thinking, Caleb?" She narrowed her eyes. Caleb expected a harsh tone, one that was telling him to stop now, but instead, Meredith seemed to genuinely be asking what was going through his mind.

Caleb glanced over to Brooke. She had taken a seat next to Greg and was showing them the photos on her phone. Helen pointed and then looked up at Brooke, whose cheeks had turned red.

"Hopefully, we can stay in contact. Email and phone calls. This is just a fling," he admitted, not liking the sound of the word *fling*.

Meredith hummed. "A fling. You may want to make sure that's okay with her."

"She's sweet," Ethan agreed.

"You don't like her," Caleb added.

Ethan shrugged. "I didn't much care for her wanting to date you, but all these ideas and changes... It's a good thing she's here to help before we lose everything. Maybe I was just being too closed minded, on both sides of the coin—business and dating related." Ethan rubbed Meredith's thigh and then jumped off the Jeep. "I want to see these pictures she took of you. She's blushing an awful lot."

Caleb sighed and watched him walk over to Brooke, sitting down next to her in the grass. He watched the group a little longer, desperately wanting to go over there with them, wanting to be done with this photo shoot to go back to the lake with Brooke. Just him and her, a pole, and her laptop. That was what he wanted to do.

"It's not just a fling, is it?" Meredith asked gently, catching his attention, placing her hand on his shoulder.

He pursed his lips and inhaled. "I'm not sure. I haven't felt this way in a long time."

Meredith slid her hand down to his, giving it a friendly, reassuring squeeze. "It's a funny feeling, isn't it?" She jumped off the Jeep. "Just make sure you talk to her before you decide it's a fling."

Caleb took a deep breath. *It's not a fling.* He turned back to Brooke, the same catching smile and sparkle in her eye. His stomach dropped. *Definitely not a fling.*

Twenty

"Perfect," Brooke exclaimed, clapping her hands and leaning back in the small chair. "I just sent these photos off to Steven, and he should have a mock-up for me tomorrow." She looked up at Caleb sitting across from her.

"That's fast," he amused, slight shock in his voice. That's definitely not what he was expecting.

"It helps when you have connections." She used her palms to push herself off the table.

It had been hours since they returned from Crystal. Ethan and Meredith had made their way home, and Helen and Greg were back at the lodge. It was just Brooke and Caleb at the office. Caleb had brewed some coffee and made a simple dinner for them. Caleb hadn't mentioned her leaving at all. Perhaps he wanted her there as much as she wanted to be there. Even though she had a fun time taking photos of Caleb and his friends, she wanted more time with just him.

"When do you need to get back to the lodge?" he asked softly, bringing his mug of coffee to his lips.

Brooke turned to him, wondering how he could have just read her mind. "Whenever, really. I'm not under any strict curfew. I think the only one who cares that I'm here is Rhonda, now that Greg has lightened up a bit."

"Rhonda?" he asked.

Brooke scrunched her nose. "I've barely seen her, but the interactions I have with her are not fun. Frank and Melinda say she's just old-fashioned. I say she's pretentious."

"So," he said in almost a whisper, "you don't need to leave just yet? I haven't even seen my solo pictures yet."

Brooke glanced at the clock behind him. The sun was setting behind the mountains, bringing warmth to the town even as the temperature dropped. The dark clouds that had rolled in during the photo shoot brought a small rain but moved on quickly, allowing the sky to turn pink.

She shook her head. "No, not necessarily." She leaned against the counter. "And I promise, your pictures are amazing. You'll see them tomorrow on the mock-up website." she sighed. "I should get back to the lodge and get those last two thousand words written for my agent."

"You could..." He stood and walked towards her, placing his hands on either side of her, leaning against the counter. He looked at her, their lips inches apart. "Write them here." Heat radiated from his voice, making Brooke's knee shake.

Brooke locked his gaze. "I could. You do have amazing internet service."

Caleb let out a light chuckle, slowly leaning into her. "Amazing service," he whispered against her lips, kissing her before she could let out any comment in return.

She ran her hands up his chest and around his neck, her fingers lacing through his hair. She broke the kiss and took in a deep breath, slowly opening her eyes, keeping his gaze.

"And what would you be doing as I work?"

Caleb thought, narrowing his eyes and looking behind Brooke. "I'm not sure." He lifted his hands on the counter and placed them on Brooke's back, pulling her as close as he could get her. "I could..." he trailed off, thought trickling across his face.

Brooke laughed. "I would say read, but you told me you're not much of a reader."

"In all honesty," he said with a sigh, "I just want to sit with you. I don't care what we're doing. I just want to be with you as much as I can before you leave. I get this feeling with you, and I like it," he whispered, pulling his eyes back to hers.

"A warm feeling?" she asked, half joking, a smile tugging on her lips

"Tingly, fuzzy, jittery..." He smiled. "All the romantic, mushy words."

"Romantic?" Brooke's smile widened. "I will say, this was not what I thought was going to happen coming to Marble. I figured I'd be locked in that lodge like the others, just trying to get an outline done. I didn't expect to find a story... or you."

"It's been two days..." Caleb began.

"Three days. We met Sunday night," Brooke corrected him.

"Three days," he repeated. "But you do something to me, Brooke, and I would like to figure out what that something is."

"With me writing two thousand words while you just sit there and watch?" Brooke asked, arching her back slightly so she could get a better look at him, leaving her hands resting on the nape of his neck.

"Well"—Caleb chuckled—"I will be trying to distract you."

Brooke laughed and kissed him again, allowing that same feeling to radiate through her body.

~

A few hours and two thousand words later, Brooke returned to the lodge, her dead laptop in her hand. She sighed in relief, knowing she had completed the task her agent wanted. Before the deadline even. Now she needed someone to proofread and edit what she wrote before sending it on its way.

She was quiet when she opened the lodge door, the old wooden door making way more sound than she wanted it to. Greg was on the couch, his laptop on his lap.

"Oh, hey," he said, sounding different than he had any other time Brooke talked to him. "How was the website building?" he asked.

She was taken aback. He wasn't asking about her writing?

She came over and sat on the couch across from him. "It was good. I was able to send a lot of pictures to Steven. We will see what he does. How was your evening?" she asked.

Greg laughed. "Great, actually."

"How many words?" Brooke asked, a soft smile on her lips.

Greg started at his screen and then back to Brooke. "Almost seven thousand."

Brooke widened her eyes. "Seriously? From blocked to book. That's amazing."

"Helen helped talk me through a lot as we sat there in the ghost town. We talked about our characters and timelines, and when we got back, it clicked for both of us. Helen has been downstairs and on the deck all evening. I've seen her maybe once when she came up for a glass of water." He laughed. Greg instantly returned to his laptop, beginning to click away on the keys. "It was a great idea to get out of the lodge. Thanks, Brooke."

"Not a problem." She sighed. "My laptop died while I was with Caleb."

"But you got everything sent off to your friend, right?"

She nodded. "Oh, yeah. We are going to work on the social media feeds tomorrow, and"—she touched her laptop as if it were a treasure chest—"I got the last two thousand words done."

Greg looked up at her. "That's great. Did you send it off?"

Brooke shook her head. "No, it's not ready yet. I need someone to read over it for me before I send it off."

"Joyce, maybe?" Greg suggested.

"I was thinking about asking her, for sure. I definitely can't ask Rhonda."

"Ask me what?" Rhonda's voice came from the upstairs landing. She was standing straight, with one hand on the railing, as if she were a queen waiting to ascend the stairs to address her people.

"Oh, um..." Brooke stammered, "I was able to get the first seven thousand words down, and I need some honest feedback before I send them to my agent."

Rhonda hummed and came walking down the steps. "It's a period piece?" she asked.

Brooke furrowed her brow. "Yeah, late 1800s."

Rhonda lifted her chin and crossed her arms across her body. "Let me read it," she said simply.

Brooke looked at Rhonda and then at Greg, who looked just as shocked as she did. Neither one said anything.

"I'll read it," Rhonda said again. This time her tone was harsh. "I am known to give fair and honest feedback for first drafts."

"Rhonda, I can't ask you to do that. You're busy working on your first draft..." Brooke began.

"And since that is almost done," Rhonda said, the same sternness as before, "let me read it."

Brooke nodded. The feeling she always had in school crept up, as if the teacher were mad and sending her to the principal's office (which happened more than Brooke would like to admit). "Okay," she agreed. "I'll see if Caleb will let me print it up."

"Nonsense." Rhonda waved her hand. "Email it to me."

"But you have a typewriter," Greg chirped.

"I always use a typewriter for my first draft. Then I rewrite the second on my computer." Rhonda spun to the entryway, grabbing a pamphlet to Caleb's business and a pen, jotting down her email and holding it out to Brooke. "Send it over tonight. I'll read it before I go to bed."

Brooke took the piece of paper hesitantly. "Thank you," she said shyly.

Rhonda nodded and then turned to go to the kitchen. Brooke's hand was frozen in midair, holding the paper. She turned to Greg, her eyes wide.

"Did that just happen?" she whispered.

Greg nodded. "You may want to prepare your soul for her review."

Brooke couldn't tell if he was joking or not. Suddenly, a fire began to build in the pit of her stomach, and her nerves shot through the roof. "It won't be that bad, will it?" she whispered back. "It's just a rough draft."

Greg shrugged. "You'll just have to email it and see what she says."

Brooke didn't know how to respond to Rhonda's offer. She held the piece of paper and looked at the email written in elegant cursive. She glanced back up to the kitchen, able to see Rhonda reach for a glass for water.

"I guess I better go email the pages to her," she stammered, standing up carefully, leaving Greg alone in the living room.

"Good luck." He chuckled.

As she went down the small hall that led to her room, Rhonda said, "Send me the manuscript. I'll read it tonight."

Brooke glanced over her shoulder at her and nodded. "I will. Right now." She opened her bedroom door and plugged her computer in, giving it life before making it work once again.

Twenty-One

- Thursday -

"The pretentious one wants to read what you wrote?" Caleb asked the next morning, casting his line into the lake. Brooke sat on a rock next to him, wrapped up in her blanket with a thermos of warm coffee hugged between her hands.

She took a sip of her coffee, causing an audible slurp, and nodded. "I sent it off to her last night. We will see what she says. I've never been more nervous about someone reading my work, not even when I was first talking to my agent. That was a piece of cake compared to Rhonda." Brooke shuffled on the rock, trying to find a comfortable place.

"Maybe she's not as pretentious as you think," he suggested.

Brooke sipped her coffee. "It would be easier if she were. I could have avoided her, or I could have just said no," Brooke grumbled. "Helen and Greg, I like. Joyce is really nice and she's helped a lot, but Rhonda... she has rubbed me wrong since the first night, and now she wants to help?"

"It's not a bad thing, Brooke." He looked down at her, beginning to reel in his line.

She squinted her eyes up at him. "I know. I'm just being off about it because it's such a new idea. I don't want her to completely destroy it."

Caleb focused back on the fishing line. "She won't destroy it. Don't authors lift each other up and give feedback? Isn't that a part of writing?" he asked.

"Well, yeah," Brooke mumbled.

"Then stop stressing about it. I know it's not a fun thought but think about where you were on Monday morning. Wrapped up in the same blanket trying to figure out *what* to write. Now you have seven-thousand words of possible pure gold. Don't stress and take what Rhonda says with an open mind." He finished reeling in the small fish that flopped in the water. Bending down to unhook it, he looked at her. "Ethan wasn't thrilled either, remember? And look what happened yesterday." Caleb stood and watched the fish swim off.

"You didn't name him," Brooke said softly.

"That was Kevin." He gestured to the lake before baiting his line.

Brooke watched him. He seemed so sure of himself at this moment, as if all his worries and fears were gone just being at the lake. Here, he didn't have to think about the company or any financial troubles he was having. All he had to do here was worry about what bait he needed to catch the most fish. He was so relaxed, so perfect in the moment.

She heaved a sigh. If only she could let go like he did and turn her brain off.

"How do you know she's not going to hate it?" she asked, still unsure of the entire situation.

Caleb sighed. "I don't." He stepped to her and held out his hand. "Come here. You're casting this one." He lifted her off the rock, the blanket falling to the ground. She took the pole from him and did the steps he had taught her the other night to cast. It landed with a *plop* in the middle of the lake. "Nice one." He rubbed her back. "Listen."

Brooke kept her eyes on the lake but concentrated on his hand on her back.

"No matter what she says, she's not the end all. You don't need to impress her. You need to impress your agent. Rhonda has published how many books?" he asked.

"Forty," Brooke mumbled solemnly.

Caleb let out a scoff. "Take her experience and comments and try to make what you wrote better. She has forty books under her belt, so maybe her wisdom can come in handy."

Brooke turned and glared up at him.

He raised his eyebrows.

"You're right," she mumbled. "I don't want you to be, but you are."

Caleb wrapped his arm around her shoulders. "Don't worry so much. It's going to be great."

She leaned into him, enjoying the warmth he offered. She gently handed him the fishing pole. He took it and set it on some rocks, keeping the line in the lake. Caleb pulled her into a hug, wrapping his arms completely around her. She fell into his embrace, breathing him in. The past few days with Caleb meant more for Brooke than she was letting on. She didn't want to scare him, yet she wanted all of him. She pulled her head up, meeting his gaze, leaning in to kiss him. His trimmed beard from yesterday tickled her skin as she sank deeper into him. Slowly, he broke the kiss and leaned his forehead on hers.

"What are we doing today?" he asked, gently kissing her nose.

Brooke pulled her forehead away and looked up at him. "We need to look at the mock website and set up your social media feeds. I wanted to write a blog post about Marble and the mill and then maybe a movie?" She smiled. "It seems to be a very busy day for us."

Caleb turned to look over his shoulder. "I need to take you to the mine still."

"The mine?" Brooke asked.

"The marble mine, the town's namesake." He turned back to her. "So I vote after we name one more fish, we head back to the office, then maybe take a trip to the gallery in town."

"There is so much more to this town." She smiled. "I love that idea, but..." She pulled away from Caleb. "I should go talk to Rhonda."

Caleb bent down and picked up the fishing pole. "After this fish."

She took the pole back and stepped in front of Caleb, who wrapped his arms around her waist, letting her lean into him. "After this fish," she repeated.

Brooke took a deep breath, smelling the crisp air mixed with Caleb's light cologne. She hadn't noticed the cologne when they first met. The thought of him trying to impress her more each day brought a smile to her lips. She leaned her head back on his collarbone and told the fish to take his dear sweet time to find the bait.

Brooke *did not* want to talk to Rhonda. Even with Caleb reassuring her that it wasn't as bad as it seemed, she had no desire to go back to the lodge to talk to where Rhonda was waiting for her. It wasn't just the fact that Rhonda was reading her work. It was the idea that Rhonda, who had made it quite clear that she was experienced, was *critiquing* her work. She remembered her words, *honest and fair* reviews. She could feel the nerves coming back, and her body tensed.

"Hey," Caleb whispered in her ear. "Get out of your head."

Brooke groaned. "It's very hard to. Maybe you should read it, or Rosie; anyone but Rhonda."

Caleb laughed. "You already sent it to Rhonda, but I'm sure Rosie would read it for you."

The line jerked. Brooke lifted her head and glared at the lake. "That better be seaweed."

Caleb's laugh grew. "It's a fish. Let's reel him in, name it, and get you back to the lodge to talk to Rhonda. I guarantee you, it won't be as bad as you're thinking." Caleb placed his hand over hers on the pole and helped her pull the fish up.

"Hi, Paul," Brooke muttered.

"Hey there, Paul. Thanks for a good catch." Caleb unhooked the fish and released him back, rubbing his back a few times before he finally took off swimming.

Caleb dropped Brooke off at the lodge, giving her a quick kiss goodbye, telling her once again, it wouldn't be as bad as she thought. She watched him drive off and then slowly walked into the lodge. She prepared herself for Rhonda to be waiting for her, but when she found an empty living room and Rhonda's bedroom door wide open with no Rhonda to be found, the nerves that followed her in the building faded.

"Hello?" she called.

"In here," Joyce said from the dining room. Slowly she made it to where Joyce was, finding her sitting at the long dining room table with a notebook and pen in front of her. Brooke glanced at the white pages, her delicate cursive writing filling the empty spaces. "Rhonda told me to tell you she would be back this afternoon, and that she has some notes for you."

Brooke swallowed. "Good notes?"

Joyce hummed. "I'm not sure, dear. Rhonda is a very good reader and editor."

"Caleb told me it wouldn't be as bad as I was making it out to be." Brooke sat down across from Joyce.

Joyce gave her the softest smile, one that went along with Caleb's words. "He's a good guy. I tried to look for information on their tours, and I noticed the pamphlets were years old."

Brooked rolled her eyes. "Yeah, we are working on that. I don't want him to lose his company. I know it's silly, but I really like him."

"It's not silly. You, my dear, are a romance writer. It's only fitting you should get your own little romance." Joyce wrote a few words on the page, then turned back up to Brooke. "It amazes me you were able to get Rhonda to read your pages. She's not fond of romance novels."

"Well, it's a historical romance." Brooke groaned, taking a deep breath. "She writes mysteries?" Brooke asked. "I think that is what she mentioned at the bonfire."

Joyce nodded. "She used to work for the FBI as a crime scene investigator. She's taken all her knowledge from the field and poured it into her books. Her husband passed away about fifteen years ago in a car accident, and she's been writing ever since."

"You've known her for how long?"

"Just three years, but she and I have stayed in contact after each retreat. We send each other things to read and give notes." Joyce kept eye contact with Brooke, giving her headway into what Rhonda was like other than the writer she came to 'know.' "She's not a mean person. She's just old-fashioned."

"You've said that a lot." Brooke sneered. "She seems to not like us."

"She does. She likes how people still have stories to tell and the world isn't being drowned out by television." Joyce took a deep breath. "All it takes is some inspiration, right?" She looked at Brooke, the same kind smile she had gotten used to seeing.

"Right." Brooke gave Joyce the same soft smile. "Thank you, Joyce,"

"I'm not sure for what, but"—Joyce picked up her pen and continued to write—"anytime, my dear."

The mock website had arrived and looked phenomenal on Brooke's computer. The banner was a wide picture of the town of Crystal, with Caleb and Ethan standing elbow to elbow in the middle. Steven had chosen a brown and green fall color scheme, which Brooke thought matched the town perfectly.

"This is beautiful," she said, clicking through all the different tabs Steven created. "I may have him remake my website after this!"

"It's fancy," Ethan said over her shoulder. "Like, way fancy."

Brooke clicked on the *About Us* tab, bringing up the photos she had taken. Ethan held onto Meredith's hand, and Caleb stood, his hands in his pockets with a slight smile.

"Oh, you picked good ones." Ethan gently punched Brooke's shoulder, making her body rock to the side.

"Do you want to see?" Brooke asked Caleb, who had kept to the counter.

Ethan stood up straight and gave Caleb a huge thumbs up. "You're going to like it."

Caleb came around and leaned over Brooke's shoulder. "Whoa," he said, taking a look at the screen. "This is not what I was picturing."

"Is that a good thing?" Brooke asked, leaning her body to look at Caleb behind her.

"That's a great thing." He took control of Brooke's small mouse and began to click through all the tabs. Steven had created a menu, complete with *Home*, *About Us*, *Tours and Pricing*, and *History*. Caleb clicked on *History*. "Why is it blank?"

Brooke bobbed her shoulders. "Well, that's where research and photos come in. I have a bunch of photos to send him, but do you have a history of the town you can gather? You two know a lot about it. I can send it over as soon as possible so he can upload it."

Caleb looked toward Ethan.

"On it." Ethan pointed up, like he was struck with an idea and then went to pull paper from the printer.

"See? He's so into it now," Caleb muttered. He turned back to Brooke and took a seat next to her, the chair scratching across the wood flooring. "How did the talk go with Rhonda?"

Brooke shrugged. "She wasn't there." She turned to her computer and clicked on the *About Us* tab, wanting to see Caleb's photo again. "Joyce said she would be back this afternoon, so…"

Brooke clenched her teeth and turned to face Caleb. "We may have to push the mine trip to tomorrow. I don't know what Rhonda is going to say about my pages."

Caleb reached over and moved a stray piece of hair behind her ear, locking her gaze. "Not a problem. That's more important than a trip to the mine." Quickly touching his thumb and forefinger to her chin, Caleb stood up, sticking his hands in his pockets. Brooke wished once again she knew him better, to be able to tell if he was hurt or not by the sudden change in plans. Smiling at him, she turned back to her computer. "But," Caleb said, making her turn back to him, "promise me we can go tomorrow?"

She leaned toward him. "It's a date." Raising her chin, she gave him a sweet, gentle kiss.

Twenty-Two

Brooke spent the next few hours with Ethan and Caleb, setting up social media sites and a blog. Caleb watched her work quickly, not entirely sure how he was going to keep everything up once she was gone. He had computer knowledge but seeing as his computer usage had gone down the past three years, he was rusty. Internet? No problem. Basic Google searches? He could handle that all day. Running a website, blog, *and* social media? He was getting a headache just thinking of it all.

All he wanted to do was grab Brooke by the wrist, pull her upstairs and watch *Hitchhiker's Guide to the Galaxy* with her, but she was so hyper-focused on everything for the company. Not that he wasn't grateful. He just wanted her...not her computer.

Ethan was now in full swing, taking in every aspect of social media. He and Brooke decided he would be the Instagram and Facebook guru, since living in Carbondale offered more cell phone service and the availability to post regularly. Caleb was happy that was off his plate, but that left him with the website.

After a few more tutorials on how to post their first blog post, Brooke gathered up her things and made her way to her car. Caleb followed her out, just wanting some time. He held her hand as she took the short few steps to the road to where her Chevy was parked. When they arrived at her car, he pulled her in for a hug and kiss, wishing it were more. Brooke promised she would be back in the morning and that she was all his the next day, excited for their trip to the mine. He opened her car door for her, leaned in for one last kiss and waved as she drove away.

Once the Chevy turned and was out of sight, he leaned his head back and groaned. His frustration with everything was finally coming out. He could let out a scream right here if it wouldn't send the entire town into a panic. The groan would have to do.

He went back inside, rubbing his eyes. It was past five, and he had completely skipped out on lunch. He stood there, like a zombie, fixated on the clock.

"Are you okay?" Ethan finally asked.

Caleb blinked. "Yeah, my head is just spinning."

"Didn't you used to be a lawyer?" he asked. "This stuff should be simple for you."

"It's not that it isn't simple. It's just all coming at us so fast. I mean"—Caleb walked over to the counter and laid his palms down on the wood—"four nights ago, I met a girl at the lake. I thought about her all night. The next day, she was there again, frustrated she couldn't write the description of a lake. So I took her to Crystal. Did I want to impress her? Sure, but I didn't expect this."

Ethan stared at him. "What exactly did you expect? Brooke has been a major help, and I think it will do good—"

Caleb waved his hand, signaling Ethan to stop. "Oh no, this is fine. Sure, the blog kinda intimidates me and the website is really advanced, but none of that bothers me. What bugs me is it's taking up my time with Brooke. She's only here until Monday." He turned, ran his hands through his hair, falling onto the chair that Brooke had claimed the past few days. "I haven't felt this way about anyone since Audrey."

Ethan looked at his friend. "Have you told her this?"

"No, Meredith told me to." He took a deep breath. "She said I needed to talk to her about what she wants from this before I label it a *fling*."

"Damn, my wife is smart," Ethan muttered under his breath. "I can tell you this, though. You've had more life in you since she walked through that door than I've seen in the past year. She's doing great things, more things than just helping the business." Ethan motioned toward the computer. "Which, by the way, once this website is up, I think we may have a shot at getting more reservations. And the social media, imagine how gorgeous that page will be."

Caleb chuckled. "She knows her stuff." He grinned just thinking about her. "When we went to dinner, we were asking each other all kinds of questions, and she asked about movies—"

"Oof, you don't watch movies," Ethan mumbled, before turning back to Caleb.

"We have the same favorite movie. We said we would watch it together and make a fire and do s'mores. I want to take her to the mine and on the loop trail. I want to fish with her again, even if she is just sitting on the rock with my coffee cup and a blanket. Just having her there, talking to her would be amazing." Caleb stopped. "I don't have much time left with her. Then what? Back to normal?"

"Except this time, we have potentially more business," Ethan joked.

Caleb scoffed, closing his eyes before Ethan got the eye roll. "Yeah, more business."

"Listen, Caleb," Ethan said softly, "I'm not one to tell you what to think or do. Hell, Meredith jokes my only romantic bone is in my ear, but I can tell you that if you really want to do all those things, then make it happen. Maybe we can hold off on things tomorrow, get that website in full gear. I can take Mer up the Loop Trail and take some pictures for Instagram, and you can take Brooke to the mine, have a cheesy picnic, and tell her how you feel."

"I don't even know how I feel. It's been three days."

Ethan shrugged. "That's all you can do. You still have time tonight. You could go up to the lodge and have that bonfire. Hell, run to Carbondale and get things for s'mores and surprise her."

Caleb's eyes lit up. "Meredith is wrong, you know."

"I know." He shrugged. "Wait, about what?"

"You have more than that one romantic bone. Here I am complaining, and you just nonchalantly remind me that I'm being a dick and that there's time tonight." Caleb stood up. "Do you mind closing up? I have to run to Carbondale."

Ethan shrugged and flashed Caleb his signature smile. "Sure thing."

Caleb grabbed a Jeep key and ran out the door, all too excited to surprise Brooke with s'mores.

"Alright, Brooke," Rhonda said, her laptop and a notebook spread in front of her on the dining room table. Brooke sat across from her and waited, the fire in her stomach rising. She quickly noted where the closest bathroom was, in case she needed it. She may have to throw up. "Let's talk about these pages."

"I'm not going to lie," Brooke interrupted. "I'm scared to death right now."

Rhonda lowered her eyebrows. "Why?" she asked sternly.

"Because you're intimidating, Rhonda. I honestly didn't think I would be sitting with you in the same room for a lengthy amount of time, yet here we are with my work in front of you, and I'm terrified." Brooke spoke at lightning speed, unsure as to how she was able to get everything out in one fluid sentence.

Rhonda nodded. "I will admit that I haven't been the easiest to get along with on this retreat, but I had work I needed to do and young writers coming in with their laptops thinking they had more gusto than Joyce and me—"

Brooke shook her head. "We never thought—"

Rhonda held up a finger, stopping Brooke. "But, after seeing how hard everyone has been working, I have decided to..." She waved her hands in front of her, sitting up straighter as if her hands were pushing her up. "Come out of my shell. I still want to get my work done, but I also know when a fellow writer needs my help."

Brooke swallowed and nodded. "Thank you, but it's still intimidating," she said sheepishly.

"Who has read your work before your agent? How did *Winter's Edge* become so popular?" Rhonda asked, lacing her fingers together and setting them on the table, much like a therapist or principal would.

"I self-published first, and I mean, I did everything. I wrote the book, I rewrote the book, I asked my mother to read it for me, and after she gave me feedback, I rewrote it again. It was a long time of writing and rewriting before I finally got the guts to hire an editor and publish. It wasn't until a few months after that I got contacted by an agent who wanted to represent me. By then, it had already sold a lot of copies and a few people had read it, but..." Brooke trailed off. "I honestly don't know why it became so popular. People like tragic love stories, I guess." She shrugged.

Rhonda shook her head. "There is more to it than a tragic love story. You put so much work into your first novel, so maybe this novel seems daunting as if you are saying 'oh, my agent will take care of that. Oh, the editor will fix all those pesky mistakes,' so it doesn't mean as much to you as your first novel."

Brooke furrowed her brow. "What are you saying?"

She tried not to let the anger pile up. Brooke knew that this book was just as important as her first, if not more. This one may set the tone for the rest of her career. She wiggled her shoulders, trying to force herself to pretend to be comfortable. Rhonda obviously didn't understand.

"I can tell in these first seven thousand words that you aren't focused on it. It's not what is living inside your heart. Did writing this bring you any joy, or any pleasure at all?" Rhonda asked, pointing to her computer screen.

Brooke thought. *Did it?*

When she thought of her new novel, what else came to mind? *Caleb.*

The first five thousand words were written after spending an entire day with Caleb, smiling and laughing with him throughout their adventure. The last two thousands were written in between Caleb's soft kisses and him trying to distract her by tickling her thighs and kissing her neck. Caleb had eventually started playing with his tackle box, but even that didn't keep his attention for long. When Brooke had hit sixty-eight hundred words, Caleb began touching her in just the right places, and she almost dropped the computer on the ground. She tightened her lips just thinking about it. Maybe the passion was for Caleb, and not the new novel.

"I mean," Brooke started, fully aware of the fact that she was blushing. "I love the idea, but maybe it is a little forced."

Rhonda raised her eyebrows. "If you're not writing this for you first, it's not going to be a good novel."

"I want to write it for me, but I'm literally being pressured to write anything. I don't think they care what it is, just as long as I write it."

"Publishers can do that to you sometimes. They need the work just as much as you do." Rhonda slid her computer to the side. "What is bringing you joy right now? Maybe we can channel that into the book."

Brooke looked at Rhonda through her lashes. "You're not going to like my answer."

"The fisherman." Rhonda nodded.

"Caleb." Her voice was noticeably more stern. Caleb was more than just a fisherman.

Rhonda sighed. "What is it about Caleb? I notice he has made his way into your novel."

Brooke nodded and looked down at her hands, her fingers picking at her nails. She fidgeted them, forcing herself to stop.

"He's different. He's like no one I've ever met before. I want to be with him all the time, and I want to help him save his company. I don't care about this book right now. I want to help Caleb. To me, at this exact moment, that's what matters."

Rhonda furrowed her brow and tilted her head. Confusion swept over her face. "Save his company?" she repeated.

"He's losing it. If he doesn't get reservations, he can't pay the mortgage, and then it's gone. He didn't tell me how much longer he has, but..." she trailed off, "I'm trying to help while I'm here. I know writing is the main goal, but I can't let Caleb lose more than he already has."

Rhonda stared at her. Brooke could feel tears...*tears*...welling up inside her eyes. She blinked once, then twice, trying to get the tears to stay put. To no avail, the few tears she had dripped down her face.

"I have no idea why I'm crying." Brooke chuckled, wiping a tear from her cheek. "Anyway, maybe my heart isn't in those pages, but it's what I have to work with until I can get a new deadline from my agent." She sniffed, taking the subject back to the novel at hand.

Rhonda sighed. "I think"—her voice grew soft, softer than Brooke had ever heard, and suddenly Rhonda wasn't the stuck-up author of forty books who lugged around her typewriter and locked herself in her room. She was a fellow writer who genuinely cared for her colleagues and was trying to help and find the voice every author needed. Brooke saw Rhonda in a totally different light. "I think there is heart and passion in this novel. We just need to find it. Here, I have written down some notes, and I think they will help you." She slid her notebook toward her and picked up the fountain pen that rested on the table.

Brooke leaned forward as the last tear dried up, finding her bearings. She sniffled and looked at Rhonda as she turned her computer screen so Brooke could see it as well. Brooke's stomach calmed, and her head began to clear.

"Let's start with *your* fisherman," Rhonda said calmly.

Twenty-Three

Caleb drove up the hill and parked the Jeep in front of the lodge. The only guiding light he had to go off of was the moon, and even then, he wasn't sure of his footing on the balcony stairs carrying a basket and blanket. He wasn't one for grand gestures, if you could consider this grand, but he did tell Brooke that they would enjoy a bonfire with s'mores.

The lodge's window had one single light shining through, and Caleb could hear the light tapping of a keyboard as he approached. He lightly knocked on the door, the basket and blanket dangling in his free arm.

The door opened, and Caleb was greeted by Greg, who gave a small chuckle and simply said, "I'll go get Brooke."

Caleb smiled at him as he shut the door. Caleb was only alone for a few minutes until the door opened again, this time by Brooke. She was wearing the same pajama pants she had on the other morning, accompanied by a burnt orange hoodie with a pumpkin on it. Her blonde hair was tied up in a messy bun with her glasses sat perched on top of her head and a smile grew on her lips.

"Caleb," she said softly, audible joy in her voice. "I wasn't planning on seeing you tonight."

Caleb shrugged and felt the smile tug at his lips. "We have a bonfire to make." He stepped back and held up the basket. "I brought things for s'mores and a blanket because I knew you would get cold."

Brooke bit her bottom lip, and her cheeks tinted pink. "Okay, just..." She sighed, her body pivoting back in the lodge. "Let me go turn off my computer."

Caleb smiled back at her as she turned, leaving him alone on the deck. He took a few steps back, patiently watching the door for Brooke to appear again. The door creaked open, and Brooke skipped out, a smile on her lips and shoes on her feet. She reached her hands out and grabbed the blanket from Caleb, and together they used the moon to walk down the sixteen steps to the fire pit. Caleb helped Brooke step over the many stones and logs that were on the ground and guided her to the wooden bench. He sat the basket next to her and began to prepare the pit for the fire.

"So"—Caleb looked up at her once he got a spark burning against the logs—"how was the rest of your day?"

Brooke let out a long sigh of relief. "It was actually really good. You were right." She kept her eyes on the wood, and the embers turned red as the fire began to grow. Caleb walked toward her, grabbing the basket and placing it at his feet.

"I know," he said on instinct. "About what?" He looked over his shoulder at her, his eyebrows furrowed.

She chuckled. "Rhonda. The talk with her was very constructive, and her notes and ideas helped a lot. In fact, I revised everything, and now I'm at thirteen thousand words."

Caleb chuckled to himself. "See, I told you. Maybe she's not as bad as she seemed." He pulled out the Hershey chocolate and the graham crackers, followed by the marshmallows "And by the sound of it, you were able to take everything she said and just"—he flourished his hand in front of him—"blossomed." He widened his grin.

"Please don't talk like that again." Brooke chuckled and lightly hit his arm with the back of her hand. "How was your afternoon?"

"Boring, but decent. I went to Carbondale and...oh!" He began to dig through the basket. "I found this at the grocery store." He sat down next to her and held a book out in front of her.

The dark mountain scape cover appeared in front of the fire. The light blue lettering could barely be seen, but Brooke saw her book's title and her name with clarity. The small silhouette of Daniel and Mira hung in the corner, the romance being felt through the cover. Even though Brooke wasn't involved in the design when the book was re-released, she did love the way the cover turned out. It was *Winter's Edge* in all its glory. Brooke laughed and then looked up at Caleb.

"You bought one?" Brooke asked through her laughs.

Caleb looked at the book and smiled. "I had to." He flipped the pages quickly through his fingers, landing on the back to show a picture of Brooke standing in the snow-covered mountains of Utah. "It seems good. Maybe I'll read it."

"Remind me to sign it for you." Brooke bumped him with her shoulder and began to unfold the blanket. "But you don't have to read it. It's more geared toward sappy romantics."

"I can be a sappy romantic." He placed the book back in the basket and then reached for the roasting stick, jabbing two marshmallows on the ends. "Are you ready for the best s'more you've ever had in your entire life?" Caleb asked, gently lowering the roasting stick over the fire.

Brooke wrapped the blanket around her shoulders and leaned into him, resting her head on his shoulder. "Totally."

Caleb took a deep breath, enjoying the warmth Brooke's body offered. "Tell me about Salt Lake," Caleb muttered. "I've never been."

Brooke groaned. "It's crowded and busy. The traffic sucks and the air quality is terrible and there are two seasons, winter and construction."

Caleb chuckled. "Okay, so tell me something good about Salt Lake."

Brooke lifted her head and rested her chin on Caleb's shoulder. She sighed. "It really is a beautiful city. Besides the air during the winter, it's clean. You can access anything you need from downtown by public transit or walking. The capitol building is amazing, and the Avenues is out of a novel. You have Memory Grove and City Creek Center. It really is beautiful. It's surrounded by the mountains, and all the ski-resorts are all right there. Pretty much anything is just a quick thirty-minute drive."

"You ski?"

Brooke shook her head. "Nope. Tried once and cried down the mountain. Vowed never again. Do you ski?"

Caleb shook his head. "I fish. Even when it's freezing outside and Rosie calls me crazy, you can find me by the lake."

Brooke grinned, resting her head on his shoulder again. "That sounds amazing though. Relaxing," she muttered.

Caleb turned the marshmallows and leaned to touch his cheek to the top of Brooke's head. Ethan's words rang through his head. *Make it happen. Tell her how you feel.*

Caleb sighed. He wasn't even sure how he felt. He liked Brooke, found her beauty compelling and enjoyed spending the days with her. Just the thought of her kisses sent chills down his back. Maybe he was scared. Maybe the nerves had just completely taken over. What was there to be nervous about? From the moment he met Brooke, nerves had only taken over once, and even then, it was short-lived. With Brooke, he just...*felt*. The feelings that he had buried from Audrey had come up again, thanks to Brooke, and he wasn't ready to let them go.

He leaned forward, forcing Brooke to sit up. He grabbed the crackers and chocolate and smooshed the perfectly roasted marshmallow in between them. He handed one over to Brooke. She dug her hand out from inside the blanket and gently took it, her fingers barely touching his.

"Oh, this is good," she said as soon as she swallowed. "I mean like..."

"I told you." Caleb took a bite of his. "Best s'more you'll ever have."

Brooke licked her lips. "Nothing will ever beat it." She turned to look at him. "Hey," she asked, making him turn toward her, "what's your favorite color?"

He lowered his eyebrows. "Favorite color? We went from your book to colors?"

Brooke licked the chocolate off the tip of her fingers and pulled her arm back into the blanket. She scooted closer to Caleb. He welcomed the shift.

"Yeah, favorite color?"

Caleb shook his head and looked up towards the stars. "Green. Yours?"

"Yellow and orange, like a sunset."

Caleb raised his eyebrows and nodded. He folded his arms. Even with the warmth from Brooke's body, he still felt the chill air. "Okay, so what's your favorite book?"

Brooke gasped. "Not that question."

"Nope, answer it."

Brooke scrunched her nose. "Well, I could go typical like *Pride and Prejudice,* or *Of Mice and Men;* which are both classics but not my favorites. My more recent all-time favorite isn't one book, it's an author."

"Okay then, favorite author." Caleb rephrased his question.

"She's a relatively new author, but I've loved all her books; Victoria Schade. She's a romance writer; slow burn romances that leave you wanting more once the book is done. I love those kinds of books."

"Is that how yours is?"

Brooke shook her head. "No, I killed my main character in the first twenty chapters so, there is no slow burn romance there."

Caleb lowered his eyes and turned his head toward her. "You killed your main character?"

"It's a tragic love story, not a happy one." She gawked. "It takes place during two timelines, so you get to see their love grow, even though you know one dies."

Caleb looked back toward the fire, trying to get it closer to her so he could ignore the chill. "Maybe I won't read it."

"But you said you could be a sappy romantic." Brooke turned her body to face him, a sarcastic tone aimed right at him.

Caleb felt a pinch in his heart. *Audrey*.

"Despite the fact that a dead spouse can sell books, it's hard to live through," he mumbled, grabbing the skewer and rubbing it against a log.

Brooke gasped. "Oh...Caleb, I didn't mean..." She stumbled over her words, and he could tell she didn't know exactly what to say. "I didn't think..." She heaved a sigh. "I'm sorry."

He shook his head. "It's okay. It's not something I talk about a lot. I miss her every day, but I also know that it's not going to change. How does your character deal with the death of her love?"

Brooke's eyes were wet. She sniffed and reached her hand through the blanket to attempt to wipe away a tear. "She doesn't."

Caleb bit his bottom lip. "I can understand that."

"I'm sorry, Caleb," Brooke whispered.

Caleb reached up and brushed the hair from her face, the same motion he had done when she first kissed him. "It's okay. Like I said, I don't like to talk about it a lot. Besides"—he smiled, attempting to lighten her mood once again—"I can be a sappy romantic," he whispered, "but I don't want to read about it. I want to live it." He leaned in, putting his lips closer to hers, gently touching them together before pulling away and sitting back on the bench, watching her every move.

"Well, that was mean." Brooke groaned, adjusting her blanket and sitting back next to him. He pulled his arm up and wrapped it around her shoulder, bringing her in close to him

He chuckled. "I'll give you plenty of attention tonight. I can guarantee that. And don't worry—I'm not upset."

Brooke looked up at him, and he could tell just from the glow of the fire that she was blushing. She heaved a deep breath and then turned away, trying to change the subject.

"Um," she stammered, "What is your favorite time of year?"

Caleb squeezed her shoulder, hoping to keep some of the emotions that caused her to blush. "I love the fall. Right before it snows. Summer is too damned hot, and spring is too muddy. Winter is beautiful but fall..." Caleb clicked his tongue. "I love the fall. Especially here."

"Agreed. The colors here are stunning. When does the snow come?"

Caleb thought. "It could be any time after September, really. The first snowstorm last year was in October."

"I love looking at the snow, but I don't like driving in the snow. I can't imagine what it's like here."

"With dirt roads, we can sometimes shut down, but almost everyone has their own plow so we get around."

"I wish Utah would shut down. Growing up, if you had snow up to the roof of your house, you would still go to school."

Caleb laughed. "Shutting down isn't all it's cracked up to be. Where were you when the pandemic started?"

"Working at the publisher. We didn't shut down. We just sent everyone home, and we figured out how to work remotely. I didn't get much 'work' done because that's when *Winter's Edge* really started to form." She shivered. "Damn, it's cold. Even under the blanket."

Caleb laughed. "I'm happy I brought it then. Just imagine how cold you would be without it."

Brooke sat up and pulled the blanket from her shoulders. "Come here." She motioned for Caleb to sit up. She took the blanket and threw it over his shoulders before settling herself back into his arms.

Caleb smiled now that there wasn't a blanket in between them anymore, and he gently ran his fingers against her shoulder.

"Okay, let's see," Brooke said softly, shifting her body slightly, getting even closer—if possible—to Caleb. "What is your…"

Caleb silenced her by placing his hand on her chin and pulling her toward him. He wanted to kiss her, not tease her again, but truly kiss her. She breathed him in and parted her lips as Caleb tangled his fingers in the stray hairs that flowed down from her messy bun. Her kiss was warm and intense as he slipped his tongue between her lips, tasting the chocolate that still lingered. He pulled away, ending the passion with a small, gentle kiss on her lips.

"I don't know what it is about you," he whispered into her neck, "but I can't get enough of you. I want you near me all day. I don't want to talk about my business, your book, or any kind of work. I just want you." He tilted his head, keeping his hand on her cheek, and locked eyes with her. "I want to know you. I want to feel you. I haven't had this feeling in a long time, and I'm not quite sure what to do."

If she wasn't blushing before, she was now. She sighed and placed a hand on Caleb's chest. She licked her lips and kept his gaze.

"Rhonda said—" She choked, trying to get the words out. Caleb raised his eyebrows at the knowledge that he caused that reaction in her. "Rhonda told me there was no passion in my words. That my heart didn't seem to be in it. She asked what was bringing me joy and said we can try to channel that in my novel. I thought of you, Caleb, and the words just flowed." She brushed her lips against his. "You were the passion I needed."

Caleb kissed her again, making sure she felt *his* passion, his want for her. She moved, straddling him on the bench. He ran his hands up her back under her sweater, feeling her bare skin against his fingertips, causing the blanket to fall off her shoulders. She ran her hands up his chest to the back of his neck, lacing her fingers together.

"I did promise you attention," he muttered against her lips, "and you, Brooke Easten, deserve all my attention."

Twenty-Four

What seemed like mere minutes after Caleb had brought heat to Brooke's freezing night, they extinguished the fire, and Caleb slowly walked her back up to the lodge. He held on to her hand as they carefully took each step and kissed her once more before she turned and went into the lodge, watching him turn the Jeep on and drive down the dirt road.

She took a deep breath of air, exhaled and turned, happy that she found an empty living room waiting for her, not one filled with people asking questions. She quietly went to her room, shutting the door behind her, suddenly wishing she had invited Caleb in.

She took off her sweater, letting the thin tank top fall back into place, and crawled into the bed. It was cold compared to the fireside with Caleb. As she lay her head down and stared at the dark ceiling, thoughts began to rush through her head.

Her new novel had seemed to find its way to life on its own, and she couldn't be more thrilled about that. Once she took

Rhonda's advice and let her heart find the way into the book, like she mentioned to Caleb, the words just came easier to her. After getting a good portion of the opening done, she felt confident that her agent would love the story. Even though that was the purpose of her trip to Colorado, that wasn't what consumed her mind.

Though she welcomed these feelings for Caleb, she was scared of them at the same time. Her last relationship ended in heartbreak after three years of being together. What she thought was going to be a proposal ended up being a breakup. It took her heart a long time to heal from that. Most of her emotions went into her writing, and she had told herself it wasn't going to be like that again. She had been on dates with men she was set up with, but now here she was, laying on a flat mattress, wishing Caleb was with her, keeping her company and helping her body regain the same warmth.

That was what scared her. She had only known him for a matter of days, but the feelings he created, the butterflies that sparked in her stomach every time she caught him looking at her... It was a new feeling, one she hadn't felt or had since she was dumped all those years ago. Caleb had said he had no idea what to do when it came to Brooke. If only he knew she had no idea, either.

She sighed, turning to her side and staring at her computer. There had to be something she could do to ease her mind. Her novel was in a good place, and she felt okay with stopping and focusing more on Caleb and his business. She had created the website with her friend. She had set up the social media sites. The only thing she hadn't done was write her blog or post to her social media.

Throwing the comforter back, she grabbed her laptop and connected to the hotspot before opening up her blog. Her fingers began to type as she thought of her trip so far in Marble, knowing she wanted everyone to know about this place. Everyone needed to see it. She wanted Caleb to thrive, not to worry anymore about the mortgage or how he was going to pay Ethan's salary that month. She knew she could only do so much, but maybe by just doing the simple things, it would all add up.

Her train of thought was interrupted by a light tapping on her door. She stopped typing and looked down at her pajamas. Her thin cotton tank top and blue sweatpants weren't exactly guest ready.

"Um...who is it?" she asked, trying to keep the cough from her throat.

"Helen. I was in the kitchen, and I heard typing..." Helen's soft voice came from the other side of the door.

She sighed. It would be okay for Helen to see her dressed this way. She saved her document and went to open the door. Helen stood with a smile on her face and held up her laptop. "Wanna have a writing race in the kitchen?"

Brooke laughed. "Sure." She grabbed her laptop and sweater, ignoring that it was well past eleven at night, and made her way to the kitchen. "I'm not writing my book though. It's for my blog; does that count?"

Helen turned back to her. "As long as we count words, and whoever writes the most in the next hour buys drinks after the retreat."

"I love the sound of that." Brooke chuckled. "I'm not much of a drinker though, so coffee if I win?"

"Coffee is ten times better, so yes." Helen took a seat at the island and opened her laptop. "What is the blog topic?"

"My trip, mainly to the town of Crystal. I hope readers will see it and then follow Caleb on his new social media sites." Brooke sat next to her, slipping her sweater back over her head.

Helen looked up at her. "How is the business consulting going with them, anyway? Have they taken your ideas?"

Brooke shrugged. "Oh, yeah. They've been excited about all the changes. Ethan is more open to it than he was in the beginning, but Caleb—" She shook her head. "He says he doesn't want to talk about it much."

Helen narrowed her eyes. "Why not? You'd think that would have consumed his mind. Having a feeling your business is going to die... I can't imagine." Helen shook her head and put her fingers on the keyboard.

Brooke looked at her, almost nervous to tell her the reason. "He says," she began, "that he wants to spend the time with me and not worry about what could happen. Just that he wants to be with me while I'm here."

Helen dropped her jaw. "Seriously?"

"Tonight he told me I deserved all his attention." She felt her heart flutter at the memory, the butterflies in her stomach returning and the heat in her cheeks.

"Oh, Brooke," Helen swooned, "every woman wants to be told that. Ditch the consulting and spend the rest of the time with him. Forget your novel too." Helen waved her hand in front of Brooke's computer. Brooke couldn't decide if Helen was being serious with the *ditch your novel* comment.

"I can't ditch my novel, but I want to help him. I don't want him to lose everything. I can spend time with him and help his business at the same time and squeeze in my novel here and there. I think I have a good plan going. I just need to write this blog and tell Ethan how to set up their blog site—"

Helen stopped her. "What's your plan for Monday morning when we all leave?"

"I hadn't thought that far," she admitted, realizing she had mostly avoided the thoughts or comments when they came up. "I was going to give him my phone number and stay in contact. I like him too much to just not talk to him anymore."

Helen shrugged and turned back to her computer. "Talk to him about that. It's gotta mean something more to him too; not just a fun week. I mean, he showed up here with a basket and a blanket. You two had a bonfire, and he didn't seem to want to leave." Helen let out a long breath. "I take it you're going to see him tomorrow at the lake?"

Brooke nodded. "He seems to go every morning, but if I plan to go see him, then we need to get this writing race on the way so I can get some sleep. He goes early."

Helen wiggled her eyebrows. "Alright then. My current word count is at twenty thousand. What's yours?"

Brooke laughed and told her the dismal word count for her blog post. Helen counted to three, and the two started typing furiously on their laptops. They had one hour to race each other on word count, and Brooke was determined to win that cup of coffee.

Twenty-Five

-Friday-

Caleb packed the Jeep early the next morning, a sense of elation in every step. The feelings and butterflies from the night before still hung in his stomach, and the more he thought about Brooke, the more prominent they became. They hadn't made plans to meet at the lake, but he had hoped she would come. He beamed at the idea of her being there.

Making sure the Jeep had everything he needed for the lake, he closed the tailgate and walked to the driver's door. As he opened the door to climb in, a horn honked, and Ethan pulled up beside him.

"Heading to the lake?" he asked, rolling down the window, his arm resting on the windowsill of the truck door.

Caleb nodded. "Yeah, just for an hour or two." He climbed in the Jeep. "Want to join?" he asked, suddenly wishing he could take it back.

Ethan shook his head, and Caleb breathed again. "Nah, I need to call the dealer in Carbondale. I am assuming we won't be selling a Jeep?"

Caleb shook his head. "I think Brooke's idea will help, so no...we won't be selling a Jeep." He flashed Ethan a large grin, turning the Jeep on. Backing up, he waved to Ethan. "I'll see you soon."

Ethan waved and turned back to the office. Caleb cranked the Jeep up and popped it in reverse. Grabbing his tackle box and pole when he arrived, he basically skipped to the lake. When he saw the camp chair with the blanket burrito sitting in it, his heart fluttered. He noticed she was reading, not on her laptop, which was a good change. She had said she found the flow to her new novel. Maybe she had decided it was enough. Maybe she had decided it would be okay to relax, possibly even enjoy her vacation.

"Good morning." He smiled once he approached her. He set his tackle box on the ground by her feet and glanced up at her. Her beanie hugged her head snuggly, and her glasses caught a slight glare from the sun, making it almost impossible to see her blue eyes. But the sun only amplified her rosy cheeks and pink lips.

"What'cha reading?" he asked, nodding to the book in her hand.

"Good morning." She flashed the book cover at him. A cartoon woman in red heels held onto a dog on a leash. The white words *Life on the Leash* hit him.

"Ah." He returned to the tackle box. "Victoria Schade, the new favorite author of yours."

"Yup, this is her first novel, and it also happens to be my favorite," Brooke stated, sticking the bookmark in the spine. "How many fish are we going to name this morning?"

Caleb shrugged. "Who knows?" He fitted the line with the hook and stuck the worm on the end.

"What, no cricket today?" Brooke asked as she watched the worm be stabbed to death.

Caleb shook his head and chuckled. "Well, when you run out of crickets, worms come in a close second." He squeezed the worm on the hook before lowering the line close to the ground. "Oh, hey." He turned to her. "I started reading *Winter's Edge*."

Brooke's posture straightened up, the blanket falling off her shoulders. "You're kidding?" she asked, with a slight shock in her voice.

Caleb shook his head. "Nope. I couldn't sleep last night so I started reading. I can see why it's so popular. I gotta ask." He stood and looked at her, his eyebrows furrowed. "Who dies?"

Brooke slouched back into the chair. "Daniel."

"You kill the guy?" he said, louder than expected. "She's pregnant, and you killed him?" He had more shock in his voice than intended, which surprised him as much as it did Brooke.

Brooke sneered and shrugged her shoulders. "It had to be tragic. Plus, I was going through a breakup at the time, so I guess I had a vendetta against men." She placed her book on the ground and stood, leaving the blanket in the chair. She slowly walked up to him and watched him cast the line into the lake. "Nice one," she muttered, looking up at him, hearing the small *plop* of the worm in the water.

"Thanks," he muttered back, twirling the reel a few times. "A bad breakup, huh?" He looked at her from the corner of his eye.

Brooke groaned. "I thought it was a proposal, but it was a breakup. But hey, that was almost four years ago."

"Well, he was an idiot," Caleb mumbled. Anyone who would turn Brooke down was an idiot in his eyes.

Brooke hummed and wrapped her arms around his waist. "Or maybe I was the idiot for thinking he was going to propose," she grumbled. "Oh, well. If it wasn't for that, I probably would have never written my novel so...it worked out for the better, I guess."

"That's something I didn't know about you, Brooke." Caleb wrapped his free arm around her waist, pulling her an inch closer to him.

"There's a lot you don't know yet. We have so many more questions to ask each other," she said softly, "But, I would like for you to ask them."

Caleb turned and looked at her with a smile. "I want to know everything."

Brooke giggled softly at him and turned to the lake. His line hadn't moved in a few moments, and he hadn't reeled it in. She reached out and spun the reel three times, just like Caleb had taught her. He smirked as he watched her spin the reel. The simple thought that he could spend the rest of his life doing this with her flashed through his mind. He could feel his cheeks blush, but he quickly pushed the sweet thought away. After all, he had only known her a few days.

"What's on the agenda today?" she asked.

"The mine." Caleb kissed the top of her head. "I thought we could go to Carbondale, grab some decent coffee and lunch, then go on the hike."

"Carbondale? Isn't that a drive?" she asked, arching her back slightly to look up at him.

"I can get some gas in the Jeep, and we can kill two birds with one stone."

"Perfect." She sighed. "However, I do need to send that email off to my agent. I've been avoiding it..." She trailed off her voice. "I've been avoiding work more than I should have."

"You said you got more done than before. Your agent should be thrilled!" he exclaimed.

"Oh, I did, and she most likely will, but I haven't sent it off to her yet." She groaned and laid her head on Caleb's shoulder. "What time do you want to go up to Carbondale? Do I have time to send an email and maybe talk to Ethan about writing a blog post?"

"I'm sure we can work that into the day. One condition though." He looked down at her.

"What's that?"

"After the work is done, no more work talk. Close the computers and disconnect from the internet. I only have you for a few more days, and I want to spend them asking you more questions." He was tempted to kiss the tip of her nose, but her blush and smile made him lose his train of thought.

"The entire day, you and me?"

He nodded. "Maybe we can end with *Hitchhiker's Guide to the Galaxy?*"

Brooke's smile grew. "That sounds perfect."

She raised herself up on her tippy toes and kissed him. Caleb breathed her in, shivers surging through his body. Her hand found his neck, and she pulled him closer, deepening the kiss. He could taste the Chapstick that still lingered on her lips, making them softer than he remembered. Each kiss was a new interaction, a new sensation, one Caleb welcomed and never wanted to end.

He was so distracted he didn't feel the slight tug on the pole. His free arm was wrapped around Brooke's waist, holding her closer to him as he slowly came up for air. She locked her gaze, a soft smile on his lips. Leaning to kiss her again, his entire body jerked forward, the pole flying from his hand and into the lake with a splash.

Brooke covered her mouth and held in a laugh. "What just happened?" she asked through chuckles.

Caleb stood frozen, watching as the water stilled, his fishing pole nowhere to be seen. "I guess I'm not fishing today." He groaned.

Brooke laughed, lowered her hand, and looked up at him. "Did you bring a second pole?"

Caleb shook his head. "I wasn't sure if you were going to be here, so I just brought the one." He gestured toward the lake.

"How deep is the lake?" she asked.

"Not very." Caleb's voice was full of disappointment. "But that was an expensive pole."

She furrowed her brow and looked at the lake and then Caleb. "I'll buy you a new one," she said softly. "I want to know what kind of fish that was, to pull it from your hands." She let go of Caleb's waist and stepped toward the lake.

"It's gone. I mean, the lake isn't that deep, but it's gone." He stood still, trying to force a sarcastic wail. "I'll never be able to fish again." He sniffed.

"Oh, stop being dramatic." She chuckled, turned back to him, placing her hands on his cheeks and pulling him toward her for another kiss. Caleb suddenly forgot about the pole that now lived in the lake.

~~~

"Okay." Brooke clapped her hands and leaned back in the chair. "I have sent my agent the first ten pages, and hopefully, she will like what she reads and I won't have this stress anymore." She closed her laptop and did a small victory cheer in her head. She knew she wasn't completely out of the water yet, but at least this was a start. Now she could focus on more important things, like Caleb.

Caleb clapped with her, proud of her achievement. Ethan shook his head and returned to the computer. Caleb knew that he was putting on a facade. Ethan was getting accustomed to and relatively enjoying Brooke's presence at the company.

"Good, you can help me figure out what to write for this blog post you assigned me," he grumbled to her. "Caleb should write the first blog post."

"Well, it's a team effort." She cocked a shoulder, brushing off Ethan's comment. "Actually, I can't." Brooke stood up and came over to the counter. "I won't be here for the others, so you need to write it. Plus, I have a date."

Caleb grinned at her, loving the fact that he was her date, and they had the rest of the day ahead of them.

"I have no idea what I'm doing." Ethan begged, "At least give me some guidance."

Caleb laughed and slapped Ethan's back. "You need more than guidance, my friend."

Brooke narrowed her eyes and glared at Caleb. "It's the first one, so introduce yourselves and the company. Talk about the different tours and just have fun with it. You have a sense of humor, so add that in."

Ethan glared at her. "You're going to read it before I post it, right?" His voice sounded desperate.

Brooke rolled her eyes and nodded. "Yes, fine. I will read it, but I have plans that I don't want to miss."

Ethan gave her a grateful nod. "Thank you. Was that so hard?"

Brooke nodded quickly while turning her attention to the clock. She glanced back at Ethan. "Give me twenty minutes to give Ethan some pointers?"

Caleb nodded, giving Brooke a grin before turning to leave. "I'll pack up the Jeep. Ethan, do we need anything in Carbondale?"

Ethan gave a smug look. "Not that I know of."

"Perfect." He gave a thumbs up. "I'll come get you in twenty minutes, Brooke."

Twenty-Six

As much as Brooke enjoyed the short trip to Carbondale, she would be the first to admit it wasn't her favorite part. The scenery was beautiful, and she allowed her skin to soak up every ounce of sun it could, but she was having the best time just being with Caleb. It was as if the pressure of her novel and the business was gone, and they were just two people who hadn't a care in the world. Carbondale was a smaller city than she was used to, it was easy to navigate and everyone seemed to know Caleb. He nodded and waved and even stopped to talk to a few locals in the parking lot.

They walked into a City Market, each grabbing a coffee from the Starbucks inside. They browsed the aisles and grabbed things they could eat on their trip to the mine. Brooke went to the books, mainly by habit, and when she spotted *Winter's Edge,* she grabbed a copy for Greg's girlfriend. When Caleb questioned her about buying her own book, she explained.

"You'll sign mine tonight, right?" he asked.

"Of course," she responded, thumbing through the cream pages.

Before they made their way back to Marble, Caleb stopped to fill the Jeep with gas. Brooke sat in the passenger seat, clutching onto her chai tea, her fingers brushing the matte finish of her novel. It hit her that she should have signed all of the copies that still sat on the shelves. She looked around the Jeep for a pen—maybe she still had time.

"Good afternoon, Caleb," A deep voice said. She looked up and saw an older man approach Caleb as he was putting the nozzle back.

"Oh hey, Mr. Spencer. How are you?" Caleb asked, a grin forming as the man approached. He was a country man through and through, even though he tried to hide it with his white button-down shirt and gray slacks. The red trucker hat with his dealer's logo that was perched on top of his head gave him away.

"Well, I'm kind of upset. Ethan was in my shop the other day and told me you were thinking about selling this beauty here." He placed his hand on the tailgate of the Jeep. "That you were having some financial troubles."

"Well, yes, we thought about it." Caleb's grin vanished.

"My offer still stands. I would love to buy the Jeep from you. It would be my own personal vehicle." Mr. Roberts looked at the Jeep with loving eyes. He noticed Brooke and nodded to her. She smiled back, mimicking the nod.

Caleb shrugged. "Well, Mr. Spencer, if our plan doesn't work out, I'll be sure to keep you in mind, but as of this moment no Jeep is being put up for sale."

Brooke shifted her body toward the front of the car, trying to ignore the two men. Mr. Spencer, however, did not want to give in.

"I'll raise my offer..." he persisted, tightening his grip on the Jeep's tailgate.

"I'm sorry, Mr. Spencer, but we are going to try a few things before we resort to selling a Jeep, or the business." Caleb closed the gas tank and made his way toward the door. "I'll keep you in mind though, and if it comes to it, you will be the first one I call." He climbed in the Jeep and waved to the man. "Have a good day, Mr. Spencer."

The man waved and turned his back, shaking his head as he walked away, clearly disappointed. Caleb looked over at Brooke and wiggled his eyebrows. "Are we ready for the mine?"

"Yup." Brooke smiled, thrilled to see that Caleb was willing to shove that conversation to the side. "It's hard to believe that two days ago you were thinking about selling the Jeep, and now you're denying offers."

"I have a good feeling about what we are doing. I really think it's gonna work." He smiled.

"Me too," she said softly. She glanced back at the store's entrance and then remembered her train of thought before Mr. Spencer interrupted it. "Oh, wait! I want to go sign all the copies they have of my book. Do you have a pen?" Her entire body bounced as she shifted in the seat.

Caleb laughed and went to park the car in front of the store, digging in the middle console for a pen.

~

The drive up to the mine was just as beautiful as the drive to the mill. The difference was the many pieces of white marble that were scattered along the side of the road. Caleb stopped a few times, allowing Brooke to get out and take pictures or to grab a few pieces of marble. Brooke watched as the town of Marble got smaller and smaller as they drove up. The lodge sat on the edge of the mountain, the lake reflecting its beauty. She took a deep breath, taking in the crisp clean air.

As much as she enjoyed her life in Salt Lake, she knew it wasn't her forever. She had hoped and dreamed of moving somewhere different, expanding her life when it allowed her to. She enjoyed the clean air of Colorado, the sights of sounds of autumn in Marble, and all the colors that enchanted the area. She watched the trees pass her, full of life as she took in every moment of it. Knowing she was only here for a few more days, she was suddenly extremely thankful Caleb had asked her to take the day with no computer and no work—just enjoy the place around them and each other.

Caleb slowed the Jeep to a stop and pulled up to a small parking area surrounded by large marble stones. Brooke leaped from the Jeep and ran to touch one of the marble pieces, completely forgetting about the food they had brought.

"It's beautiful, isn't it?" Caleb asked, approaching her with the plastic bags full of food. "I mean, for being a mine."

"When you said mine, I pictured something *in* the mountain, like the silver mines in Utah, but this..." She looked down at the small creek that ran in between the rectangle pieces of marble and trees. It led up to a large white cliff, and a hiking path followed it. "This doesn't look like a mine."

A suddenly loud grunting sound pulled her attention back to the road where a back-hoe passed them, his front claw full of rock. Caleb waved to the driver and turned back to Brooke, her eyes wide as if she'd been caught somewhere she wasn't supposed to be.

"It's one-hundred percent a mine." He dug through the bag and pulled chips and strawberries, placing them on the large marble stone. "Oh, your tea." He balled up the plastic and went back to the Jeep, only to run back seconds later with the remainder of Brooke's chai tea.

"We're going to eat here?" Brooke asked, pointing a finger at the rock.

"Why not?" He stepped in front of her, lightly placed his hands on her hips, and lifted her up on the marble. "It's a great view, and no one is here, besides the mine employees."

Brooke looked behind him as another car pulled up and a few people got out, making their way up the hiking trail. Caleb shrugged.

"Well, not that many people are here."

Brooke chuckled as Caleb pulled himself up on the marble, sitting across from her grabbing a bag of chips. Brooke reached for the strawberries, opening the plastic container. "They won't get angry if we are eating on the marble?" she asked.

Caleb shook his head and reached for a sandwich. "No, people eat up here all the time. It's a quiet place to relax." As Caleb uttered the words, there was a loud groan from one of the mining equipment, and a *beep, beep, beep* from something backing up. Brooke raised her eyes and looked at Caleb. "Well, kinda quiet," he added. "Just ignore the mining equipment."

"Compared to the parks in Salt Lake, this *is* peaceful." Brooke bit into a strawberry and licked her lips. "Mining noises and all." The beeping in the background continued. "Are we going to take the hike up?"

Caleb smiled, locking her gaze. "If you want to."

"I'd love to," she responded.

They ate in silence, just enjoying each other's company. Brooke snapped pictures of the surroundings, even jumping off the marble to climb down to grab a few bigger pieces she saw scattered in the dirt. Caleb kept close to her, saying he had seen people slip many times. Just as Brooke was assuring him she would be fine, she lost her footing and slipped in the dirt, Caleb catching her elbow and pulling her up. Just his touch made her body tingle. She wasn't sure if it was Caleb or the thought that she could have fallen down the side of the ravine. She looked at Caleb, his eyes full of worry—yet with a hint amusement—as he pulled her back toward him. She clung onto his biceps and followed his movements through the marble. Her heart began to beat faster. It wasn't fear. It was Caleb.

All the fears she had about him seemed to be fading away. She wanted to spend the time with him and learn all about him, ask him as many questions as he would allow. It wasn't that all the nerves and fears had completely vanished. There was still the lingering one that ate at her when she thought of it. She was only visiting Marble. What would happen when she left?

She had told Helen that she would stay in contact, that she liked him too much to just let this be a small fling. By the way Caleb talked to her and acted, she guessed he felt the same, but was he on the same page as her? Did he want to keep up a relationship or simply a friendship once she returned to Salt Lake?

Her mind tried to shove the thought away, to just enjoy the time and focus on Caleb, not on what could or could not happen. But her heart told her she should probably address the situation. She held onto him, feeling his muscles pulse under her touch as he walked farther out into the road.

"Hey," she said before she could stop herself, "can I ask you a question?" She grasped onto his hand.

He clutched it, twisting his body to lead the way to the hiking trail. "You can ask me anything," he responded with a smile, tightening his grip on her hand.

She cleared her throat. "What are we exactly?"

Caleb raised his eyebrows and swallowed, focusing on his feet. "Well," he stammered, "I'm not sure, to be honest with you. I've been enjoying spending time with you, and you make me..." He shook his head. "...happier. As if nothing else matters while I'm with you. I feel stable, and the world seems clear." He looked over his shoulder to her, catching her gaze, "Which is kind of strange to say aloud because I've known you a total of five days."

Brooke pursed her lips. "The fact that I'm leaving Monday doesn't bother you?" she asked.

"Oh, it bothers me." He looked forward, taking more steps up the hill, her hand still firmly in his. "But I don't want to lose contact with you. I *hope* you feel the same. I know there are going to be hurdles, but we can still talk and get to know each other, even if we are six hours apart."

Brooke blushed. "You knew it was six hours?"

"Seven with stops. I may have Googled the drive." Caleb chuckled. "All I know is I'm not nervous or afraid of whatever this is, and I'm willing to keep it going as long as I can."

Brooke pulled him to a stop. "You are a sappy romantic." She grinned as he jolted to a stop, turning to face her.

Caleb took the few steps to close the gap between them. "You like it," he joked.

Brooke leaned in and brushed her lips over his. "I really do. If you are willing to stay in contact, then I am." She paused, already hating herself for her next words. "I've never done anything long distance. I'm not sure how it would work."

Caleb gently touched her cheek. "We don't have to be in a relationship." He heaved a heavy sigh. "We can just see where things go. But I will say, I am going to spend these next few days treating you like you are the only woman in the world."

She blushed and rested her head on his chest. "Why do you have to be so perfect?" she grumbled.

Caleb laughed and began walking up the trail, pulling her back. "Come on, you're gonna love this view."

Brooke grinned as she followed him back up the path, suddenly no longer nervous or afraid of anything.

Twenty-Seven

"Hey, you're back!" Ethan exclaimed as soon as Caleb opened the door for Brooke, allowing her to walk through first. "I need your help."

Caleb shook his head in annoyance. "With?"

"Posting this." He waved at the computer screen. "It's typed up, Meredith read it, and spell check doesn't underline anything, but I need to post it."

Brooke came up behind Ethan and looked at the screen. Her eyes moved quickly across the screen, reading the blog post at lightning speed. Her narrow eyes grew larger as she read on, her face beaming with joy. "Oh, that's a decent first post! I love it." She stepped closer to the computer, reaching her arm around Ethan to take hold of the mouse. "Here, let me show you."

Caleb watched as she guided him in the posting process, explaining it in simple detail that even a third grader could understand. Ethan nodded along with her as she clicked, and then raised his hands and widened his eyes when Brooke shouted, "Voila!"

"It's that easy," Brooke declared. Caleb smiled, just watching the joy that radiated from her. He really loved her smile. The way it lit up her face, and her cheek bones turned a slight shade of pink. Everything about it made Brooke more beautiful than she already was.

He glanced at the clock. It was almost five. *Almost time for Ethan to go home,* he thought to himself.

"That's way easy," Ethan repeated. "I can do that on a regular basis."

"If you get stuck, you can always call me, and I'd be happy to read and proof any posts before you publish them." Brooke reached for a pen and a sticky pad, scribbling her phone number down and sticking it to the edge of the computer screen.

"Publish," Ethan said sarcastically. "Makes it sound so formal."

"That's what we're doing," Caleb walked up to the counter, craning his neck to see the yellow note on the screen. "Other than the blog, how was your day? Mr. Spencer came up to me at the gas station. He really wants the Jeep."

"But," Brooke chimed in, "Caleb told him no."

Ethan's glance went from Caleb to Brooke and then back to Caleb. "He didn't seem too happy on the phone. He thought I was calling to accept the offer, but then I turned him down." He shrugged. "Other than that, it was a great day. We got two reservations from the website."

Caleb's eyes widened, and he straightened his back. "Wait, what?" he asked with shock in his voice.

"That's something you lead with, Ethan." Brooke groaned, trying to hold back more excitement.

"You're serious? Two bookings?" Caleb repeated. "But the website just went live yesterday."

"Steven is a genius," Brooke muttered.

Ethan nodded. "Yea, one for next Tuesday—a group of four. They paid half and want to do Crystal Mill and town. The other one is for Friday. King's Loop, group of seven."

Brooke cheered and clapped, jumping in place. "It's working, you guys. It's working!"

Caleb's grin grew as he watched Brooke's enthusiasm. "This is fantastic."

Ethan tilted his head and raised an eyebrow. "Looks like we may be able to make the mortgage after all next month without dipping into our savings." He sighed.

"Now we just gotta get your paycheck," Caleb reminded him.

"Just imagine," Brooke piped up. "Once the social media sites are full, have tons of followers, and the blog is posting regularly, this will be a daily thing!" Brooke chuckled and shook her head in disbelief. "It's happening," she mumbled. "It's really happening."

Ethan looked over at her. "Thanks to you," he remarked. "You manifested it."

Brooke smirked at Ethan, and then looked at Caleb, her cheeks still blushing from excitement with a soft smile on her lips. She shook her shoulders and head, jostling herself back to reality. "What's for dinner?"

Caleb chuckled. "I'm pretty sure I have a frozen pizza upstairs." *Frozen pizza...* He had an amazing day with Brooke, and all he could offer her was frozen pizza. He scrunched his nose and raised his eyebrows, waiting for a reaction from her.

Brooke scrunched her nose. "A frozen pizza? That's all?"

Caleb shrugged. "I sadly don't get to the store that often." He furrowed his brow, looking as if he was contemplating all his life decisions over a frozen pizza.

"Didn't I catch a fish the other night?" Brooke suggested.

"You did," Ethan barked, "and it's in your fridge. I should know. I put it there."

Caleb looked over at him. "It is, isn't it?"

Brooke cocked her shoulder. "Well, is it edible?"

"Yeah." Caleb laughed at her. "Maybe we can do fish tacos." He quickly thought of all the things in his pantry upstairs. Did he have everything he needed to make fish tacos? Seasonings, tortillas... Did he even have cheese? He raised his eyebrows and looked back over at Brooke, whose smile pulled his train of thought completely off the rails.

"Mmm," Brooke hummed. "Delicious."

Ethan laughed at them and then stepped away from the counter. "I'm gonna head out since you two seem to still be on your date..."

"It's an all-day date," Caleb interrupted. "Of course we are."

"Meredith is off at six tonight, so we will just go have a better at home date."

"I doubt that," Brooke said softly, locking eyes with Caleb. "We are watching *Hitchhiker's Guide to the Galaxy*."

"A classic," Caleb agreed

Ethan shook his head. "Maybe for nerds..." He patted Caleb on the back and then said his goodbye to Caleb and Brooke. "I'll see you in the morning." He waved, leaving them alone in the office.

Brooke turned to Caleb and pursed her lips. "Fish tacos and popcorn?" Her hair swung onto her shoulders, falling in the right way to make her look irresistible.

"Is there any other way to have a movie night?" Caleb walked over to the counter, grasped her hand, and slowly guided her up the stairs.

∽

Brooke had seen Caleb's apartment that sat above the office once, but that particular day, she didn't pay too much attention to the decor. He flicked on the light, showing the living room. A large leather couch sat in front of a small cabinet and TV. Bookcases sat on either side of the TV, holding very little books but more knick-knacks and photos. It had a very rustic and woodsy feel to it, almost like the lodge but with more of a sense of home.

Caleb left her standing in the living room and went to the small kitchen, digging through his refrigerator for the fish Ethan had fileted a few days prior. He placed the fish on the counter and went to find the other ingredients—happy and elated to find he did indeed have everything he needed.

"The only thing I don't seem to have is a tomato," he called from the pantry.

Brooke turned to look at him, seeing his back as he was half in the pantry. "That's okay. Cabbage, cheese, sour cream... Do you have an avocado?" she asked, feeling hopeful.

"As a matter of fact..." He turned and pulled an avocado from the fruit bowl on the island. "I do."

She smiled. "Well then, who needs tomatoes?" She turned back around, once again looking toward the decor.

Brooke walked over to the bookcase to look at the bent spines that told Brooke that he did, in fact, read. Stephen King and James Patterson, all classics that she would expect most people to own but sitting next to them was *Winter's Edge* with a bookmark sticking out of the top. She smiled, then darted her eyes toward the photos.

She assumed they were of his family all back in Chicago. There was one of a young, clean-shaven Caleb in a cap and gown, standing next to a younger girl and possibly an older boy.

"Was this high school or college?" she asked, pointing to the picture and turning to him.

Caleb looked up, grabbing a frying pan and turning his stove on. "College, right before law school."

"Are these your siblings?" she asked again, turning back to the picture, stopping herself from picking it up to get a closer look at a young Caleb.

"They are." He sighed. "My older brother, Devin, is a lawyer too, and my younger sister, Maria, owns a dress shop in Chicago."

"Two lawyers in the family. Your parents must be very proud." She left the bookcase and walked over to the kitchen counter, sitting on one of the high-top chairs he had pushed up against the countertop. She leaned her elbows on the counter and leaned in toward him.

"They are." He shrugged, cutting up the frozen fish and placing it in the pan. "My dad, Richard, he's a retired lawyer, and he owns his firm. Devin took over once he graduated, and slowly, my dad just stopped working. My mom, Penny, was a high school teacher. She retired last year."

"Your dad," Brooke began, "was he upset you left the firm?"

He tightened his chin. "Yes and no, I think. He was hoping Devin and I would run the firm together, but he also understood I needed to change my life. They've been as supportive as they can be." Caleb set the knife on the counter and leaned against his counter, closing the gap between him and Brooke. "I think they would have wanted me to stay in Chicago, but they get it." He locked eyes with Brooke. "What about your parents?"

Brooke groaned, rolling her eyes into the back of her head as far as they could go. "My mom, Heather, is a dentist. She's big on teeth. I haven't had a single cavity, thank you very much."

"Impressive." Caleb nodded, pushing himself back up to continue cooking the meal, putting the frying pan on the stovetop.

"My dad, Michael, is a pilot. He retired about two years ago. He liked to go fishing too, but his way. Which was on a boat and giving us direction in our lives."

Caleb listened as she spoke, every now and then pushing the fish around in the pan, which made her sigh and continue, even though Caleb could tell she didn't really want to. He turned toward the pan, thinking it would be easier for her to talk if he wasn't looking directly at her.

"I have two younger brothers, Shawn and Andrew, and they are still in college. My dad is very proud of them," she mumbled. Her head loomed down as she began to pick at her fingernails.

"But not of you?" Caleb asked, the fish beginning to sizzle.

Brooke shrugged. "I mean, he kind of is. But I didn't become the *publisher*. I'm just the *writer*. He came to all my events when *Winter's Edge* was released, but I don't think he owns a copy."

Caleb turned back to the counter, letting the fish cook. He grabbed two new knives and a cutting board, placing all the taco fixings on the counter. Brooke grabbed the knife and avocado, slicing it in half while he began to chop the lettuce. The smell of the cooked fish began to waft through the air.

"Are they in Salt Lake? Do you see them often?" he asked.

Brooke nodded, stabbing the pit of the avocado with the knife. "Yes, they are. I live about twenty minutes away. They are on the benches, and I'm downtown. They have *learned* to be supportive."

Caleb furrowed his brow. "Learned to be. Well…it's something, right?"

Brooke heaved a sigh. "I guess. They're supportive in their own way."

Caleb's furrowed brow raised, and he heaved a long sigh. He set the knife down and turned back to the fish, which was looking almost ready to enjoy. He left Brooke alone at the island as he went back to the pantry to retrieve the leftover ingredients, coming back with her, looking more somber.

"Okay, so…" he said, breaking the silence. "Parents are all well and nice but tell me something that no one else knows about you." He stirred the fish and turned off the stove, bringing the pan to the counter.

"Something no one else knows. Going bold now, are we?" Brooke asked, dropping her hands still holding half an avocado and a knife on the counter in front of her. Her jaw dropped, and her eyebrows raised.

Caleb locked her gaze. "Yeah." He grinned. "I want to know everything about you."

The conversation took a turn once the fish was done cooking, and they each made tiny tacos for one another. They sat next to each other on the island with their knees touching. The room became lighter once they began eating. Caleb told stories from high school, some of the adventures he had with his friends, which mainly ended up in detention. Brooke learned that even though he had a foolish side, he was able to keep his grades to be able to become a lawyer. He did admit once he landed his acceptance into law school, he settled down.

The more he shared about his life, the more she felt inclined to share about hers. Digging into how she was the "nerd" in school, always hiding behind books and spending her time in the library. She had her friends that stuck by her, but mainly, she and Caleb were from two different sides of the coin. College was important to her, but since she didn't know what she wanted in life until her late twenties, she's studied the most basic degree you could, landing her the job in publishing.

"Don't get me wrong. I loved my job, but I love writing more. That is when I can actually put words to the page." She laughed. The plate in front of her had nothing left except crumbs as she reached for her water to take a sip.

"You found the right path, obviously." Caleb took the final bite of his fish taco, glanced up to Brooke, and wiggled his eyebrows. "Should we start the movie soon?" he asked, grabbing both plates and standing up.

Brooke smiled. "I'd love to." She stood, grabbing her glass of water and making her way toward the leather couch. "You have popcorn, right?"

"Do I have popcorn?" Caleb repeated sarcastically.

Brooke chuckled and settled herself down on the big leather couch, lifting her legs under her, sinking into it. She heard plastic being ripped open and the microwave beeping. As she waited for Caleb, she looked around the room for a blanket. The same one she spotted from the other morning was draped across the La-Z-Boy chair, just a bit out of her reach from the couch. With a groan, she moved to grab it, noticing his bedroom door wide open, seeing his empty, plain bedroom.

"Movie theater butter," Caleb said loudly from the kitchen.

"Perfect!" Brooke shouted back, turning her body back toward the kitchen, forgetting about the bed in the next room. She plopped back on the couch again, draping the blanket across her lap, purposefully leaving enough for Caleb.

Minutes later, he arrived with a large bowl of popcorn and began to fiddle with the TV and DVD player.

"I really love your place. It has a great feel to it." Brooke smiled, watching him as he bent over to grab the DVD.

Caleb looked over his shoulder at her. "Lettie lived here for a while, and then she moved out when she couldn't do the stairs anymore. It sat empty for a good two years before I came."

"Is this Lettie's furniture?" She looked at the leather couch and the brown recliner chair.

"No," Caleb interjected quickly, "Ethan helped me pick out things when she passed. I had to make it my own, right?"

"The only thing missing is one of those singing fish plaques," Brooke joked.

Caleb stood and turned to look at her. "Oh, I have one. In the bathroom." He smiled back at her. "Keep in mind"—he laughed—"this TV is older, and the DVD is from when the movie was first released..."

"Caleb," Brooke stopped him, "I'm extremely excited to watch this. Now hit play and come over here." She smacked the side of the couch.

Caleb grabbed the remote and came to sit down next to her, his leg touching hers. She grinned and placed her hand over her cheek, leaning her elbow on the back of the couch. She hoped the slight movement would hide her rosy cheeks.

∞

"I don't care what anyone else says," Brooke retorted. "The whale falling from the sky giving its train of thought is by far the best part of that movie." The credits began to roll, and all the popcorn had been eaten. Brooke glanced over at Caleb, seeing the night sky from his window behind him. She stretched out her arms in front of her. She had thoroughly enjoyed her night, and she had completely lost track of time.

"Forty-two," Caleb responded.

Brooke shook her head and laughed. She still, even after fifteen years of the movie and even more of the book, didn't understand why "forty-two" was the answer to life. "I hadn't seen that in years. It's been even longer since I read the book." She looked at the black credits rolling on the screen. "Please tell me you've read the book," she said, remembering he "wasn't much of a reader."

"Of course I have. Back in 2005, this was the movie event of the year for seventeen-year-old me." Caleb leaned forward, resting his elbows on his knees.

The soft blue glow of the light of the television enhanced his features. Brooke noticed the edge of his cheekbones and the curve of his lips under his beard. His jaw line—even with the beard—was sharp and defined. She had to stop herself before she reached out and touched him. She could see his long eyelashes—a part of him she had never noticed before. They fluttered when he blinked; making the butterflies that rose in Brooke's chest fly higher. She blinked a few times to keep herself from staring.

He glanced over at her, making Brooke turn her head. "I still love that movie." He turned back to the television.

"It's a classic." She smiled. "I think it needs to be watched every year."

Caleb looked over his shoulder at her once more. His eyes were hot on her, and she could feel them. "Only if you watch it with me." He plopped back on the couch next to her, his hands resting on his thighs. "Via phone, video chat, or in person. Your commentary was by far the best part of the entire film."

"Who else is going to tell Beeblebrox he's being an idiot?" Brooke asked, resting her arm on the couch behind her.

She and Caleb had kept close contact through the movie. Caleb had slipped his arm around her, and she'd snuggled in closer at one moment. Now that the movie was over, they had drifted apart on the couch. Brooke hoped they could get closer but knowing she should probably head back to the lodge, she kept herself from inching closer. The night sky covered the windows and having only the glow from the TV as the light source, it seemed later than it really was. Brooke's logical mind and body were fighting against each other, and she hoped that Caleb had the same thoughts running through his head.

Pursing her lips, she sighed, moving off from the couch to grab the bowl of popcorn kernels.

She wouldn't assume he felt a certain way. Even if she wanted to, she wouldn't assume.

"I had a wonderful time today," Caleb finally said, breaking the void that filled the room.

Brooke turned and smiled at him. "Me too. It was great to not think about work for a few hours and just enjoy the day." She stood. "I should get going though. Back to daily life at Marble Lodge."

"Stay," Caleb muttered. He reached out and softly grasped her hand. "Stay," he repeated, a whisper to his voice.

She laced her fingers around his hand and gently glided her thumb against his skin. She wasn't sure how to respond. She knew how she *wanted* to respond, but the logic was screaming at her. He tightened her grip on his hand and softly said, "I should really probably go..." Her voice was almost in a whisper, fighting the urge to stay, but so desperately wanted to give in.

"I don't want you to," Caleb whispered. "Stay with me tonight."

As if all thought left her brain, Brooke's body won the fight. She allowed him to pull her close. She lifted her legs on the couch, straddling him once again. Their lips met, and the fireworks began. All senses amplified as she kissed him. His beard was soft against her skin, a feeling she had gotten used to and craved. She could taste him, and he smelled like firewood. He parted his lips, deepening the kiss as Brooke breathed him in.

She ran her hands over his chest, slowly playing with the buttons on his shirt. She had done this motion several times, and each time, she wanted to unbutton them. Finally, she allowed them to move. Once her fingers touched his bare chest, Caleb broke the kiss and bent his head, lightly kissing her collarbone. Brooke tilted her head back and let out a soft gasp. His fingers slid up her shirt. Her back feeling the icy touch, she arched slightly.

"Brooke," Caleb muttered against her skin. "I can't tell you how much I want you." He lifted her head, locking his eyes with hers. His cheeks were flushed, and his breathing was deep. He moved his hands to her side, keeping them under her shirt. Brooke twisted with his movement, raising her arms in the air as he lifted her shirt over her head.

"Caleb," she responded, her voice shaky as she felt his fingers slide up her bare skin. "I'm yours."

She glided her hand up his chest, lacing her fingers together behind his neck. Feeling his hands explore her body. He grasped her waist and stood from the couch as if she weighed nothing at all. Kissing her, he carried her to his bedroom. Brooke let all logic leave as she followed his motions, knowing she had all night to embrace him.

Twenty-Eight

-Saturday-

The sun crept through the window, and Brooke slightly opened her eyes. The digital clock on Caleb's nightstand told her it was barely six a.m. She inhaled deeply, aware of the fact that she was more comfortable than she had ever been, and she was one hundred percent positive it was because Caleb's body was pressed against hers. His arm draped around her side, and his breath lightly touched the nape of her neck. She grinned at the memory of the night before, having Caleb all to herself. They had slept in each other's arms, the heat of their skin causing more than just sleep to happen. Brooke was the one to wake him up the second time. The way his skin felt against her fingers and the touch of his lips against her collarbone was enough to send Brooke over the edge.

She could feel the shivers up her spine just thinking about him. Trying not to wake him, she gently moved her body away, feeling the chill of the sheets hit her bare back as she left the warmth of his arms. She scooted toward the edge of the bed, ever so slowly pulling the blanket from her body.

"Hmm." She heard a slight hum. "Good morning," Caleb muttered.

Brooked stopped and turned to face him, instantly giving back into the warmth of the bed. "I'm sorry," she whispered, cuddling up next to him once more. "I didn't mean to wake you."

"You didn't." He smiled, keeping his eyes closed. "I've been awake for a few minutes, trying not to wake you."

Brooke giggled. They both had the same thought once waking. It wasn't the first time he had seemed to read her mind. The fact that they had the same thought made her body warm. She reached her arms up and cupped his cheek, feeling his beard under her palm. Their bare bodies being back in close contact again was making Brooke want to claim him.

"I hope you slept well," she said, holding back her urge, running her fingers through his hair.

Caleb shifted against her and pulled her closer. "The best I've ever slept," he responded. "And you?"

"I feel very refreshed," she mumbled, lifting her head slightly to kiss his neck. She felt his skin twinge as her lips touched him.

"Hmm." He hummed, gliding his hands up her bare back. "You better stop, or we won't be getting out of this bed today."

"Maybe I don't want to. We can spend all day in bed."

Caleb pulled his head away and raised an eyebrow. "I'd figured you would jump on the website and blog. See if anything hit during the night."

She scrunched her nose. "I mean, yes. A part of me wants to do that, but the bigger part wants to stay here." She turned, causing Caleb to roll on his back as she slid on top of him. He wrapped his arms around her waist and held her steady.

"Maybe just a little longer in bed," he said with a smile.

Brooke's corners of her lips raised, and she kissed his neck, gently nibbling on his ear lobe as she moved her body against his once more.

Caleb had finally convinced Brooke to climb out of the bed, making their way to the kitchen where Caleb began to make Brooke breakfast. Once the coffee was made, he cracked the eggs and gently placed the sausages on the skillet, while Brooke traveled back to his bookcase, looking at all the photos once again.

She had a blanket draped over her shoulders and her coffee mug wrapped in her hands as she scanned the photos, passing the one of Caleb and his siblings, coming to one that she assumed was his parents. She gently touched the photo with her fingertips, took a small sip of coffee, and tore her gaze from the photo, landing on another picture. She furrowed her brow, looking at the wedding picture with care, desperately wanting to ask Caleb about it, but unsure how he would react.

Clearing her throat, she kept her eyes on the couple in the photo. "Is this your wedding day?" she asked softly. The couple in the photo looked blissful. A younger Caleb with his forehead resting on a brunette's temple. The smile on Audrey's face was pure happiness, and the daisies that rested against her modest dress brought the pop of color the photo needed. Lifting her eyes from the photo, she turned to look at Caleb.

He watched her, his hands resting on the island, and the eggs and sausages cooked behind him. A small grin tugged at his lips. "Yeah, that's my Audrey," he said simply.

Brooke turned, leaving the bookcase and going back to the island, the same motion as the night before. She sat on the high-top chair and placed her mug in front of her gently. She tugged at the blanket and wrapped it around her body. "Tell me more about her. What was she like?"

"I told you." Caleb laughed. "She was a pain in the ass."

"Judging by that photo, she wasn't a pain in the ass all the time." Brooke raised an eyebrow at him, wanting to know more about the woman that had his heart before she was taken from him.

Caleb heaved a sigh. "No, she wasn't, really. She was my everything." Caleb pushed himself from the countertop and went to the food that sizzled. "Audrey was my first *real* love. The one I knew I wanted to spend the rest of my life with. It wasn't easy getting the news of the cancer, and then just like that, she was gone."

With his back to her, he poked at the food. "It all just happened so fast. One day she was fine, and the next…she just started to feel off. Then next thing I knew, the doctor told us she was dying. Our entire world was thrown off course, and all the things we wanted didn't seem important anymore."

"So you came to Marble? Did she die here?" Brooke watched him, gauging if the conversation was going to be welcomed or if he was going to close off.

He shook his head and turned toward her, leaning on the counter. "It was a vacation. We came here as kind of a last hurrah. She found the Beaver Lodger, and we stayed there. I fished, she read. We relaxed, one day not even leaving the room." He gave her a soft smile, "We did the hike up to the mill, and that was when I noticed a change in her health. Once we got home to Chicago…" He trailed off, taking a deep breath, "That's when it took a turn. She was gone shortly after that."

"Did you talk about it at all with her? What would happen? What she would want for you?" Brooke asked cautiously.

"We talked about possible treatments and what would come from them, but we never had time to talk about other things. Once she refused treatment, we focused on the time we had left." Caleb turned back to pull the eggs from the stove. "I've seen in movies and in books where the dying spouse always says 'move on and find happiness,' but Audrey and I never had that talk. I didn't want to think about life without her…until I had to live it. The first few days, I was a wreck, but I pulled myself out of it to handle funeral arrangements and try to get everything in order. I tried to go to work, but life just seemed pointless. It wasn't until her parents had told me to find life again and be happy that I actually made the moves to do so."

"Her parents—do you still talk to them?"

Caleb nodded and handed Brooke a plate of eggs and sausages. "I do. I'm still close to them and consider them family. They've come out to visit a few times and always let me know how proud they were of where I've ended up. They always say that Audrey would have wanted me to have this life."

"A happy one." Brooke smiled, taking her gaze from Caleb to her coffee mug. "I'm sorry you lost her too soon. I can't imagine what that was like and then changing everything to grieve in your own way. It does bring me comfort to know you haven't lost her completely, that her parents still love you the way I..." She paused, taking a deep breath. Pursing her lips, she raised her coffee to her mouth, stopping herself from talking.

Caleb furrowed his brow at her silence and made his way over to Brooke, wrapping his arms around her waist and pulled her close to him.

"She would have liked you." He relaxed his forehead, the creases leaving as his brows returned to his normal, caring glance. "I like to bet that if her parents ever met you, they'd like you too."

Brooke raised her chin up to him, closing her eyes and loving the gentle brush of his lips on her forehead.

Twenty-Nine

After breakfast, Brooke had begrudgingly left Caleb alone in his apartment to return to the lodge. He was feeling completely different than he had the day before. His spirits were lifted, and his mood was high. He showered, trimmed his beard, and brushed his hair, channeling his Chicago days until he placed the flannel shirt over his white t-shirt. He smiled at himself in the mirror, enjoying the Colorado Caleb much more than the one he left behind in Chicago.

He made his way downstairs to the office, passing the front desk being hit by the morning light and headed toward the kitchen. He brewed another pot of coffee and snagged a banana from the counter, the grin from the mirror still on his lips.

Brooke had made him feel whole again, as if that one small puzzle piece he had been searching for was found under the table and pressed into place. He only had her for two more days, but with the promise of a friendship and long-distance contact, he wasn't worried about what *had* happened. He was more focused on what *could* happen. Caleb saw light in his future with her. He could see them spending holidays together, building a life he didn't know was possible again. It all seemed so close, yet so far. The distance of the future didn't matter to Caleb. All that mattered was keeping Brooke in his life somehow.

Once the coffee was in his mug and the banana was peeled, he headed toward the front office, setting his mug on the counter. He turned the computer on and took a bite, watching the screen come to life. He opened the internet browser, sipping his coffee.

Auto pilot kicked in, and he opened his email inbox. The morning offered a few spam emails, but in the mix, he saw a titled email that, if possible, lifted his spirits even higher.

Reservation, Group of eight.

Eight people. *A group of eight!* That would require both Ethan and Caleb to drive a Jeep. He covered his smile with his hand, in shock he was even reading the subject correctly. With a chuckle, he opened the email and saw the generic website reservation form Brooke had shown him.

It was indeed a group of eight, but the reservation was for four weeks from now. Caleb's hand that was covering his mouth moved to his hair. He couldn't believe it. Someone had visited the website and decided they were worth the reservation for four weeks ahead.

He heard the key in the front door, pulling his attention from the computer. He saw Ethan pushing through the door, a sense of urgency in the air.

"You marry her," Ethan announced, the door banging behind him.

"What?" Caleb asked, a hint of happiness still in his voice.

"Brooke. You marry her. She's a miracle worker." He pulled his phone from his back pocket and swiped the screen, moments later, putting it on the counter in front of Caleb. "We already have over five hundred followers on our Instagram, and our Facebook page isn't far behind. When I went to bed, we had sixty followers, and now…we blew up overnight."

Caleb looked at the phone, noticing pictures that Brooke had taken of him and Ethan, the building with the Jeeps in front, and the Crystal Mill and town. Next to the small circle that was their profile picture was a black and bold number *537 Followers*.

"Damn." He gasped.

"All this that she's doing is working. We have two reservations for next week, and I bet you there is more coming. All thanks to Brooke." Ethan pointed at his phone, the screen turning black. "I was skeptical at first, but, Caleb...you marry her." Ethan's eyes were wide, and his voice was full of excitement.

Caleb shook his head, his smile still growing on his lips. "I don't believe this," he muttered. "Here." He turned the computer screen to Ethan. "We got another reservation, a group of eight."

"That will definitely save us next month!" Ethan opened his arms, his excitement growing.

"It's in four weeks," Caleb added.

"Did they pay a deposit?" Ethan asked, stepping forward again, looking at the computer.

Caleb heaved a sigh. "I didn't see. I just opened the email when you came in. I bet if I go to the bank with this kind of information, they will give us an extension on some debts. Then we will be able to catch back up in no time if we keep this up." Caleb gestured to the screen. "I need to talk to Brooke about the upkeep on the site before she leaves. I know her friend did everything, but we are going to have to manage it from here."

"Where is Brooke? I figured she would be here by now. It's late." Ethan glanced at his watch and back at Caleb.

"Um," Caleb stammered. He wanted to keep his time with Brooke simply that: *his*. Ethan didn't need to know she had spent the night. "She left late last night, so she is most likely sleeping in. Hell, I missed the lake this morning. I was *that* tired," he lied.

Ethan narrowed his eyes. "Alright. I wish she had service. I would text her and tell her to come here now so we can share the news."

Caleb turned and glanced at the clock, then to the small ten-digit number stuck to the computer. It was nine. She had left a little over an hour ago. "She'll be back soon," he added.

"Again, Caleb. Marry her."

"I've only known her since Sunday."

"Hey, when I met Meredith, I knew after the first date she was the one for me. I see the way you two look at each other."

Caleb grinned, feeling his cheeks heat up. He was thankful he had a beard to hide the blush. "We will keep in touch, but who knows from there?" He shrugged. "We both don't want to lose contact, so long distance."

"Like a long-distance boyfriend/girlfriend relationship?"

"We didn't specify. Again, Ethan, we've known each other for a week." Caleb took a deep breath. "Let's plan these reservations. We have two next week, so we can split it."

Ethan rubbed his palms together, ready to start the business day. "Let's get to it. Back to normal," he said enthusiastically.

∽

"Where were you all night?" Helen asked as a freshly showered Brooke stepped out of her room, running her hairbrush through her hair.

"With Caleb." Brooke smiled. She set her brush on the island and looked over at the full mug of coffee. "Oh, yes! You made coffee." She reached for a mug and poured herself a cup of the fresh brewed coffee Helen had made.

"With Caleb?" Helen responded. "What did you do?"

"We watched a movie," she said softly, bringing the cup to her lips, hoping the large mug would hide the truth in her eyes.

Helen raised her eyebrows. "Mm-hmm. Well, I'm glad you had fun." Helen wiggled her eyebrows at her, making Brooke scoff and roll her eyes. "Did you email your agent and get the blog posted?"

Brooke nodded and swallowed her coffee. "I posted the blog after we had our race, which you still owe me for."

"We will go to Starbucks on the way out," Helen interrupted, disappointment from her loss filling her voice.

"And I did get my email sent off. I haven't seen if she replied or not. I promised Caleb I wouldn't do any work yesterday." She tapped her fingers on the tile counter, the slight memory of his skin against her fingertips made her bite her bottom lip.

Helen lowered her eyebrows. "But that's why we are here."

Pulling her hands away and blinking back up at Helen, she shook her head. "Okay, *Greg*." Brooke glared at Helen. "I've gotten a lot more done than I thought I ever would, in more aspects than just my novel." Brooke set her mug down, still holding onto the porcelain. "It's been a crazy week."

It had been one that Brooke wasn't soon to forget.

Helen smiled. "I bet you didn't expect to save a business and fall in love, did you?"

"I didn't say I was in love." Brooke stopped her, her voice falling flat. "Caleb is...different. He's fun to be around and cares about his town. You can see it when he talks about the mill and the way he interacts with the people here, even in Carbondale." She bit her bottom lip again, trying to find the exact words to describe how she felt. When it came to putting words on paper, she was brilliant, but describing them in person—her mind always drew a blank. "I don't know what I feel, but I definitely feel something."

"It helps that he's extremely good-looking." Helen's lips formed a grin, and she looked at Brooke with her eyebrows raised.

Brooke chuckled, taking another drink, rolling her eyes, trying to ignore the comment that was just thrown out in the open.

"Who's good-looking?" Joyce entered the room, followed by Rhonda.

Helen stiffened at the sight of Rhonda, but Brooke smiled at her, actually excited to see her new friend.

"Caleb," Brooke said softly.

"Oh, the tour guide," Joyce spoke, her eyebrows lifting, widening her eyes. "Yes, I agree. He is very good looking. Enough to catch your attention." She smiled at Brooke, reaching over to grab the carafe.

Brooke blushed, choosing not to answer, but to keep Caleb to herself for a little longer.

"How is his business?" Rhonda asked, sitting down next to Helen. Helen raised her eyes and stared at Brooke. Brooke made a face at Helen, telling her to let loose, but Helen's posture didn't reflect that.

"It's okay, I think. They got some reservations for next week, but I don't know if it's enough to help them make the month. Yesterday, in Carbondale, he had a man come up and say he will raise his offer on a Jeep. Caleb turned him down, so that's a hopeful sign."

Rhonda furrowed her brow. "He was going to sell a Jeep?"

Brooke shrugged. "I told you they were close to selling the business. If he had an option, I think he'd rather sell a Jeep than the entire business."

Rhonda nodded, pursuing her lips. "Excuse me." She stood from the table and left the kitchen. Brooke watched her head back upstairs before turning back to the island.

Helen let out a long breath. "That was the longest she's been next to me, and that was nerve wracking."

Brooke knew exactly how Helen felt, but letting out a small chuckle, she said, "She's not as bad as we thought. She's nice."

Helen scoffed. "Yeah, right."

"No, really. She helped me with my first few pages. She was able to give a lot of insight, and she's different than we thought. We were quick to judge."

"Who? Rhonda?" Greg appeared. "Oh, yeah. She's really interesting once you get to talk to her."

Brooke watched as Greg made his way around the kitchen, excited that someone else was seeing Rhonda in her true light. Helen shook her head, clearly not believing anything Brooke was saying.

"I guess I need to talk to her when she's not busy banging on her typewriter." Helen took a long drink of her coffee.

Brooke looked at her new friends, knowing that these were people she hoped to keep even after they left. She watched Greg pour a bowl of cereal and settle himself in the chair Rhonda had just left.

"Oh, Greg." She turned, quickly heading into her room to grab the copy of *Winter's Edge* she had purchased for Greg's girlfriend. She grabbed a pen and ran back to the kitchen. "I bought this yesterday in Carbondale for your girlfriend." She opened the book and readied her pen. "What's her name?"

"Seriously!" Greg sat up straight. "Her name is Kelly."

Brooke smiled and signed the first page for Kelly. "You're in Utah, right?" she asked, sliding the book toward him.

"Yeah, St. George," Greg replied, taking the book in his hand, holding it as if it were pure gold.

"Maybe we can meet up someday. I'd love to meet her." Brooke smiled. "Helen, where do you live?"

"Idaho." Helen smiled. "Rexburg."

Joyce hummed, listening to their conversation. "It's great to have support, especially since you are all closer than you think."

"Where do you live?" Greg asked, gently placing the book back on the table.

"I'm in Wyoming. Rhonda moved to Montana last year."

Brooke smiled. Bringing her coffee to her lips, she muttered. "We are all closer than we think we are."

Thirty

Caleb was hunched over the counter when the door opened, having him quickly fix his posture. *Look professional.* An older woman walked through the door, her arms at her sides as she came up to the counter. Caleb, still on the high from the night before and this morning, smiled at her.

"Hi, how can I help you?" he asked, his customer service smile shining through.

"Are you Caleb?" she asked, placing her hands on the counter, lacing her fingers together in front of him.

He nodded, keeping his customer service smile on. "That's me."

She nodded. "My name is Rhonda. I am staying at the lodge with Brooke. She's told me a lot about you."

He began to raise a finger. The pretentious one was in his shop. He stopped himself and just kept his smile. "Nice to meet you, Rhonda. Brooke has told me about you as well."

"Probably not good things. Until recently, hopefully." She sighed. "Brooke has told me a fair amount about your company, how she's worried you're going to lose it."

Caleb raised his eyebrows. He wasn't expecting *that*. "No, that's not going to happen."

"Well, of course not. But I also know she didn't help enough to suddenly bring in enough money to save everything before the end of the month." She had one eyebrow raised, and her tone was steady—like a schoolteacher, one who was about to scold their student.

As she talked, Caleb could understand why Brooke was intimated by her. Her entire demeanor screamed business. Even though Caleb could tell she was here to possibly help in some way, he even felt intimated.

"Well," he stammered, "we have reservations, thanks to Brooke's website, and I'm confident that with our savings we will be ok—"

"Caleb," Rhonda stopped him, holding a palm in front of her, "what I'm asking is what do you need for the month to make your mortgage and pay your employee without using any savings?"

Caleb stared at her, unsure on how to answer. Sharing finances with a woman who he just met was not on his to-do list, ever. "Um..." he stammered. How did he answer this?

"This morning, Brooke said you were close to selling a Jeep, that if it came to it, you would rather lose a Jeep than the business, which I can understand. I looked at her blog yesterday. Her new post is about this company and the tours it offers. She spends a good amount of time talking about how much you have influenced her life." Rhonda looked Caleb in the eye, freezing him on the spot. "You even made your way into her new novel and have changed the way she feels about writing in general, for the better. You mean more to her than someone she met on vacation."

She lowered her hands, bringing them up seconds later, carrying a small bag that Caleb didn't notice before. "I want to treat everyone at the lodge to the best tour you have. I don't care about the cost. I want to be able to help you make the month in order to see those new reservations next week with no stress. I am not here to offer financial guidance or to be the stuck-up writer Brooke most likely told you I was. I just want to help in a way that will work, and that is by booking a tour for everyone at the lodge."

Caleb dropped his jaw as Rhonda pulled out her wallet, pulling a credit card out and placing it on the counter. He looked at her, a smile forming on her thin tips.

"Do you think you and your employee could come pick us up at the lodge? I'd like to surprise everyone."

Caleb gently took the card off the counter, holding on to the plastic with great care. "Ethan and I would be ecstatic to pick everyone up. The Loop trail offers everything, only it's a five-hour or more adventure, but you get to see the beauty of everything."

"That sounds perfect." Rhonda nodded. "No matter the cost, that sounds lovely."

Caleb smiled, shaking his head at her. "Are you positive? How many are at the lodge? Five?"

"Seven, including the hosts," Rhonda added.

Caleb cleared his throat. The Loop trail cost for a group of seven would cover the mortgage for sure, and then the two reservations the following week would at least help Ethan get a small paycheck. He looked up at Rhonda and nodded. "Group of seven for the Loop trail. You got it."

∽

Brooke stared at her computer screen, looking at the email with the subject matter *B. Easten New Proposal*. Her agent had read the pages and responded, quicker than Brooke thought she would, and she was hesitant to open it to read the notes.

She placed her forehead in her palms and glared at her screen. "Just open it," she muttered to herself.

Slowly moving her finger across the mouse pad, she clicked on the email. It took longer to open with the hotspot and not Caleb's wi-fi, which only amplified her nerves. The screen finally loaded, and she furrowed her brow when she saw the email.

Brooke,

Thank you for emailing me the new pages for your new proposal. I knew this retreat would be a good idea, and even though it's taken a bit longer than I expected, it was worth the wait. I have read the new pages, and I will say...I'm intrigued. I looked into the town, and I think if you do it right with the correct research, we may have another bestseller on our hands. I can't wait to see the rest. Let's set a deadline for the first draft—end of November? Let's shoot for a release next fall. Call me when you're back on Monday.

Talk then,

Angela.

All of Brooke's nerves faded. Her agent accepted the new idea, and she called it a potential bestseller. She chuckled and leaned back into the chair. There was no more pressure. She responded back with a positive attitude, knowing that she had two full days with Caleb when she wouldn't have to worry about her novel at all. She hit send and then switched windows, taking a look at her blog before she closed the screen.

She had posted the blog about Caleb's business the day before, attaching pictures of her first tour with Caleb and pictures of them in the town. She noticed a lot of the comments from her readers, saying they followed their socials and went on their website. There was even a comment stating they were visiting Colorado in a month, and they would definitely book a tour in Marble.

Her heart soared.

It was working. Everything was working.

Caleb would be able to keep his business.

She wrote a quick response to the comment, telling them they wouldn't regret it and that they were in for an adventure of a lifetime before she closed her computer and grabbed her coat. It was closer to ten now, and she had the rest of the day to see Caleb.

She flung open her door, grabbing her keys to her car, only to be stopped by Rhonda and Joyce in the living room.

"Guess what!" She beamed. "My agent loved it. My deadline has been pushed to November for the first draft." She walked up to Rhonda and wrapped her arms around her neck. To her surprise, Rhonda hugged back. "Thank you for helping, Rhonda—and Joyce! Really, I'm not the best at research."

"We were happy to help." Joyce smiled. "And Rhonda has a little surprise for all of us."

Brooke looked at Rhonda, her eyebrows raised. "Really? What?"

"Caleb and his employee will be here at eleven to take everyone on the Loop tour." Rhonda's face formed a thin smile, and her eyes actually beamed, something that Brooke didn't think she would ever see coming from her.

Brooke smiled, stunned. "Seriously, you got us a tour?"

Rhonda nodded once, a light smile growing wider. "I wanted to make sure they made the mortgage this month. All seven of us will go. Frank and Melinda will be there as well. He said it's a five-hour tour, so we need to get ready and pack food."

"Greg and Helen?" Brooke pointed her thumb to the kitchen, knowing her colleagues would want to hear the news.

Joyce placed a hand on Brooke's shoulder and walked past. "I'll go help them pack some food. I think they are making sandwiches."

Brooke bit her bottom lip and looked at Rhonda. "Thank you," she whispered.

Rhonda gave her signature nod. "You're welcome. I've come here for the past three years, and I've never done the tours or seen this town. I can't wait to see what your inspiration is."

"You're gonna love it." Brooke's smiled amplified.

Later, the two Jeeps pulled up the drive, Caleb and Ethan jumping out of the seats to open the doors for their passengers. Everyone came out onto the deck, anxiously talking about the afternoon. Greg and Helen talked about their short trip, but they were more excited to see what else the mountains had to offer.

Brooke pushed past them and ran up to Caleb, wrapping her arms around his neck. "We're going on a tour." She smiled.

Caleb chuckled and wrapped an arm around her. "Everyone's going on tour. The...uh..." He looked over his shoulder at Rhonda, then lowered his voice. "The pretentious writer you always talked about is one of the nicest ladies I've ever met."

"I may have misjudged her," Brooke answered.

Caleb kissed her forehead. "It's all day with me again. Are you prepared for that?"

Brooke tightened her grip on his waist. "I can't wait. Can I sit shotgun?"

"Who else would?" Greg came up behind them. "I, for one, am excited to take this tour again. I didn't get to hear about the history last time."

"So much history. Okay, everyone!" Caleb let go of Brooke and stepped in front of the Jeep. "We can fit four in one Jeep and three in another. Ole' Red, which is piloted by Ethan"—he turned and gestured toward Ethan, who stood in front of the Jeep and waved—"is a bit roomier, so I'd suggest four people ride there and three with me in the silver. I do have some safety rules to go over before we head out, and this is a five hour—or longer—tour. So we have water bottles and snacks, but I told Rhonda to have you prepare a lunch. We can eat when we get to the town of Crystal."

Brooke stood close to him as he talked to her new friends. She enjoyed this side of him, and she was thrilled knowing that it wasn't going to fade. That he had many more tours ahead of him.

Thirty-One

The drive, like Brooke expected, was flawless. Caleb and Ethan took their time with the drive up to the mill, stopping at points along the way so the group could step out of the Jeeps and marvel at the beauty. Brooke gaped at Lizard Lake and Angel Falls, wishing she and Caleb had time to join the fishermen who were standing in the river. Every chance she got, she snapped a photo, perfect for her blog, or Caleb's website—or simply her memory.

This was more than the little tour she had a few days prior. This was what the Jeep tours should have been. This was what it *would* be.

Everyone seemed to enjoy the time spent in Crystal with Ethan and Caleb spouting off facts about the town, the mill, and the paths. They settled in the middle of the town to eat their lunch they had packed, each taking turns taking pictures of the group or the area. Caleb and Ethan even let them relax more than they normally would have. After all, the retreat was going to end in a few short days. The new friendships that were forming needed time to stew a bit longer. Brooke was thankful they saw that the group of writers needed to get to know each other more so than just the authors they were introduced to.

"I think this is amazing." Rhonda smiled, looking around at the town. "It's so much different than I imagined; the perfect setting for your new novel. I can see it."

Brooke grinned and looked over at Rhonda, her mind more at ease when it came to her novel. "I can't wait to get home and see where it goes. I need to work on an outline, but I think this is absolutely beautiful. I wish I could have seen it in its heyday."

She looked around the small town, just as beautiful as she remembered from her two previous visits, but this time she caught her attention on Caleb. He led Melinda, Joyce, and Greg around, telling them about each building and what it was used for. She noticed his trimmed beard and his combed hair, his flannel shirt was buttoned up, leaving the first few buttons undone to show the white tee underneath. His jeans were not worn or filled with holes, and his shoes were not covered in mud. The smile on his face proved just how much he enjoyed his job, how much this small Colorado town meant to him.

She tried to picture him in a suit and tie, stiff and carrying a briefcase, being the lawyer he once was supposed to be. No matter how hard she tried to imagine it, it never came. This was Caleb Turner. He belonged in this town doing exactly what he was doing. She blushed and looked at her feet, kicking a small rock to the side.

Shifting her focus, she looked at the mountains around her. The sun hit the trees and the tips of the mountains perfectly, illuminating the colors of the fall. She closed her eyes and breathed in the clean air. She had never felt more alive than she did here. She enjoyed her home and the city, but as she has told Caleb before, she didn't see herself in Salt Lake forever. Maybe here, maybe Marble, was where she belonged too?

Brooke opened her eyes, noticing that Rhonda had left her to follow Ethan, Frank, and Helen on their small tour. The entire scene was picturesque and perfect in every way.

"Hey." Caleb came up to her, his eyes locked on hers. "You didn't want the full tour?" His smile was one she had seen before, one she had tried to memorize. This smile, however, was different. It was filled with more passion than she had seen. The small crinkle in the corner of his eyes only added to his perfect features. Brooke reached up and gently touched his cheek, brushing her thumb against his beard.

"I've had it. A personal one." She gave him a soft smile. "Nothing can beat that."

∽

Caleb wasn't sure if this was love he was feeling or just pure happiness. When he watched Brooke as he showed the two around, he stumbled over his words, having to correct himself a few times. When she climbed in the Jeep next to him, he instinctively grasped her hand, feeling shivers when she squeezed back. His breath shuttered as her thumb caressed the top of his hand. He lifted his fingers to lace them with hers, in his opinion a more intimate connection.

He glanced over at her for two seconds, her focus completely on the mountainside. He didn't want this tour to end. He reached for his walkie and hit the button for Ethan. "Let's head up to Devil's Punchbowl. That will only take thirty minutes."

"You got it." He heard Ethan's mumbled voice and cheers coming from the Jeep behind them.

Brooke turned to him. "Devil's Punchbowl?" She furrowed her brow, and her mind began racing. The Devil's Punchbowl had to be something...not fun...right?

Caleb grinned and cocked his shoulder as he met her gaze. "You're gonna love this."

∽

Caleb was right. Brooke loved every second of the tour. Each stop they took was just as beautiful as the first, and her phone was now full of more pictures of mountains and rivers than anything else. She wanted to remember every second of it.

After all the snacks were gone, and both Jeeps were running low on gas, Ethan and Caleb made the descent down the Loop trail and arrived back at the lodge. Everyone jumped out, talking about how amazing the adventure was and how great it was to forget about their projects for one afternoon.

"I even got a perfect idea for a scene!" Brooke heard Greg exclaim. She chuckled at his announcement. He was the one who was convinced he couldn't write, that he would never be able to get it out on paper, and now here he was, outlining a new journey for his characters to take.

Frank and Melinda shook hands with Caleb and Ethan, thanking them for the tour. Brooke noticed Frank slipped Caleb a tip, which made her emotions grow larger.

"Thank you, thank you," Caleb said over and over. Brooke watched as he fumbled with the tip he was just handed, trying to be polite and not look at it. "I'm glad you enjoyed yourselves. Next time you have a retreat, reach out to us, and we will be sure to give you just as great of a tour, if not better."

"We will." Frank slapped Caleb's shoulder. "We definitely will."

Frank and Melinda turned and went into the cabin. Their small dog was barking and losing its mind in the window. Brooke walked up to Caleb and slid her hand in his, pinning his arm against her body. She smiled up warmly at him, tempted to pull him away. He turned her and kissed her temple.

"It's safe to say they all loved the tour," she said softly, leaning into him slowly.

"All thanks to you," Caleb muttered, resting his forehead against hers.

"Well, and Rhonda," she added.

"She wouldn't have come for a tour if you hadn't grown closer to her," Caleb mumbled, pulling his head up, turning his head toward Rhonda.

Brooke turned to look at the lodge behind her, resting her chin on Caleb's shoulder. "It's sad to think I only have one day left here," she said softly. "I've really enjoyed my week here, getting to know everyone."

"What are you going to do?" Caleb asked, the dorky grin on his face telling Brooke he already knew the answer.

Leaving her chin on his shoulder, she looked up at him. "Spend it with you."

"Fishing and a picnic it is."

"Brooke! Caleb!" Greg called from the deck. "We have things to make s'mores tonight, and we all know Caleb is a master at building bonfires!"

Caleb chuckled. "Smores tonight, us tomorrow." He slowly let go of Brooke's hand, quickly kissing her cheek before he turned to Greg. "S'mores sound amazing. We can cook hot dogs over the fire too. Ethan!" Caleb turned to Ethan, who was still talking to Joyce. "Can you run to the office and grab the hot dogs and buns?"

Ethan nodded and waved. "Sure thing. Can Meredith join?"

"If Meredith didn't come, I would be offended," Brooke joked, a small laugh escaping as she turned her back to Ethan.

"I'll call her." Ethan's tone was nothing short of giddy, making Brooke turn to see him quickly finishing his conversation with Joyce to jump in the Jeep.

"Oh, tonight is going to be a blast," Brooke muttered to herself, grabbing Caleb's arm and pulling him into the lodge to grab all the things needed for a bonfire. "What else do we need?" She laughed.

"Well," he began, "Ethan is grabbing hot dogs and buns...so let's grab plates and some condiments." Caleb walked in sync with Brooke to the kitchen, her fingers releasing his arms as he began to rummage through the fridge. Brooke began to pull down the paper plates. "Do we have things for s'mores?" he asked, setting the mustard and ketchup on the large island.

Brooke smirked at him and nodded. "Tons." She spun and grabbed the roasting sticks, setting them down next to the ketchup. "These too."

Caleb smiled up at her, placing his hands on the countertop, leaning toward her. "The sun is going to set, and you get cold..."

Brooke popped up, tilting her head to the side with narrow eyes and the cutest smile she could muster. "Sweater and blanket. Got it. What about you?" She dashed from the kitchen, heading down the small hall to her room.

Caleb pushed himself from the counter, following her to her room. Brooke instantly made her way to the dresser where she pulled out the same orange sweater from the other night and turned to grab a blanket.

"Oh, I have a coat in the Jeep. I always come prepared," Caleb said making his way into the room.

"That's true." Brooke smiled, pulling the sweater over her head. "I guess you never know what you're going to run into on the trails." She pulled her hair from the sweater, letting it fall on her shoulders.

Caleb gave a small smirk and took a step toward her, reaching out and grabbing the pocket of her sweater with his fingertips. "You're adorable," he muttered under his breath, pulling her closer to him.

"I'm warm," she responded. Brooke placed her arms on his chest and slid them up to the nape of his neck. "I think I'll need to invest in some flannel."

He kissed the tip of her nose. "I like the pumpkin sweater." He kissed her cheek, slipping his lips down to her neck.

She tilted her head for him. "It's probably for the better, I couldn't pull off wearing flannel anyway," she said breathlessly.

"You can pull anything off, but I'd prefer you with nothing," Caleb whispered in her ear, gently kissing her neck once again.

Brooke used her hands to bring his lips to hers and kissed him with all she had. He inhaled sharply as his hands ran up her back, arching her toward him. She hummed lightly and broke the kiss, locking eyes with him.

"As much as I love that," she whispered, "we should probably head back down—"

Caleb stopped her with a kiss, taking a quick step to fall on her bed. "Ethan is going to be at least forty minutes to get Meredith." He used his foot to shut the bedroom door. "We have plenty of time."

Brooke giggled, wrapping her arms around him and kissing him again.

Thirty-Two

Caleb laughed and smiled more in the last week than he had in the three years since he'd moved to Marble. He sat around the fire, next to his best friend and a woman he was hoping to keep in his life forever, near people he knew nothing about; but he was having the best night he'd had in a long time. Brooke sat close to him, twirling the hot dog in the fire, her leg gently touching his. The fire created an orange glow in the dark sky, the smoke drifting off into the atmosphere. The cracking of the wood was the perfect background noise to the light conversations that surrounded him.

Being around experienced and inspiring authors made for interesting topics. Frank and Melinda took the opportunity to talk to everyone about their projects. He had learned more about Greg and his novel than he thought he would ever know, actually gaining an interest in it.

"Will you beta read for me?" Greg asked with enthusiasm, his eyes wide as he leaned forward. Caleb could have sworn he would have fallen into the fire if he hadn't stopped.

"Sure," Caleb answered, not really sure what he'd agreed to, but it seemed to make Greg's evening.

Brooke lightly nudged his side with her elbow, giving him the sweetest grin when he turned to look. She leaned her chin on his biceps, her blue eyes glancing up at him over the rim of her glasses.

"Do you know what a beta reader is?" she whispered.

"No idea. But look"—Caleb nodded toward Greg, who was talking to Helen with a great look of excitement on his face—"he's thrilled."

Brooke chuckled and weaved her arms through his, holding onto his bicep and leaning her cheek on his shoulder.

The night went from hot dogs to Caleb teaching them his recipe for the perfect s'more. He watched as everyone gave the same satisfied look as Brooke had just a few nights before. He grinned, enjoying the idea that he had a group of friends.

The fire slowly died down, and one at a time, starting with Rhonda and ending with Greg and Helen, the group retreated back to their rooms. Ethan and Meredith said their goodbyes to Caleb and Brooke, leaving them alone together in front of the dwindling fire. Caleb poked at the wood while Brooke stayed nestled next to him, her arms still linked onto his.

"I think I love it here," she mumbled. He turned to look at her. Her gaze was fixated on the night sky. "You don't see the stars like this in Utah."

"I'm sure you would if you got out of the city," he defended.

Brooke shook her head and gave him a "uh-uh" noise. "You don't. I've been to other camping sites with my dad, and it's never like this. The closest I can think is Mirror Lake, there's not a lot of light pollution there, but this is what I imagine heaven to be like."

Caleb looked up, seeing the stars he had enjoyed for the past three years high above him. He sat under them and gazed at their wonders every night since he moved, but for the first time, they seemed brighter. A few clouds glided over the moon, but its light was still fierce, shining through the thin clouds. Caleb sighed and leaned his head on the top of Brooke's.

"I see why you stayed," Brooke said softly.

"You'll come back, right?" Caleb asked. "I'll see you again?"

Brooke raised her head and sighed. "I will. It's so beautiful here. I've fallen in love with everything about Marble. You're just a bonus."

Caleb gave a silent laugh. "I'm the bonus."

Brooke laughed, reached her arms up slowly to cup his cheek, turning him to her for a kiss. "The best bonus," she mumbled against his lips. She smiled at him, the sweetest smile he had ever seen, before gently resting her head back on his shoulder. "I really, really love it here." She sighed.

Caleb grinned, feeling the shivers down his spine and the butterflies rise in his stomach. He glanced back up at the stars. Brooke's body was warm against his, her breaths matching his perfectly. He didn't want this moment—this week—to end. The moon caressed her skin and gently fell upon her eyelashes under her glasses.

Just as before, he wasn't sure if what he was feeling was love or simply happiness. Whatever it was, he wanted it to last forever.

Almost as if she could read his thoughts, Brooke groaned and lifted her head from his shoulders. "I should probably go inside. It's late." She arched her back in a stretch, only to settle back down next to him.

Caleb moved his arm to wrap it around her shoulder, pulling her even closer to him. "We can stay out longer." He kissed her temple.

She hummed. "As much as I want to"—Brooke's groan got deeper—"we have tomorrow."

"One more day," Caleb said softly. "One more day."

Brooke shifted her body, scooting to the edge of the bench. "We will make the most of it." She stood and pointed to the fire. "I hate to admit I don't know how to put that out."

Caleb laughed. "Good thing I do. I'll meet you by the Jeep." He stood and wrapped his arm around her waist, not wanting to let her go.

She hugged him, slowly and hesitantly pulled away, then made her way up the creaky steps.

Caleb didn't like saying goodnight. It felt too much like a goodbye. He wished he had a way to keep her longer. The thought of crashing into her car flew through his mind. But then the thought of him having to pay for repairs killed that idea really fast. He shook his head and poked at the soft wood that was still burning in the fire pit, spreading out the ash that remained. He doused it with water and poked at it again, his brain still trying to find the perfect excuse to get her to stay with him longer.

Satisfied with the now settled ash in the fire pit, he shook his head, getting all thoughts of Brooke staying out of his mind. He kicked the dirt, piling some on the ash, and turned to make his way up the steps after her.

Brooke waited for him patiently, resting against the hood of the Jeep. When he approached, all the lights in the lodge were off, and the small cabin where Frank and Melinda were staying was just as dark, if not darker. The lodge at least had a porch light on for Brooke. He walked up to her slowly, his hands in his pants pockets, fishing out the key. He caught Brooke's gaze and locked it as he closed in on her.

"Hi," he mumbled.

"Hi," she responded. "Um," she stammered, "have you ever taken the drive up to the town at night? Is it different?" She fiddled with her fingers.

Caleb smiled. "Do you want to go see the town at night?" *Yes,* he thought.

She tightened her lips and smiled with her eyes. "For research."

Caleb laughed at her. Here he was, trying to find a way to keep her from walking in the lodge, and here she was, trying to find a reason as well. "The drive can be kinda scary at night."

Brooke pushed herself off the Jeep and opened the passenger door. "It's a good thing you know the roads like the back of your hand." She climbed in the Jeep and shut the door. "Come on."

Caleb shook his head at her, the shivers returning. He laughed as he took the extra gas can in the back and filled the Jeep. He climbed in and turned to her and met her halfway for a kiss. "Full tank of gas again. Are you sure?"

Brooke nodded and kissed him swiftly once again. "Positive. I'd love to see more of the stars."

"Okay, but listen. I'm gonna take it slower..." He gripped the wheel.

"Even better," Brooke interrupted.

"Because even the headlights won't show everything in the trees. There will be more animals and weird noises..." he continued.

"Just go." Brooke laughed. "I don't want the night to end yet."

Caleb turned the Jeep on and then headed up the hill, passing the turn to the touring company and then heading back up the bumpy dirt road to the ghost town. Any normal day, the trip would take twenty minutes but taking the trip during the night, Caleb took the road slower, shifting the Jeep when needed and trying to pay as much attention to the bumps as possible. He would move his hands from the gearshift to Brooke's knee, blushing at the fact that she allowed it to sit there as she kept her eyes on the night sky.

He stopped for a moment once they reached the mill. Brooke got out and listened to the river hitting the sides of the rocks, gently flowing around them. It was black, only the glow of the moon giving them any light. Caleb walked up behind her, wrapping his arms around her shoulders. It was hard to believe that just on Monday he had brought her up here for the first time, giving her the tour script he had done so many times in the past. It was different with Brooke. It felt as if he had known her for longer than six days, that she had always been a part of his life somehow.

She leaned her head back and inhaled, resting on his shoulder.

"I can't see it very well, but it's still perfect," Brooke said softly. "The shadows of the moon make it look even more enchanting."

"The town will look even more so." Caleb stepped back, forcing Brooke to pull her head up. He ran his hand down her arm, gently tangling her fingers with his. "It is a ghost town, you know. Maybe we can catch something on your phone and send it to *Ghost Hunters*," he joked.

Brooke laughed. "I don't believe in ghosts. Plus, if they are real, I have you to protect me."

Thirty-Three

Brooke definitely believed in ghosts, and there was a small twinge of fear that was creeping in her stomach as they got closer and closer to the ghost town. She wouldn't even go through the fake haunted houses during Halloween. What made her think she could set foot in an abandoned mountain town in the middle of nowhere? If it weren't for Caleb's hand firmly on hers, she would have gotten back in the Jeep and told him to go back to the lodge.

But 'she wasn't afraid of ghosts.'

They turned the corner, their feet crunching the gravel under them, and the small town came into view. It was just as breathtaking as during the day. The shadows of the moon and the low light from its glow made the buildings look a hundred times older than they really were, and Brooke could have sworn she saw shadows in the old post office. She kept her eyes on the old doorway, trying to see if it would move again. She tightened her grip on Caleb's hand and placed her free hand on his bicep, protecting herself from whatever shadow was there.

Caleb let go of her hand, stepping in front of her. "See?" He opened his arms. "Not scary at all."

"Not scary." Brooke smiled, realizing that Caleb most likely couldn't see her expression. "But still, no ghosts around."

"The post office"—Caleb dropped his left arm, leaving his right pointing at the building— "that's said to be haunted."

Brooke jerked her head in the direction of the building, suddenly wishing Caleb was still standing within inches of her. Off in the distance, there was a rustle in the grass, movement that neither one could see or explain. Brooke gasped and took a few steps toward Caleb. It most likely was an animal, but Brooke didn't want to find out.

"You do believe in ghosts." Caleb laughed, stepping forward and reaching out for her hand. Brooke didn't even think. She grasped it and stepped closer to him.

"Maybe a little," she muttered.

"Look." Caleb pointed out to where the rustling came from. Brooke squinted her eyes and saw the outline of a deer step from behind a building and into the open area. It looked at them, its eyes glowing in the moonlight. "Just a deer."

Brooke's jaw dropped. Never had she been so close to a deer before. She watched as it looked at them, making a quick decision they were not a threat. The small deer lowered its head to bite some grass before it slowly walked away, crunching the grass with every step.

"Wow," Brooke whispered.

Caleb squeezed her hand. "Are you still nervous there's a ghost in the post office?"

Brooke shook her head, glanced one last time at the building, and then slowly nodded. "It's creepy looking."

Caleb laughed, pulling her along the open walkway. "It is not."

"You said it was before we left." Brooke chuckled. She reached up and held onto his arm again, letting him lead her toward the end of the town. "I still wanted to see this town one more time. I have a feeling this was my last chance. Tomorrow is Sunday."

"And what is on the agenda for your last full day here?" Caleb asked.

She shrugged her shoulders. "Not sure. I think I just want to read by the lake all day while you fish. Or take a hike. Or maybe have a picnic up here…"

"All the normal things we do in Marble, Colorado." Caleb sighed. She felt his body move, shoving his hands in his pants pockets. "Fishing will happen, but you'll need to cast a few. There are so many fish in that lake that have no names that are just waiting to be caught."

Brooke chuckled. "I think the weather is supposed to be nice. Maybe we can spend all day at the lake." She looked up at him, the moonlight making his features more prominent. The thought of spending all day with Caleb again brought extreme happiness to her heart. All the possibilities flashed through her head. Reading while he fished. A small hike and walk around the lake. A trip to the general store to say goodbye to Rosie and dinner at the Slow Groovin' BBQ. Oh, wait. The farewell dinner at the lodge.

Brooke stopped walking, halting Caleb to a stop. She had completely forgotten about the farewell barbeque Frank and Melinda were hosting. Her day with Caleb suddenly seemed daunting and sad.

"What?" Caleb asked, turning to look at her.

"There is a farewell barbeque tomorrow night. Frank and Melinda are ordering from the restaurant, and we are going to talk about our accomplishments and all that jazz." She groaned. She didn't want to go. She wanted to play out her fantasy with Caleb.

"Okay, so we will have the entire day to ourselves, and then we will say our goodbyes before you have to be 'Author Brooke Easten' again." He stood in front of her once more and placed his hands on her shoulders. "We will have a fantastic last day together."

Brooke smiled, but the smile quickly faded once she looked into his eyes. "We won't really be saying goodbye though, right?"

she asked. "We are going to keep in touch. Plus, I'll be stalking you on all your social medias I created for you... It won't really be *goodbye*."

Caleb rubbed her shoulders and pulled her in for a hug. "It will be until next time. How about that?"

She wrapped her arms around his waist. "I like that better."

Caleb lifted her chin to meet her gaze, gently pressing his lips against hers. Each new kiss was a new feeling inside Brooke, one that she wanted to last for a lifetime. She inhaled, breathing him in, trying to memorize his scents. As the kiss grew more passionate, she longed to be wrapped in his arms again. She ran her fingers through his hair, tangling the tips on her fingers into the longer hairs on the nape of his neck.

Caleb was the one to break the kiss, lifting his chin up to look at her. She kept her fingers in his hair, wanting more.

"You're something else, Brooke Easten."

She grinned. Using her fingers, she lowered his lips to hers again, kissing him softly. "You, Caleb Turner, are more than something else." She muttered against lips, kissing him again with all the fire she could muster.

―――

Once they were back in Caleb's bed, he left her breathless and shivering underneath him. She was close to begging for more. He collapsed on top of her, his mouth resting on her shoulder. He kissed her bare skin, sending the same shiver down her spine. She could feel him trembling, his shaking matching hers, just as their breaths and bodies had. They were in sync with one another, something Brooke hadn't felt before.

Sooner than she wanted, he lifted his head and locked her gaze.

"You're absolutely amazing," he said breathlessly.

She heaved a sigh, grasping the back of his neck, feeling his hair in her palm. She looked at his eyes, trying to memorize them just as she had with his scents. His beard had a few stray gray hairs that she found irresistible the more she studied him. He had trimmed his brown hair at some point, but a few more stray hairs fell down, covering his eyes.

She tucked hair back into the folds of the others. She chuckled to herself as she watched him, his breaths starting to calm.

"I never would have thought this would happen," she muttered, sliding her hand up his side to cup his entire face in her palms.

"Well, it was amazing the first time. I had to up the game," Caleb joked, kissing her neck.

She laughed and pulled her head to the side, moving her body from under him. Twisting to her side she faced him, his bicep becoming her pillow, his skin still pressed against hers.

"That's not what I meant." She placed her hand on his chest, feeling his heartbeat.

Caleb closed his eyes and adjusted his head on his pillow. "I know." He chuckled at himself. He looked tired—relaxed—but so tired. Brooke tried to find a clock, but the only clock around was an analog on the wall, and the shadows in the room covered the numbers.

She sighed and scooted closer to him on the bed. "I'm happy I found you," she whispered.

Caleb hummed, hopefully in agreement with her. She watched as his breathing returned to a normal rhythm, falling into a pattern of sleep. She ran her thumb against his chin, gently kissing his lips before closing her eyes to fall asleep next to him.

Thirty-Four

- Sunday -

The afternoon sun hit Brooke's skin as she lay in the grass next to Caleb. He fished while she read her book, and then they took a walk around the lake. When the afternoon sun rose above the mountains, letting warmth overtake the town, Caleb dragged her to a Jeep and drove her up to Crystal once again. He said she didn't get enough inspiration from their previous visits. She just had to go again.

Caleb lay with his arm behind his head, his green flannel shirt acting as a pillow. His eyes were closed, his breathing was slow. Every now and then, Brooke would turn from her book to look at him. He hadn't moved or talked much but just being with him was enough.

She felt the grass beside her for her bookmark, shoving it in the book and setting it on the ground. She turned to look at him and lowered her glasses from her eyes.

"How are you sleeping?" Brooke asked, louder than she expected. "It's so warm out here. You need to be enjoying the day."

"I am enjoying it." Caleb groaned next to her, not opening his eyes. "The sun feels great, you're reading, and I caught some fish this morning. It's a great day."

Brooke narrowed her eyes at him, hoping the sting from her glare would cause him to open his eyes.

It worked. He opened one eye first, then the other, before turning to her with a smirk on his face. "What?" he asked.

Brooke looked at him over the rim of her glasses. "Nothing."

Caleb chuckled and turned back to the sky, closing his eyes again. "Okay." Caleb took a deep breath. "What was your favorite thing that happened this week?"

"So many things." Brooke smiled. "I want to go see Rosie before you take me back to the lodge."

"I'm sure Rosie will enjoy that. When's the farewell shindig?"

Brooke took a deep breath. "It starts at seven with dinner and then the bonfire at sunset." Truth be told, she didn't want to attend the bonfire. She was pretty sure it wasn't a requirement, but Frank and Melinda thought it would be a good idea for the writers to talk about their week and all the writing they accomplished.

She thought back to a week ago, during the first bonfire she had at the lodge. She and her fellow writers all sat around the fire talking about who they were and their goals for coming here. Brooke had questioned the entire trip upon her arrival, and now she was lying next to Caleb, her new novel in the works and a new adventure ahead of her.

"Did anyone else get anything done?" Caleb asked, making her turn back to him again.

"I'm sure everyone but me got things done."

"You did everything this week." Caleb opened his eyes and turned to look at her, shifting his head slightly on his arm. "You figured out your next book, you helped a dying business, and you learned to fish." He turned back to the sky, closing his eyes and taking a deep breath. "You're living in your own romantic comedy movie."

She chuckled and shook her head. "In my defense, I already knew how to fish. You just made it fun."

"I'm glad I could convince someone that fishing is fun. Ethan doesn't like to fish."

Brooke shifted. "Oh, I made new friends!" she said with enthusiasm. "I honestly thought Ethan hated me there for a few days."

"Oh, he did," Caleb said very bluntly.

Brooke dropped her jaw, furrowed her brow, and glared at Caleb.

He smiled and laughed.

"I won him over, I think."

"You did; Meredith too. They are already asking when you're going to visit again."

Brooke pursed her lips. She had thought about coming out to Marble again, but she also knew it wasn't any time in the near future. "I'll definitely be back," she said with uncertainty in her voice.

Caleb raised his eyebrows and turned to look over at her. "We know." He wiggled his eyebrows at her. "It's been an amazing week, Brooke."

"It has, hasn't it?" Brooke paused, glancing at Caleb once more before turning to look at the sky. The Colorado weather during this week had been interesting. Today, she was lying on the grass wearing a tank top, her coat underneath her. Her shoes were kicked off and her bare feet were enjoying the feel of the grass, but two days ago, she'd sat on the bench wrapped in a blanket, wishing for warmth.

It was giving her one last day of perfection before she traveled back to the muck that was Salt Lake. It truly was perfect.

"We still have yet to do one thing," Brooke said softly, thinking back to all the time spent with Caleb.

"What's that? We've done almost everything there is to do in Marble." Caleb kept his eyes closed, answering her question.

"We haven't had a fight," Brooke said simply.

Caleb furrowed his brow and looked at her. "Excuse me? Isn't that a good thing?"

"There has to be some conflict, right? We have had zero conflict. It's like we walked into a dream." Brooke turned back to the sky. "Say something to make me mad."

"No." Caleb turned and leaned up on his elbow. "Why would I ruin this?"

"Because we need conflict," Brooke repeated. "Be honest. How many times did you and Audrey fight?"

Caleb narrowed his eyes. "More than I'd like to admit. But it was over simple things that every married couple argues over, but that doesn't mean anything." He took a deep breath. "You've been spending too much time thinking of your next plot. Not everything in life needs conflict." Caleb tilted his head but kept her gaze. She smiled softly. "I love that you are a writer and that you are always thinking of the next step and the next plotline. You are worried about your characters and the people around you; always wanting a happy ending-"

"I killed my main character..."

"Yes," Caleb added, "but I'm assuming you gave the others a happy ending."

Brooke shrugged. "Somewhat."

Caleb laughed. "Conflict." He laid back down, closing his eyes once again, resting his hands on his chest.

Brooke placed her palm on his chest and scooted closer. He lifted his free arm and wrapped it around her shoulders, and she rested her head on his shoulder. She couldn't help but grin to herself. She knew her week had been perfect and there was nothing that could take the moments away from her, but Caleb was right. Her writer brain wanted the conflict and drama that occurred in everyday life. Once she returned to Salt Lake, she knew it was going to happen every day. But, in Marble, conflict didn't exist.

She chuckled, just with one thought.

"What?" Caleb mumbled.

"I have it." She grinned.

"Have what?"

"Our conflict."

"Brooke." Caleb drew out her name, not even bothering to open his eyes.

"No, you'll love this." She laughed. "I..." she trailed off, taking this one simple form of information and trying to make it sound worse than it really was. "I don't think *The Hitchhiker's Guide to the Galaxy* is *that* great of a movie," she admitted, a smile on her lips.

"Excuse me?" Caleb opened his eyes and stared at the sky.

Brooke pursed her lips, tightening her grin, waiting to see how he would react.

"You love that movie." He lifted his head and jerked it toward her.

Brooke raked her teeth against her bottom lip and shook her head. "The book is amazing and sure I've seen the movie, but it's nothing to brag about. Definitely not 'favorite movie' material."

Caleb sat up, flopping her head from his arm to the grass. "This whole week has been a lie," he mumbled. He turned his head and glared at her. His voice said one thing, but his look said another. The smile on his face grew, and his eyebrows wiggled. "I don't think I can talk to you ever again." He turned his body and playfully climbed on top of Brooke.

She laughed, holding her arms out as a barrier. "Oh, come on. That was not as bad as it could have been." She giggled, trying to push him away, but he crept closer.

Caleb kissed her neck, her cheeks, her nose, her forehead, and finally her lips. He broke the soft embrace and pulled up on his palms, looking down on her. "We don't need to have the same favorite movie or book or color or anything like that, and we don't need to fight about it." He smiled. "I just want to force you to enjoy it all with me." His smile widened, his sarcastic comment hitting her like rocks.

Brooke pursed her lips into a grin, reaching up behind his neck, pulling him down to her for more kisses.

∽

Caleb took the drive back to the lodge slowly, knowing it was his last moments with Brooke. He held onto her hand as tight as he could, pulling it to his lips and gently kissing it every now and then. He didn't want this week to end.

They went to the general store where Brooke gave Rosie a hug, thanking her for the advice. Then asked if she would be willing to stay in touch. You could see the small woman's heart explode.

"Oh, nothing would make me happier!" she exclaimed, pulling Brooke in for another hug. "I do hope you come back, dear, and please"—Rosie pulled her away, holding her at arm's length—"when your new novel is ready, I'll carry it here. And your first novel—I've already ordered some to keep in stock."

Brooke smiled, tears welling in her eyes. "You have no idea how much that means to me." Holding Rosie at arm's length, Brooke sniffed. "Can I..." she stumbled. "Can I buy that photo of the mill?"

Rosie's eyes widened. "You don't even have to ask, honey. It's yours." Rosie left the counter and went to retrieve the photo, handing it to Brooke. Catching glances with Caleb, she gave him a small grin. "He needed you, you know. Probably more than you needed him."

Brooke's lips tugged into a grin. "It's been one hell of a week, Rosie. I'm so happy he introduced us." She set the photo on the ground and wrapped her arms around Rosie again.

Caleb watched as the two women hugged and spoke about a hopeful future for Brooke. He smiled, hoping he was a part of it.

The short ride back to the lodge seemed to be the longest part of the day. He pulled into the lodge's parking lot and turned the Jeep off. When Brooke didn't instantly jump from the cab, he mimicked her motions, sitting still. The clock on the dashboard told him it was almost time. The day had gone by so much faster than he wanted. Last Sunday felt like yesterday. Why did time move so quickly?

"What time is your dinner again?" he asked softly, knowing the answer, but wanting to hear it again.

"Seven." Brooke glanced at the mountain. Her voice was soft.

He laced his fingers through hers. "And what time are you leaving tomorrow?"

"Early," she mumbled. "I need to get back in time to have dinner with my parents. They want to know all about the trip. You know"—she looked up at him—"learning to support me."

He nodded. "Do you think you'll have time to stop by the lake?" he asked, a hopeful tone in his voice.

Brooke met his gaze and gave him a soft smile. "I may be able to manage that."

He nodded again, a shy grin hiding behind his beard. He looked down at their hands, still laced together. Maybe if he didn't let go, she wouldn't leave. "I think we figured out our real conflict," he muttered.

"Hey." Brooke took his face in the palm of her hand, forcing him to look back up at her. "It's not goodbye, remember? It's 'until next time.'"

He smiled and kissed her softly. "Until next time." He leaned his forehead up against hers. "You better get to your dinner. I will hopefully see you tomorrow morning at the lake, and if I don't, call me when you get to Salt Lake?"

Brooke nodded, kissed him once again, tightening her grip on his hand, before leaving the Jeep and walking slowly up to the lodge. Caleb watched her as she climbed each step and turned the door handle. When the door shut behind her, he placed his hands on the steering wheel, trying to tell himself that everything would go back to normal.

Normal.

Caleb didn't want "normal." He wanted Brooke to stay, to call out to her again and take her back to the mill. He wanted this to be his new normal.

He drove back to the office, furrowing his brow when he saw Ethan's truck in the driveway still. He climbed out and went inside, ready to climb in bed—maybe Brooke's scent would still be tangled in his sheets—only to see Ethan quickly flipping through a notebook, a pen in one hand and a phone in the other.

"I figured you would've gone home by now," Caleb mumbled.

"How can I when people keep calling to make reservations?" Ethan exclaimed. "We are booked up this week, two or three tours a day! Our first one is tomorrow at nine... Can you believe it!?" Ethan shoved the notebook across the counter towards Caleb.

Caleb looked at the financial book that was now in front of him. Last Sunday—just seven days ago—it was empty with a bleak future. No mortgage payment, no paychecks for either him or Ethan, and the possibility of selling a Jeep, but now it was full of names and phone numbers, group sizes and prepayments.

He chuckled and looked back at Ethan. "She did it." He sighed.

"I'll say it again." Ethan tapped the book with his pen. "Marry her."

Thirty-Five

Brooke grabbed a blanket and headed down to the fire pit. The warmth of the afternoon had left, and the chill of the night crept in. Her beanie sat on her head as she wrapped the blanket around her shoulders. Greg and Helen were sitting on the long bench facing the lodge; Rhonda and Joyce were sitting next to one another on the other side. A week ago, she would have sat next to Helen, but now she felt as if she could sit and be welcomed by anyone.

"How was your last day?" Joyce asked.

Brooke gave a faint grin. "Perfect," she said. That word, *perfect,* had been used a lot today, but for Brooke, there was no other word to describe it. "Is everyone bummed to be leaving tomorrow?"

"I can't wait to get home," Greg answered quickly. "This was great and all, but now I have to share everything with my girlfriend and start to find an agent. Brooke, what's yours like?" he asked.

"She mainly does romance novels, I'm afraid." Brooke shrugged.

"I know just the person," Rhonda said, reaching out toward Greg. "Before you leave, we will talk, maybe exchange phone numbers."

Greg had wide eyes, and his jaw was dropped. Helen elbowed him in the side, and he seemed to snap back to reality. "Yeah, no..." he stammered. "That would be amazing."

Brooke's heart glowed. She didn't think the others would open up to Rhonda as she did but seeing the interaction between Rhonda and Greg, brought her happiness. The two continued to talk, exchanging phone numbers, and Greg started to explore his book with her. The small smile on Rhonda's lips grew as she nodded. Brooke knew she most likely had no interest in his sci-fi book, but the pure fact she was paying attention was all Brooke needed.

Frank and Melinda made their way down the rickety stairs, bags of food in their hands.

"Hello, writers!" Frank exclaimed, holding up his free hand, which wasn't 'free' since he waved the paper plates in the air. Brooke couldn't help but think he looked as if he were surrendering. "Food has arrived!"

Everyone let out a loud cheer. After a week of eating sandwiches and SpaghettiOs, they were excited to finally be trying the local barbeque. Brooke smelled the smoked meat flying through the air. She grinned, the scents bringing back a memory that now felt so distant.

The simple evening she spent with Caleb at the barbeque now seemed so long ago. Asking Caleb questions and answering his. The messy finger food, the drinks, the laughs. Her mind wandered to Caleb. He had been back at his home for a few hours now. Brooke had packed her bag and made sure all her things were gathered and ready to head home in the morning. She would go to the lake before heading out to spend one last morning with Caleb.

They agreed it wasn't goodbye. Caleb wasn't gone from her life. It was until next time. Brooke held back tears she had been keeping in all day. The fact that she didn't know when that time would be pulled at her heart. Maybe that was a discussion for tomorrow. When was the next time? She heaved a sigh. Why hadn't they talked about that before she left for the night? It was a big thing to discuss. *Wasn't it?*

"This place is absolutely amazing," Melinda said loud enough to snap Brooke back to the group. She bit the inside of her cheek and shook her head.

"I hope everyone likes pork and chicken," Frank added, setting everything up on the spare bench that sat farthest away from the bonfire. "We also have coleslaw, rolls, corn and mac and cheese."

Brooke waited as everyone stood to get their helping of the food before she created a small plate for herself. Her plate was almost identical to her dinner with Caleb. The only thing missing was Caleb himself.

"Now that everyone has food on their plates"—Frank clapped his hands to get everyone's attention again, sitting next to Melinda—"let's chat about our weeks. Tell me what happened with your projects and your goals. "

Helen sat up straight and grinned. Brooke could tell just by looking at her she was proud. Brooke's heart gleamed. "I was able to bust out the first forty thousand words...which for a week is phenomenal. I'm so excited to go home and start the second draft..." Helen counted. She spoke with so much enthusiasm that it radiated off of her, so much different from the Sunday before when she said she was having difficulty with her genre. "Everything came together so well once it started flowing. It was interesting to see it all come out."

"Hmm," Rhonda hummed, turning everyone's attention her way. "It seems, Helen, you have proved me wrong. Your two genres do mix together."

Helen shrugged. "I didn't do mystery and comedy. Brooke gave me the idea to branch out, use a new pen name, and go all out thriller. So I did, and I now have forty thousand words of pure terror that I can't wait to get out in the world."

"You changed your plan?" Melinda said, clapping her hands together with joy. "Sometimes, all we need is a new, blank page to get our mind rolling again. That's exciting. Rhonda." She turned her head. "Your goal was to complete your first draft on your new novel. How is that?"

"Completed," Rhonda said, the stiff tone returning to her voice.

Frank raised his eyebrows. "That explains why we haven't seen you much this week. You have been busy."

Rhonda gave a slight nod and then glanced over at Brooke. "I may have finished my first draft, but I also have been able to step out of my comfort zone and help my fellow writers. Something I haven't done here before."

"You do mainly keep to yourself," Melinda added. "I am thrilled you were able to reach your goal and help your colleagues. On to the second draft then?"

Rhonda nodded. "Already started. Hopefully, that will be completed this month."

Greg furrowed his eyebrows. "Why does it take you one week to write the first draft, but a month to write the second?"

"The first draft is a rough sketch of my book. I go through and add more detail, more dialogue, fix errors I may have missed. It's more concentration than just getting the words on the page."

Brooke smirked and looked down at her feet. Her writing process was the same. Words on the page, read through and second draft. Readers and a third draft, editor, then ultimately publishing. She let her mind wander back to Caleb. If she thought of this as a writing process, where would they be? The first draft, with hopes of a reread and a second draft in the near future.

Greg sighed. "It was always so daunting to get the words on the page for me. That blank computer screen glaring at me with a simple header on the top."

"But..." Brooke edged him on.

Greg turned his head and gave her a slight glare. "But it helped to leave and get away from the screen. Once I relaxed my mind, I was able to pull from it and find what I needed. The two trips up to the ghost town helped."

"Oh, me too!" Joyce exclaimed. "It was so nice getting out into the fresh air, away from everything. My hope was to get my manuscript ready for my editor, and even though I had distractions along the way..." Joyce paused and looked at the fire. Brooke's heart sank. In her mind, she was the distraction. "I was able to finish it, and I'll be sending it off first thing tomorrow to my editor."

"What do you mean by distractions?" Frank asked.

"This trip was different from the others, and I'm not saying the distractions were bad. It was pleasant to step away from my work for a few hours each day. It was also a joy to help Brooke with her new piece." Joyce smiled over at Brooke.

"It seems Brooke was able to accomplish a lot with everyone's help." Melinda smiled, scooting closer to her husband.

Brooke mimicked her smile. "I will admit, my mind was more focused on other things, but I did get an email back from my agent and she really likes my proposal. So I just need to finish writing it now. Then the second draft, and third..." Brooke rambled.

"How did you find what you needed?" Frank asked.

"Well, the town of Crystal gave me the setting. Joyce helped me learn how to do research for a period piece. Rhonda was amazing enough to read what I had written before and gave me a lot of pointers, and Helen and Greg were always there to talk it through. They were the support I didn't know I needed, even if Greg just tried to pressure me into writing." Brooke chuckled as she looked over at her new friends. "A lot happened on this trip I didn't know would happen."

"Like writing." Greg pointed at her, a smirk on his lips.

"Especially meeting your fisherman." Helen gawked.

Brooke glared over at her, shifting in her seat. She wanted to keep Caleb to herself, and her emotions.

"We never asked you," Frank began again, sitting back on the seat and wrapping his arm around Melinda. "How did you meet Caleb? Did you call the touring company?"

Brooke shook her head. "I took a walk around the lake the first night and saw him naming a fish. Then the next morning, I went out there to write. Writing about..." She swallowed. *No tears, Brooke...no tears.*

"A fisherman," Rhonda finished her sentence for her. "It's a good thing she met that man. Without him, her new novel wouldn't have come to fruition."

Brooke shrugged. "Well, it was because of the town of Crystal..."

"Oh, yes." Melinda leaned forward, resting her palms on her knees. "I can't believe we've never done that trip before. For the past five years, we've come up here, and we've never once called them for a tour."

Brooke sighed. "I'm just happy he will be able to keep the company. I was nervous there for a minute...."

"You did spend more time helping Caleb than writing your book." Frank raised his eyebrows and looked at Brooke through the fire, almost as if he was sending the flames her way for not writing.

"But I got what I needed to get done...done." Brooke brought her arms closer to her body, wrapping her fingers around her hips. Brooke pursed her lips. She was unaware she was going to be graded on how much she wrote during this trip. If she was, she was going to include her blog post, the website, and socials for Caleb, and editing Ethan's blog. She may not have written her entire first draft, but she definitely didn't feel as if she wasted anytime.

She looked at her new friends for comfort. Maybe, if she tried hard enough, Caleb would appear and whisk her away.

"I did try to tell her every day we were here to write," Greg mumbled, noticing her look of desperation. "In all honesty, she probably wrote more than I did. I found myself sitting on the blank document forever, rewriting the same sentence over and over. It wasn't until I talked to Brooke and actually got out of the house that I finally I found something."

"Inspiration," Brooke whispered. *That's what she was here for,* and she was able to find it in ways she wasn't expecting.

"I think we all found inspiration in places we least expected." Joyce smiled.

Brooke glanced at her, her lips forming a tight smile. Her gaze went back to Frank. She wished she could read his mind.

Frank sighed and kept his gaze on Brooke. "Did you find the inspiration you were looking for? I remember last week you were hesitant to even begin to write, afraid it would turn into a sequel to your first novel."

Brooke took a deep breath. She thought of the Crystal Mill, the water lapping around the rocks below. She thought of the small town of Crystal. It's many buildings that were slowly falling apart and being taken over by the wildlife around it. She thought of the lodge, the lake, the entire town of Marble and how she had reservations when it came to leaving. She smiled when her mind went to Caleb. Caleb was the inspiration she didn't know she needed. She wasn't sure of these feelings that crept into the pit of her stomach as she thought of him, but the grin gave her away.

She looked from Frank to the fire, the heat rising in her cheeks, and the flames rose in the air.

"I did. I really did," she said softly.

Thirty-Six

-Monday-

Caleb woke early the next morning, the thrill of knowing he had an entire day of reservations in line for him and Ethan. He brewed his coffee and quickly made himself a bowl of oatmeal. His stomach was in knots. He couldn't eat it. His to-do list grew as he ran from side to side in his small apartment. He made sure he had plenty of time before the first trip at nine.

The thought of fishing on the lake didn't even occur to him.

Ethan agreed to take the nine, and Caleb would take the noon trip. The four pm trip would require both of them, and the idea that it was a fact brought jitters to his brain. He was close to jumping for joy. If only Lettie could see him now, see what had happened for the business in a matter of a week.

Even with the sky still dark and the stars still shining, he climbed into the red Jeep and drove to Carbondale to fill it with gas. He ran it through the car wash, gas station and made sure the seats were vacuumed. Once he returned to the office, he did the same for the silver Jeep, both ready for people to fill their seats and get dirty again.

After the sun had risen, Ethan pulled up, a large smile on his face.

"We're back in business!" he exclaimed.

"Make sure you take a camera and document the trip. It will make for a great blog post," Caleb called over his shoulder as he walked back into the office.

Ethan followed him. "I have my phone too and the Instagram is ready to go. Brooke trained us well."

Caleb stopped in his tracks, looking at the clock on the wall. It was closer to eight—past fishing time and well past when Brooke was most likely on the road already. He had completely forgotten to watch for her car, and his mind was too jumbled with reservation preparation that the lake became a passing thought. He took a deep breath, wondering if Brooke had gone to their spot with a blanket and a book, only to notice he wasn't there.

He let out a long breath and rubbed his forehead. He missed it. It was too late now.

Ethan walked past Caleb, a skip to his step. "Do the Jeeps need gas? You could go to Carbondale... Wait...what?" Ethan stopped, looking at Caleb's expression.

Caleb shook his head. "Nothing, nothing at all." He exhaled through his mouth and took another deep breath through his nose. "I took Red and Silver up to Carbondale this morning. They've both been vacuumed and washed, and they both have a full tank of gas."

Ethan furrowed his brow. "Are you ok?" he asked, throwing a curve ball at Caleb.

Caleb heaved a sigh. "I forgot to go to the lake. To say goodbye to Brooke."

Ethan shrugged. "If she leaves without coming here to say goodbye...." He groaned. Caleb could tell he was unsure of where to take the conversation, seeing as the night before he told Caleb to marry her. "I'm sure she's still in town. It's barely eight. She is probably still sleeping."

Caleb smiled at his friend, thankful for the words of hope, but yet that pit in his stomach was still there.

"Did you say you took Red and Silver to Carbondale?" Ethan asked, suddenly returning to the conversation at hand. "What time did you wake up?"

"Four. I couldn't sleep." Caleb leaned on the countertop. "My head was racing. I couldn't get it to stop. I kept thinking of all the things we had to do to get ready for the tours today. I started thinking of all the posts we could do, and the blog... we need to make these tours be the best we've ever done because I was going to ask the clients for reviews on our website." Caleb's mind began to race again, the lingering thought of Brooke still there, but overruled.

"They can do that?" Ethan asked, seemingly shocked. "I had no idea! There's more to that website than I thought."

Caleb chuckled at his friend. "I hope for our sake we make enough money that we can hire someone to run the office and social media pages."

"Man." Ethan tilted his head back as if in a daydream. "Wouldn't that be something?"

A small tap on the glass pulled Ethan back to reality and made Caleb's heart skip a beat. He knew it was Brooke, yet he didn't want to turn. Ethan raised his eyebrows and nodded toward the door.

"She came."

"She came," he repeated, his voice shaking.

"Just propose and tell her to stay. Get it over with." Ethan sighed.

Brooke tapped again on the door. Caleb glared at his friend and turned to look at her.

Her glasses sat perched on her nose, a sweet smile on her lips. The same beanie sat upon her head with her blonde hair sticking out, and her coat was zipped to her chin. Even though he could tell she was cold, she looked comfortable. Comfortable enough to sit in her car for seven hours.

He smiled, his heart fluttering, as he walked to the door. He unlocked it and stepped outside, wanting more privacy from Ethan. He noticed Brooke was wearing lounge pants, another sign of a long drive ahead.

"You weren't at the lake," she said softly, a break in her voice.

"I know." Caleb rubbed the back of his neck. "I forgot. I'm sorry. I didn't get much sleep last night, and I woke up extremely early to get ready..."

"Ready for what?" Brooke asked, cutting him off.

Caleb smiled. "We have three reservations for today. Our first one is in an hour."

Brooke's eyes lit up, and her smile radiated. Caleb was certain the entire town of Marble could see it. "You're kidding! That's fantastic!" She did a little jump and wrapped her arms around Caleb's neck. "It's only going to get better from here," Brooke muttered in his shoulder.

Caleb rubbed her back, memorizing the way she felt in his arms. When the realization struck that she was here to say goodbye, he pulled back, locking her gaze.

"Are you ready for your trip?" he asked softly.

Brooke groaned. "Somewhat." She exhaled. "Helen is meeting me at City Market to buy me a coffee, and then it's our separate ways."

"You got everyone's information. You'll be able to keep in touch?" Caleb asked, locking his fingers behind her back, wanting to keep her close and in his arms forever.

She nodded. "Oh, yeah. There's no way Greg and Helen...hell, even Rhonda...can get rid of me that easily."

"What about me?" he asked.

Brooke took a deep breath and moved her hand from his shoulder to the nape of his neck, lacing her fingers in his hair. The last time she did that, Caleb couldn't contain himself, but with Ethan clearly watching, he just kept her gaze, not wanting to look away.

"I don't think you'll be getting rid of me anytime soon," she said softly.

Caleb grinned and leaned down, pressing his lips against hers. These kisses were going to be something he missed most. The way her lips felt against his, the way she seemed to fit him in every way. These were the kisses he would wish for until she was in his arms again.

Brooke leaned her forehead against his, her eyes closed. "Thank you, Caleb, for everything this week."

"No, thank you."

Brooke sniffed. Caleb lifted his head to look at her.

"I have your numbers and emails," She sniffed again, opening her eyes to lock gazes with him.

Caleb licked his lips. "And I have yours."

"I'll miss you," she whispered.

"Hey." Caleb placed his palm on her cheek, and she leaned into him. "Until next time."

Brooke kissed his palm. "Until next time." She began to step away, inching closer and closer to her Chevy. "I'll call you when I get to Salt Lake."

Caleb nodded, shoving both of his hands in his pants pockets. "Please, let me know you got there safely."

Brooke nodded, pursing her lips. She sniffed again. Caleb noticed a single tear fall down her cheek. She gave a small wave, blew him a sweet kiss, and then climbed in the driver's seat, turning the engine and driving away. Caleb watched as the Chevy grew dust trails as it traveled down the dirt path.

"Did you propose?" Ethan asked from behind him.

Caleb turned and saw him leaning against the door, most likely watching everything. He didn't answer. He kicked the dirt and walked back into the office, past Ethan, and to the computer.

"Well?" Ethan asked.

"The next time I see that woman," Caleb answered, picking up a pen from the counter and grabbing the financial book, "I'm going to ask her to marry me."

Thirty-Seven

Helen had the coffee ready for Brooke when she arrived at City Market. She pulled up next to her and gave her new friend a hug.

"A victory chai tea just like you requested," Helen said, handing her a warm paper cup. "Also, I bought this, and you signed them!?" Helen held up a copy of *Winter's Edge*, a large wide grin on her face.

Brooke laughed, taking a small sip of the chai. "I signed all of them. The employees thought I was so strange taking all the books to the counter and asking for a pen."

"That's awesome." Helen leaned against the hood of her small Toyota. "Did you go say goodbye to Caleb?"

Brooke nodded. "Yeah, it was a lot harder than I thought it would be." She scoffed. "I've only known the man a week."

Helen shrugged. "My boyfriend and I were official after one date. When you know, you know."

"But how long did you know each other before you were 'official?'" Brooke asked, using her fingers to air quote, holding her chai with care.

Helen chuckled. "We met on Tinder..." she said softly, her cheeks blushed with embarrassment. "Then one date, and I knew he was it. Five years later, we are living together, have a dog, and going strong."

"Marriage in the cards?"

"Someday, but at this moment, we are just happy being with each other." Helen grinned and lifted her cup to her lips. She looked at the ground, and Brooke could see the love in her eyes, just thinking about her boyfriend. "He's my person," she said before taking a sip.

"Helen has a person!?" Greg's voice appeared from the parking lot, making both of them turn and see as he approached them. "I was getting gas and saw the party; thought I'd come join for one last goodbye."

"Don't you have an eight-hour drive ahead of you?" Helen shouted at Greg.

"Yours is longer. Plus...coffee." He pointed to store's entrance behind them, and they laughed.

Brooke was going to miss this little group they'd created. When she signed up for the retreat, she didn't expect to make new friends or find Caleb. Yet here she was, wanting to stay here forever.

It's not goodbye...

It's until next time.

"When Frank and Melinda do another retreat, you and Greg should come," Brooke said softly, holding back tears.

Helen looked over at her. "Oh, hell yeah. I have Frank's information, and I will be stalking him."

Brooke shook her head, holding in the same tears and a new chuckle. "As will I."

The seven-hour drive seemed to take longer on the way back to Salt Lake than it did going to Marble. *Isn't it supposed to be the other way around?* The view on the road changed from mountains to passing cities to the vast emptiness of eastern Utah. She passed the alien jerky stand on the freeway and almost stopped. Then she considered stopping at Arches National Park. She had never seen the Delicate Arch. Perhaps now was the time to take that hike. In the middle of the day. On a Monday.

Then her phone dinged, a sound she hadn't heard for a week, and she realized she hadn't missed it. Her Chevy's dash screen blinked a small red circle. Tapping on it, she heard the automated female voice read aloud...

I hope your drive is going well. Dinner will be ready at six. See you soon, Brookey.

The text was from her mother, a simple reminder for dinner tonight. She sighed, pulling herself back to the drive and away from an adventure in Arches.

Maybe Caleb would go with her to Arches one day.

Maybe Caleb would take her camping somewhere she'd never been. He could fish, and she could write, and then they would laugh and talk in their tent until they ended up getting tangled up in a sleeping bag.

Maybe Caleb would visit Utah one time. But then he'd probably remember why he hated the city and quickly run back to Marble. Maybe he would take her with him.

She exhaled a huge sigh that no one could hear, even though it was louder than she even expected it to be.

"I'm an idiot," she mumbled to herself.

Five hours later, she pulled into her parents' driveway. She could see her cat perched on a windowsill, her ears pulling back when she looked Brooke in the eye. Brooke stayed in the driver's seat for a moment more, thinking about all things she could tell her family about the trip, not particularly wanting to go inside. She rubbed the steering wheel and groaned, grabbing her phone and turning the Chevy off, begrudgingly setting foot on the driveway, the cool Salt Lake air hitting her.

The first thing she noticed was that it smelled.

Like the lake had salted over, the wind carried a foul smell to every inch of the mountain.

Marble didn't have that smell.

She locked the car and opened the front door to her parents' house, hearing the hustle and bustle of the inside come to life. She could hear her mom talking to one of her brothers about college and her dad watching a sports game on the television louder than anyone would care to hear. She quickly closed the door and took her shoes off. The modern decor of the house made it seem bare and dull compared to every place Brooke had recently been. The family photos on the wall did pop out against the white walls, but there was little to no color in her parents' house.

Brooke inhaled, missing the log lodge she had just lived in.

She shook her head.

She needed to get her mind off of Marble and back to reality. It was a retreat she'd gone on, not a life-changing sabbatical.

Although, it did feel that way.

"Hey, everyone," she shouted, hoping to gain everyone's attention before appearing in the doorway.

"Brooke!" her mother shouted back. "Just in time, honey. Come help me with dinner."

Brooke groaned. "Coming, Mom."

The kitchen was full of life and way too clean to be in the middle of dinner prep. Her brothers were sitting at the kitchen island, both listening, or pretending to listen, to their mother. Brooke rubbed each of their backs and then circled to her mom. Giving her a quick side hug, she reached for the closest utensil and started to stir the pasta that boiled on the stove. She glanced at the living room. Her father sat in front of their large TV, his arm draped on the back of the couch, watching the football game.

"Hey, Pops," Brooke said.

"Hey, Brookey."

She rolled her eyes at the nickname.

"How was Colorado?"

"It was great," she responded, not wanting to go into full details of her trip. "My agent accepted my new book idea."

"That's great," her dad added mindlessly. "I'm glad you had a good time."

"Margie didn't cause you too much trouble, did she?" Brooke asked her mom, turning to stir the water again. "She didn't look too pleased to see me pull up."

"She likes the space," her mom mumbled. "She kept to herself, ventured outside a few times."

"Mom." Brooke groaned. "You know she's an indoor cat. She can't leave the studio once I take her home."

"Mom wants you to leave her here," Shawn interrupted. "She enjoyed the cuddling."

"Not gonna happen," Brooke's father bellowed from the living room.

"She's coming home tonight. No more worries about my cat tearing up your furniture. Thank you for watching her."

"No problem, sweetie." Brooke's mom nodded and smiled at her daughter. "Now, tell me about your retreat."

∞

Margie meowed and whined the entire drive back to downtown Salt Lake and into the Avenues, where Brooke's studio apartment sat. Brooke did love the atmosphere the Salt Lake Avenues gave, even if it was hell in a winter storm. The trees covered the roads, and the small apartments and houses lined the streets, giving it a charm that couldn't be found anywhere else.

Yet it didn't compare to the beauty that was the town of Marble.

She pulled into the underground parking, stopping her car in her designated space and grabbing all of her things before heading up into the elevator, her cat still meowing as if she were dying. She unlocked her door and felt the stale air hit her like a rock.

Her studio was more colorful than her parents' house, but the white walls still blinded her. Her purple sofa sat untouched, and her small TV showed the reflection of the living room. Her small kitchen was cleaned before her trip, welcoming her back, and her bed was still unmade from the morning she rushed out the door.

She opened Margie's cage and let her out, instantly running to her cat tree, away from Brooke.

"You did like the open air, didn't you?" Brooke walked up to her pet and lightly pet the top of her head. Margie lifted her head and began to purr. "Missed you, girl."

She turned and looked at her small apartment, which she once took pride in. It was hers, the first thing besides her car she had bought with the money she earned from a career she always wanted.

The small clock on the stove blinked a few times. At one point, she must have lost power. She furrowed her brow, reached in her back pocket for her phone to check the time, then gasped—almost dropping her phone as she realized she never called Caleb.

Thirty-Eight

Caleb flicked the lights to the office off when the phone rang. Ethan had just left for the day, and they both were drained. When he first moved to Marble, he was doing three—if not more—tours a day, but now that he had months of slow days and no reservations, just doing a full day of work seemed to tire him out. Of course, he loved every second of it, even though in the back of his mind he kept thinking it would have been better if Brooke were sitting next to him.

This was what his life used to be like after he moved to Marble. He went from being a lawyer with a goal to be involved in politics to a mountain tour guide, and he never regretted any of it. With every turn of the wheel, it would bring a spark of joy to his body, a sensation in his fingers that he was yet again showing people the beautiful mill and town. But even as he talked and told the history, he could see Brooke's face, her smile as he talked about the haunted post office and the time he and his friend came up in the middle of the night, only to see a deer and absolutely no ghosts.

He so desperately wished she were with him on every single tour.

He tried to keep his mind off the fact that she hadn't called him in the seven-hour timeframe it took to drive to Salt Lake. He told himself she was busy and would call when she could. He knew she had a dinner with her parents and a cat to tend to. She was probably happy to just return home and be able to plop in her own bed again.

So when the phone blared through the dark, quiet office, to say Caleb jumped toward the phone was an understatement. He cleared his throat and answered.

"Marble Touring, this is Caleb," he said as professionally and happily as he could.

"You sound so professional." Brooke's voice hit his ears like a harp.

He sighed, as if a weight was taken off his shoulders. *She called.*

"Well, it could have been a new reservation." He smiled.

Brooke chuckled, and he could see her smile.

"How was your drive?" he asked, not sure what to say.

She sighed. "Long and tiring. I stopped in Grand Junction for lunch and then came straight home." Brooke stammered, "Well, no, I went to my parents first. I had to get my cat. Now I'm home."

"Is your cat happy to be back with you?"

"Ha, no. She's a brat." Her voice sounded strained. She was tired. There was the sound of fumbling of drawers in the background and cat food hitting a porcelain bowl. She had so much going on since she had gotten back to Salt Lake, and yet she was here with him, even if not in person. Even though there was a six-hour distance between them, hearing her do daily tasks made it feel like she was just in the other room.

Caleb walked around the counter, settling himself down on the small table in the lobby. "You should trade in your cat for a dog," he commented.

"I'm pretty sure it doesn't work that way." Brooke laughed. "Tell me about the reservations today? How many did you do?"

"Three. Ethan and I did one solo, and then we went up together on one." Caleb relaxed into the chair, resting his feet on the chair Brooke would have been sitting in. "Two to the town and one photography tour. It's felt good to be doing that again."

"Any tomorrow?"

"Two, as a matter of fact. Ethan will be doing them. He's gotta earn his paycheck."

"His back pay, you mean." Brooke chuckled. He heard another rustle and a cat's meow. "I'm trying to unpack..." she muttered. "...and feed my cat. She's *not* having it. I think my parents treated her like a queen or something because she is very disappointed."

"When did you get home?"

"Oh...." her voice trailed off. "About ten minutes ago."

"And you're already unpacking? Go to sleep." Caleb glanced at the clock and then outside to the dark sky above the clouds. The stars twinkled above them, and the moon was brighter than he had seen in days. No clouds overlapped the darkness that was the night. "It's a clear sky here tonight, perfect for night fishing," he murmured.

"It's hazy here." There was disdain in Brooke's voice. "No stars to be seen."

"The moon?"

Brooke was silent for a moment, then her voice returned, soft and still. "It's bright enough that I can see it, but the haze makes it look red."

Caleb was quiet. He wasn't entirely sure how to respond to her. He knew what he wanted to say. *Come back to Marble. Write from here and fish with me every day.* But he decided to keep those thoughts to himself. It didn't feel like it was this morning that he kissed her goodbye, watching her drive away. It felt like eons ago, possibly more. The twelve hours in between a kiss and a phone call put the distance in perspective. Caleb could tell by Brooke's silence she could feel it too.

"Marble misses you," he finally said, breaking the deafening silence that hung in between them.

Brooke sighed. "I miss Marble."

Caleb mimicked her sigh and changed the subject, keeping it rolling until late in the night. He had made his way upstairs and climbed in his bed, Brooke still telling him about the dinner with her family and how her cat had decided she wasn't who she wanted to live with anymore. Caleb rested the phone on his cheek, and they talked until Caleb closed his eyes and his breathing slowed.

"You're falling asleep," Brooke mumbled in his ear.

"No, I'm not."

She chuckled. "Yes, you are. It's late. We both need to go to sleep. I even climbed in bed." Her voice was muffled, as if the pillow was smooshed up against her.

"Me too." He groaned. "As much as I don't want to hang up, we need to. I have reservations tomorrow."

She hummed. "Goodnight, Caleb,"

"Goodnight, Brooke."

∾

The next morning, Caleb helped Ethan prep the Jeeps and then spent the afternoon in the office. He wrote a quick blog post, thumbed through all the pictures Ethan had taken on the tours yesterday, deciding which ones would be the best ones to post, and then he checked the email for any new reservations.

There were six.

The excitement he felt with each new reservation would never get old. The feeling in his chest rose as he wrote down information and began to call the first reservation. While the phone rang and rang, he picked up his cell phone. He had never given his cell phone a huge thought after moving out to Marble. Since there was no service, he relied on the wi-fi to send any messages via text, but he mainly used the office phone for any calls.

He opened his new Instagram app, finding Brooke's profile and quickly typed her out a message.

Six new reservations today, all from the website. Please tell your friend in person your fisherman thanks him.

Her fisherman.

Whether she knew that or not, he was hers.

He hadn't considered himself belonging to anyone since Audrey. He was always Audrey's. Even after her death, he had a hard time envisioning himself with anyone else. He was certain he was going to live a bachelor's life in the mountains. But then Brooke had appeared.

His phone made a ding, a new notification from Instagram.

I will make sure he knows. I'm seeing him today. I hope you have a wonderful day, MY fisherman.

He re-read the message a few times before setting the phone down and returning to the books. With these new reservations, the ones from yesterday and the writing group, he would be able to cut Ethan a check tonight, making up for the back pay he missed.

The phone rang, pulling his attention from the notebook.

"Marble Touring, this is Caleb," he answered, then proceeded to take another reservation.

Thirty-Nine

Brooke's favorite coffee spot hadn't changed in the week she was gone. Not that she was expecting it to change but just walking in gave her the first sense of *home* since getting back. The music was still the same, and the mood lighting was as dim as it always was. Shelves of used books lined the walls, and worn, very comfortable couches were scattered around. This was the place where her first novel came to life, and as she entered with her laptop stuffed under her arm, she knew this new novel would find its way here.

She approached the counter to see the owner with a smile on his face.

"Brooke!" Steven exclaimed. "How's my new website going?" His jet-black hair was slicked back, matching his black apron perfectly. His apron was ragged and worn, but had silver markings, signatures of all his favorite customers, scattered around it. It was

Steven's trophy in a way, and even if it got to be nothing but frays, he wouldn't get rid of it.

"Hey, Steven." Brooke smiled. Steven had become a close friend of Brooke's while she sat everyday writing, and she always knew she could rely on him. When a website was needed for Caleb, she instantly reached out to him. She knew he designed it while making drinks for his many customers. "It's doing fabulous. Caleb told me to tell you that he had six reservations from it today." Brooke set her laptop down on the counter and leaned on her palms. "Really, thank you for doing that. How much do I owe you?"

"For my best customer and friend? Absolutely nothing." Steven grabbed a large white mug and began to make Brooke's favorite chai tea. "Besides, I saw their website before I jazzed it up. It was in desperate need of my assistance." He smiled. "What's your schedule like today? Are you meeting Angela?"

"Not today. My meeting is on Thursday, so I plan to sit in that chair and write all damn day if I have to." Brooke pointed to her normal table and chair near the window.

"Wasn't that what the retreat was for?" He lowered a single eyebrow and glared at her. "I seemed to remember you sitting at that table talking about how you were going to write so much your fingers would be numb by the end of the trip."

Brooke clenched her teeth and looked at him. "Yeah, that didn't happen."

"I can see that." Steven placed the mug in front of her. "Are you going to give me details?"

Brooke slid her laptop off the counter and grabbed her mug. "Possibly, but I have to write."

"I'll come bother you after the rush. You know I will." He pointed at her as she turned her back, making her way to the small table by the window.

As promised, Steven was sitting across from her forty minutes later, his chin resting on his knuckles as she told him about her retreat. She started slow, talking about all the writers and how she found friends in Helen and Greg, but then, once her story turned to Caleb, that was when Steven's interest piqued.

"And you just left him there?" he asked.

"What was I supposed to do? Handcuff him and put him in my car?" Brooke asked in return, jumping to the extreme.

Steven dropped his hands on the table. "Well, no, but you could have at least made plans to see him again. None of that 'until next time' mumbo-jumbo."

She furrowed her brow at him. The 'until next time' moment, even though she didn't know when that exactly was going to be, was what made the distance easier. "We talked about it. We agreed we would keep in contact and not label anything. We enjoyed each other's company and really had a wonderful week, but it wasn't about that." Brooke ran her fingers against her keyboard. "My heart just went out to him, you know. I mean, he was going to lose everything. Even after he already lost everything and built himself up from the ground up. Marble is Caleb's home, and I wasn't about to let him lose it."

"So you focused on his business and not your own?"

"Hey, I got my book started, and my agent loves it." Brooke looked at him through her eyelashes. "I found what I was looking for and got part of my job done while helping a new friend. I'd say the trip was a success."

"You did seem to break through the writer's block, and that one writer...Wanda?"

Brooke chuckled. "Rhonda."

Steven rolled his eyes. "You said she liked it, and with her experience, that's great news. Helen and Greg seem fun, but this Caleb..."

Brooke began to click through the photos on her laptop, trying to ignore whatever was going to come from Steven's mouth.

"He seemed to be more than just a good time with how you were talking about him." He sat back in the chair, stuffing his hands in his apron pocket.

Brooke looked up at him. "I don't know what he was. Like I said, we didn't label it. I didn't want to label it—I just wanted..." She shrugged. What did she want? She scoffed. "I just wanted *him*."

She could feel the heat coming from Steven's eyes. He had seen her through her worst break up and even a vow to never date again. She knew what he was thinking, but she didn't want him to put it into words. She didn't need to hear how stupid it was for her to meet a random man naming a fish in the lake and then spend the next seven days pining after him. She didn't want to hear that he could have been a serial killer, or that it wasn't what she thought it was—especially just after one week.

Caleb, to her, was so much more than—as Steven put it—a *good time.* She blushed when she thought of his message this morning.

Your fisherman.

She bit the inside of her cheek and looked up at Steven, preparing herself for whatever he was going to throw at her.

"Do you want to know what I think?"

She quickly shook her head...but slowly turned it into a nod.

Steven leaned forward and locked her gaze. "I think you should have stayed in Marble with Caleb." Brooke blinked and stared at her friend. Did she just hear him right?

"Okay, that's not what I was expecting you to say."

"To be honest, I wasn't going to say it either. My first response was going to be forget about him and focus on the here and now, but then I kept seeing how you would light up whenever he entered the story. He obviously left a mark, enough to inspire your new book. Sometimes a whirlwind romance and spontaneous move can bring out the best in people."

Brooke shook her head. "I can't just move to Colorado. He was able to because, well, like I said, he lost virtually everything when his wife died. He wanted to form a new life and start over. I don't have a need for that. My entire life is here..."

"Except for him," Steven added.

Brooke took a deep breath. "We promised we'd stay in touch, and I'll go back to Marble again to see him and..." she trailed off. "We will make it work."

Steven nodded. "I hope you do. He seems like a great guy." He sighed. "I'll be rooting for you, and if you up and decide to move to Marble, you know who to ask to help you pack."

Brooke chuckled. "Gee, thanks."

"I bet it's beautiful there," he said, changing the subject.

"It's absolutely gorgeous, and that doesn't even do it justice." She smiled. The excitement returned to her voice as she began to talk about the small town that had stolen her heart, pulling up all the photos she had taken, pausing a little longer on the ones that included Caleb.

Forty

-Five Months Later-

"Hello, world!" Caleb's voice rang through Brooke's phone, leaning it up against her computer screen to clearly see the video Caleb had posted the night before. "It's been an interesting winter, but we are happy to announce that we are back full time and will be opening for tours on March 1st! December and January were quite stormy here, so we are thankful we closed those two months, but we were able to take some amazing trips in February. So keep a look out for more posts and blogs up on our site." He was beaming. His excitement was radiating through the small screen.

He seemed so confident now in front of the camera. She remembered back in September when he refused to have his picture taken, and now here he was, smiling and waving his arms like he knew exactly what he was doing. Like he belonged in front of the camera. She chuckled, just envisioning Ethan behind the camera, still getting used to all the buttons and features it offered.

She had been following their journey since she had gotten back to Salt Lake. She was excited to see that their entire fall season booked up, and they didn't have a free slot through December. They had closed to special request reservation only during winter, which according to their many phone calls and texts was a harsh one, but they were able to open back up three days a week in February. Now that spring was making its way into Colorado, they were planning to open their schedule back up.

Every day, Brooke's heart grew as she watched his business thrive. She had followed his blog closely, even editing a few for Ethan, and helped them make the perfect captions for their Instagram feed. They were both busy with their own projects, and even though they had attempted to meet, it never worked. It was a hope to visit for Christmas, but Caleb's parents begged him to come to Chicago. Then at New Year's, Brooke had to attend a gala. No matter how they tried to see each other, something always got in their way.

No matter how busy their schedules seemed to get, each night, they spoke to one another. They spent hours and hours on phone calls and video chatting, ending each call with "until next time."

Each day, Steven's words rang through her ears. *You know who to ask to help you pack*. The thought of being closer and closer to Caleb was sounding better each day, but Brooke still hadn't made that leap. The distance was starting to weigh on her after the months apart, and likely Caleb felt the same. She sighed and turned back to her phone screen.

"We are happy to welcome a new person to our team," he shouted through the speakers. "Phillip is a Carbondale native, and he is going to be manning the front desk and helping us with reservations and our social media feeds. He's a great guy, and we can't wait to bring him on, starting in March."

Brooke smiled as the camera turned to a brown-haired man who was wearing the signature flannel, and he waved at the camera.

"Hello!" he shouted, a large smile showing off pearly white teeth.

"We will see you on the mountain!" Caleb waved and turned to run into the office. The shot ended, and Brooke was tempted to hit replay.

She sipped her coffee and tried to focus back on her laptop. Her second draft was almost completed. Her agent had enjoyed every update she had given her, and she was more confident in this story than she was with *Winter's Edge*. The more she edited and wrote, the more she fell in love with her characters. But even though she loved her new story, she wasn't ready to hand it off to her editor yet. There was something that wasn't there, and she couldn't place it.

She groaned and placed her forehead in her palms.

Writing is hard...

Her phone dinged, forcing her to slide her face up and look at the small screen. A text from Helen blinked across the screen.

Just finished my third draft! Off to the editor's desk!

Brooke smiled, sitting up straight and grabbing her phone. She had kept close contact with Helen and Greg. Helen more so since the retreat and was excited to see their goals coming to life. She even had Greg's document waiting to be read and commented on sitting in the background of her computer.

She typed a quick response. *That's amazing! Second draft is still chugging along for me. Agent needs it by Friday, so I'm pushing!*

How many more edits do you have to make? Helen asked, her response coming through before Brooke had time to set her phone down.

Four more chapters.

You got this. Keep it going.

Brooke didn't respond. She put her phone next to her and stretched her back, standing up from her kitchen table and circling her way back to the counter to pour herself a fresh mug of coffee.

Margie sat on the countertop, eyeing every move Brooke made with what she took to be disdain.

Sitting in the middle of the table was a very large contract Brooke had yet to read over and sign. She had finally agreed to make *Winter's Edge* a movie, and the only things she'd asked was that she be a consultant on the script and be involved in the casting process. The production company had been very cooperative, and her agent was thrilled, but yet she couldn't bring herself to sign the papers. She didn't know what was stopping her. She knew she was ready and excited for the next step—but signing that small, dotted line scared the shit out of her. So much was riding on it.

What would happen if she didn't sign? Nothing, really. Her life would stay the same. She would continue like normal—but did she want normal?

And what would happen if she signed? Everything would change.

She flipped through the pages, Margie watching every page flip, reaching her paw out to swat at the sound.

"What do you think, Margie?" Brooke sighed and looked up at her cat. "Should I sign it now or wait another fifty years?"

The cat meowed.

"You're right," she spoke back, as if Margie had answered every life question Brooke had ever had. "I should just sign it."

She turned and rummaged through a drawer, finding the perfect black pen to sign the contract. Her phone gave a slight ding from the table, giving her a sense of relief as she set the pen back down on the contract, happy she could ignore it for a bit longer. She needed a distraction anyway.

An update showed on her Instagram, one from Marble Touring. She quickly opened it, wanting to see Caleb's face once more, as if he had all the answers in his eyes. But to her dismay, the photo showed no person, just a beautiful ghost town covered in snow. Footprints could be seen on the white blanket, and a moose was off in the background. It was stunning in every way.

How badly Brooke wanted to be back there.

She liked the photo and shared it to her Instagram, then set her phone back down and glanced at the pile of papers on her countertop.

Normal.

Did she want her life to stay normal?

She knew what she wanted.

And it wasn't normal.

She quickly turned and picked up her phone, her mind finally making a decision that she should have made five months ago. Opening her messages, she clicked on Helen's name.

I'm signing that damn contract.

Helen's response was instant. *FINALLY!!!!*

Brooke chuckled, grabbed the stack of papers and sat down at her table. The small tabs where she needed to sign were sticking out. Gripping the pen, she signed her name on the first line. Then the next and the next, until finally the stack of papers was completed, and it was official. *Winter's Edge* was going places she always hoped it would.

But now for the next part.

March 1st—that was Caleb's opening day. That gave her two weeks to figure out exactly what she was going to do. Her computer sat on the table; the word document open. She had two weeks to finalize everything. *I got this.* Pushing the contract to the side, she gripped her phone again, tapping on Steven's name.

I'll need help packing soon.

When his response came through, Brooke couldn't help but smile. She laughed out loud and looked at Margie.

About damn time!

"Well, girl…this is happening. Trust me." She walked up to the poofy cat and stroked her fur. "You're going to love Marble."

Forty-One

-March 1st-

Caleb all but jumped down the stairs on opening day. The snow was still sticking to the ground all around them, but with the sunshine shining down and warming up the ground with each passing day, he knew it wouldn't stick around. Today was the opening day of the new season, and nothing—absolutely nothing— could bring him down.

Phillip was already there when he landed on the wood flooring. Phillip was a good choice for a front desk and social media hire. He was in his mid-twenties with a degree in recreation, and he was always glued to his phone. When Caleb and Ethan started to get back up on all the tours, they couldn't keep up with the new website, blog, and their profiles. They knew they needed help. Putting the ad out was easy. Choosing from the massive amount of applicants was even easier. They clicked instantly with Phillip, and they hired him on the spot.

"G*ooo*d morning, Phil," Caleb sang, slapping Phillip's back and making his way toward the kitchen. The smell of coffee permeated the air, and with how many tours were on the books today, he was going to need it.

"Morning!" Phillip called from the front desk, not even looking up from his phone. "We have a full day today. A great start of the season."

"How many tours are we doing?" Caleb poured his mug and walked back over the counter, looking at the new fancy computer program showing him a day full of tours ahead of him. "Holy, whoa…"

"I told you. Great start to the season. Ethan has four tours. You have five."

"Five?" Caleb almost spit out his coffee. "We're double booked. You made sure we weren't doing the same trail at the same time?'

"Yes, sir." Phillip nodded. "All the Jeeps got filled last night, and the extra tanks are full and ready."

"Good, because we won't have time to head to Carbondale if we are doing nine tours," Caleb said. "Are the satellite phones charged and ready to go? Just in case?"

"Yes, sir." Phillip looked up from his phone. "And before you ask, so are the cameras. Everything is ready to go, and I have our first blog of the season written and ready to be reviewed by Ethan."

Caleb smiled. Yeah… Phillip was the right choice. "Awesome."

A small red blinking light caught Caleb's attention from the office phone. A voice message was waiting for them. His adrenaline jumped. Another reservation? A quick look at the computer told him he was booked out for three weeks, not another slot until the end of the month—which made him giddy.

"We have a message." He looked over at Phillip.

Phillip looked at the phone and then up at Caleb. "Yeah, it's for you. Some chick. I listened to the first second and then decided you needed to hear it, not me. So I left it."

"Was it Brooke?"

"I'm not sure," Phillip replied, not taking his eyes from his phone.

The front door chimed, and Ethan made his way inside. "Happy first day of the season!" he exclaimed, his arms wide.

Caleb laughed at his friend and then hit the message button on the phone. The automated voice rang through his ears before Brooke's. He smiled. He still loved hearing her voice. It always brought chills down his spine. *Until next time...*

"Hey, Caleb." Brooke's voice sounded different. Shaky, and she was sniffing. Was she crying? "I'm sorry, I know it's early and we usually talk at night and you're most likely at the lake anyway." She paused, taking a deep breath and sniffing. "I just needed to call you sooner rather than later. Just call me when you get back from your reservations. Listen, I..." she stammered. "I just don't know what to do. I thought I had everything figured out with the movie deal and new books and...I just...I can't, Caleb. I don't know if I can do this distance thing anymore. I hate not talking to you, and I haven't seen your face in months. I mean, I know it was only a week. I shouldn't be getting worked up over a week we shared. A week out of hundreds.... Caleb...is this worth it? Are we ever going to have that next time? I just...can't anymore." She was crying now, her voice shaky and fumbling from what Caleb had assumed, wiping tears from her cheek. "Just...just please call me when you're done with your day, and we will talk. Ok...ok...bye." He heard the click of the phone.

He felt the pit in his stomach. There was an instant ache in his heart. Sure, there was the distance and trips had never seemed to work out, but he was planning on taking a week to go see her, surprise her and spend time with her in her home. By the sound of it, she wasn't interested anymore. Just a week, she had said...it was just...one...week.

Caleb snapped himself back to reality, noticing that Phillip and Ethan were both looking at him as he stood still behind the counter, his mug of black coffee still tight in his grip.

"Well then," he stammered, wishing he had taken that message in private and not on speaker phone. "I guess..." He coughed. "I guess that's that." He cleared his throat and pounded his chest, keeping emotions locked inside.

"Caleb," Ethan muttered.

"Nope." He shook his head. "She was right. It was just a week...out of the entire year. It was just one week. So..." He took a deep breath and turned to Phillip. "We have a lot of tours today."

Phillip nodded. Caleb could tell he was trying his hardest to just ignore what had just happened. "Right, so..." He walked behind Caleb and grabbed the computer mouse. "Ethan, you're doing three mine tours and one King's loop trail." Ethan nodded. "Caleb, you have one mine tour this morning while Ethan is on the loop, and the rest to Crystal—oh, except your last one. That's a single rider photography tour."

Caleb groaned. Out of all the tours, that was his least favorite. He could distract himself giving tidbits about the town and the mill—hell, he could even talk about the mine all day, enough to pull his attention from the voicemail that was going to haunt him all day, but a photography tour...that meant he had to hold a conversation with the photographer to find out exactly what they wanted from the trip.

"Can't Ethan take it?" he groaned, taking a sip of his coffee—ignoring the pit that still sat in his stomach.

Ethan and Phillip shook their heads at the same time.

"They requested the owner," Phillip mumbled.

"Oh, great. Okay, what's the name?" Caleb tried to make his voice calm as possible, hiding all annoyance or heartbreak that could come through.

Phillip side eyed Ethan and clenched his teeth. "I don't have that—just a photo tour."

Caleb turned that hurt in his stomach to a small amount of rage. Phillip knew he needed to grab names and phone numbers before even taking a reservation. "Phil, you know this..."

"She paid in full—more than the suggested price. She said she wanted it personal."

Caleb groaned. "I can't make it personal if I don't know her name, now, can I?" He set his coffee down, feeling bad for snapping, but also not caring one bit. He left the front desk, making his way back to the kitchen. He needed to give himself a pep talk. Pull himself back together. This was a normal day, the start of a new season for him. He couldn't let a voicemail bother him.

It didn't matter if it was from the woman he had fallen in love with and had imagined spending the rest of his life with her.

No...that didn't matter at all.

He rubbed his eyes and held onto the back of his neck, looking up at the ceiling. He let out a long sigh, closing his eyes hoping all feeling and emotions left with his breath.

"Pull yourself together, and then after the tours, you can call her and talk. It will be okay." He talked to himself. "Until next time..." he muttered. Then he left the kitchen and returned to the front desk. He had a Jeep to prepare and tours to take.

∞

All that was left of Caleb's day was the photography tour. He had managed to keep a smile on his face as he talked about the town and mine, but the thought of Brooke was still lingering. He had almost called her multiple times during his breaks, but she had said to call after his day. That was considerate enough. At least she didn't want to ruin his entire day. Just his morning.

He pulled the Jeep up and climbed out, opening the doors for the tour group and thanking them all for coming, asking if they could leave him a review. They all waved, promising they would go on his site, all leaving with smiles on their faces.

Caleb smiled back and waved, hoping they couldn't tell how fake it was.

Once their car had left, he made his way back inside. Maybe he could call Brooke now and convince Ethan to take the photography tour. Who cared if they requested the owner? Ethan could pretend to be the owner.

"Nope," Ethan said the second Caleb walked in the door. "I'm not doing the photography tour."

Caleb let out a loud groan. "I need to call Brooke. Phillip can take it."

"Phillip is not trained on the tours yet. Besides, he's done for the night. He did his job, and now you have one last tour and then you can call Brooke." Ethan's eyes were heavy on him, seemingly trying to force out any heartache that sat with Caleb.

Caleb glared at his friend. He leaned against the counter and dropped his head. "Fine. When does it start?"

Ethan was silent. Then, after a few moments, Caleb heard a front door close behind him.

"Now." Ethan nodded toward the door. "They just got here."

With one last glare at Ethan, Caleb flashed his fake smile and turned to greet his client. His heart stopped.

Brooke stood there, her blonde hair waving past her shoulders and her glasses bringing all the light to her eyes. She looked as beautiful as he remembered.

He was frozen, unsure if he should take her in his arms or ask about the voicemail. He felt his body shake, fighting all the emotions that stirred inside him.

"I told you I couldn't do the distance anymore," she said softly.

Caleb let his breath drop, not realizing he was holding it.

"How...um...what?" he muttered. He took a step toward her. "You're my single rider?"

She chuckled. "How else was I supposed to see you? You're so booked up I had to pay to just get you to myself."

"Um, excuse me," Ethan said from behind Caleb. "You didn't pay a cent."

Brooke shrugged. "Okay, that's true..." She smiled, taking a step closer to Caleb, closing the gap that still filled the void between them. "I just couldn't do the distance."

"But your voicemail...." Caleb mumbled, reaching his hand out to grab and touch her arm, making sure she was really there.

"Fooled you, huh?" Her smile grew as she stepped closer to him, sliding her arms around his waist. "Turns out I can fake cry and read from a script just as well as I can write. You can thank Steven for that."

Caleb's body relaxed. He pulled her closer, cupping her face in his palms and kissed her. He missed his lips against hers, the feel of her warmth up against him. He could feel her body relax against him as their kiss grew deeper, his lips lightly parting, taking her in. He missed her. He didn't realize how much until this moment.

He broke the kiss and looked at her, her cheeks blushed, a slight grin still lingered on her lips.

"How long are you here?" he whispered.

She took a step back and moved her hands to his arms. "Well, see..." She stepped away from him, gripping his hands and taking him to the window. He looked out, and down the street. There, sitting against the trees was an ugly red-and-yellow moving truck. A sore thumb in the scenery. "I kinda did something drastic. Sold my studio and made my cat really mad."

Caleb looked at the cab of the truck, making out a small brown-haired cat sitting on the dashboard.

"You're..." He paused. "You're moving here?"

Brooke nodded. "I don't have a place yet, but with the movie contract and my next novel being sold, I knew I had to. I didn't want to be in Salt Lake anymore. I wanted to be here with you. So"—she tightened her grip on his hand, turning to face him once again—"I have a hotel room in Carbondale until I can find a place to rent there. The hope is to be here—but...baby steps."

Caleb pulled her to him quickly, pressing his lips against hers. "You're staying."

"Forever," she muttered.

"Did you ask her yet!?" Ethan shouted.

Caleb turned to glare at him, remembering what he had said when she left in September. Ethan wiggled his eyebrows and smiled.

"Ask me what?" Brooke asked, a nervous shake in her voice.

Caleb turned to her, his face growing hot. He laced his fingers through hers and locked his eyes with her.

"I love you, Brooke," he muttered, saying the words he had wanted to say since he first met her. They came naturally, slipping from his tongue as if he had told her a million times, as if she were always the one he was going to say it to.

She kissed him slightly. "I love you, Caleb."

He took a deep breath. "Marry me?"

Brooke's smile grew, a sweet soft laugh escaped her lips as she wrapped his arms around his neck, giving him the tightest, warmest, hug he had ever felt. "Does that mean I can stay here tonight, because I lied. I don't have a hotel room or a plan or anything for that matter." She laughed.

Caleb wrapped his arms around her waist and rocked her back and forth. "Is that a yes?"

"It wouldn't be any other answer. I love you." she smiled, "So much."

He kissed her. Breathing her in, still not believing she was really here. She was here to stay. He was hers, and she was his and suddenly, nothing else mattered.

He was full again.

It was no longer until next time....

It was now until forever.

Epilogue

-Six months later-

"Your phones are charged?" Ethan asked, following Caleb as he packed up the Equinox.

"Yes, Ethan, the phones are charged." He threw his duffle bag in the back of the car, his new tungsten wedding ring glittering in the sunlight.

"And you have a satellite phone, just in case?" Ethan followed even closer.

"Yes, Ethan. We have a satellite phone and it's charged, and I have its charger." Caleb checked the trunk once again, making sure Brooke's bag was there, along with the many things she insisted on bringing, before he shut the hatch door to the Chevy. "We're only going to Arches, and we will be gone for three days. I think we will be fine."

"Crazier things have happened." Ethan stuck his hands in his pockets. "Just making sure you have everything you need."

Caleb sighed and looked at his best man. "Arches isn't Marble. There is cell phone service and a lot of people. You have all the information for the hotel we are staying at and any kind of emergency numbers, but Ethan..." Caleb placed his hand on Ethan's shoulder. "It's three days."

Ethan grimaced.

"What is he complaining about?" Brooke flew from the office doors, jumping down the steps and making her way toward the boys. Her hair was in a tight ponytail, bobbing with each step she made, pulling Caleb's lips into a smile.

"Do we have phones? Do we have a satellite phone? Do we have our pillows? Do we have blah...blah...blah," Caleb mimicked.

"Oh!" Brooke gasped. "My pillow!"

She began to turn, but Caleb reached out and grabbed his wife's hand, playing with the small ring that fit her finger perfectly as he grasped her fingers in his. "It's in the car," he said, twisting her toward him.

She leaned up against him and placed her palm on his chest, kissing his chin. "You grabbed my pillow?" she asked sweetly.

"An adult never goes to a hotel without their own pillow." Caleb looked down to her and wiggled his eyebrows.

"I mean"—she stepped back—"that's facts."

Caleb watched as she slinked around them to the passenger side of the car, opening the door to make sure her bag and book were ready for the three-hour drive. He turned back to Ethan, his eyebrows raised. Ethan's expression was that of an annoyed third wheel.

"Are you sure you have absolutely everything?" he asked for the tenth time.

"Yes, Ethan. We have everything." Caleb smiled at his friend.

Things had fallen into place since Brooke's first visit to Marble. Since then, Marble Touring had more reservations every day. They even were in the process of hiring another tour guide. Brooke's book *Winter's Edge* was in production to be made into a movie, and her new book, which she had titled *Crystal Sky,* sat on an editor's desk for a November release. Everything was perfect.

The night before, he and Brooke were married at the lake where they met almost a year ago. Only a few people were in attendance. Ethan was the best man, and Helen stood next to Brooke as her maid of honor. Brooke chose a simple, sweet, cream dress with her hair pinned back with pins that looked like rocky mountain columbines. The blue of the flower popped in her blonde hair, and for the first time since Caleb had met her, she wore contacts—promising him hours later it was a one-time thing and for him not to get used to seeing her without her glasses. Caleb wore simple gray slacks and a blue shirt that matched the flowers in her hair, Ethan matching him.

It was the perfect personal and intimate wedding they both wanted. It was the ceremony they needed. One they could remember forever.

They spent their wedding night together in their now-shared apartment, talking about their future together and what they were going to accomplish. Then they worshiped each other all night, not thinking about the road trip they were going to take the next morning. The only thing that mattered was each other.

"And you're sure you're okay with Phillip taking your tours?"

Caleb furrowed his brow. "Just let me go on my honeymoon," he begged, a laugh of annoyance in his voice.

Ethan shrugged.

"Phillip will be fine. He knows what he's doing." Caleb looked at Brooke on the other side of the SUV through the Chevy's rolled-down windows and beamed. "Are you ready? We need to get out of here before Ethan duct tapes me to a Jeep."

Brooke laughed and climbed into the passenger seat, adjusting herself and placing her book on her lap. "Ethan." She leaned toward the driver's window as Caleb opened the door and climbed in, shutting the door with a bang in Ethan's face. "Three days. We will be back in three days."

Caleb started the car and rested his arm on the window. "We will let you know when we get to Arches, and we will see you in three days."

Ethan nodded, shoved his hand in his pants pockets, and waited.

Caleb shook his head, turning the engine over and waved to Ethan. He watched as he got smaller and smaller in the side-view mirror, giving them a small wave before turning back into the office.

"He's acting like you've never left before." Brooke chuckled, reaching over and grabbing Caleb's hand, forcing him to change hands on the steering wheel.

"Well, I haven't had the need to." He turned to look at her, wiggling his eyebrows. "I don't think he thought we would actually go on a trip. Plus, he's always been like this. Always making sure we have everything."

Brooke shook her head, settling back into the passenger seat as they passed the general store, waving to Rosie as they rounded the corner.

"We're going to take the long way home, right? Through the mountains?" she asked.

"Anything for my wife." He leaned over quickly and gave her a kiss. "We can even take that way there if you want. Five hours instead of three."

"More time for reading?" Brooke asked, a grin on her lips as she held up the book that sat on her lap.

He chuckled. "More time for reading. So, you tell me. Do I go right...or left?"

She leaned on the middle console, taunting him for another kiss. "I love you," she said sweetly.

"I love you," he said, turning his head to kiss her again.

"Go left," she responded.

"Left it is." Caleb smiled as he turned the Chevy off to the left, taking the more beautiful, scenic route to Arches, where the rest of their life would begin.

The End

A Note from the Author

Hello My Wonderful Reader,

I unfortunately do not get to travel much honestly. Nor do I want to, unless I can reach the destination by car. The traveling I do is in books. Sure, I've been around, but I'm not one to willingly go to Hawaii. (Scandalous, I know!) In 2021, I was invited to a wedding...in Colorado. My friend was marrying her best friend in a small town called Marble. It would be my first vacation in YEARS, so I was actually very excited to go.

My husband and I saved money, and we left our kids with a babysitter (Thank you, Michelle!) and left for a glorious week away. The seven-hour drive (we stopped a bit in Grand Junction) was fun, and I got to see a state I had never seen before. But once we passed Carbondale and entered the mountains, losing all cell service and coming into the small town of Marble, Colorado, I knew...I just *knew* my next novel would take place there.

All Because of Elowin was in its second draft phase, and I edited while my husband fished—and as the chill mountain air hit my skin and the beautiful views got embedded into my brain, a new story came to life.

Caleb and Brooke's story is fictional, one hundred percent. Caleb's business, Marble Touring Company, is based off a real company called Crystal River Jeep Tours—taking people up to the gorgeous Crystal Mill and town. The Marble Lodge is real and an *amazing* place to stay. If you ever go to Marble, I suggest you look at staying there. It was so comfortable and homey and amazing in every way. The Slow Groovin' BBQ was smoking meats every night and is just as amazing as I described. The small church Brooke admires—I admired and knew it was going to be in the story even if just a glance.

For as much as I don't travel, I would travel there again and again. It was truly amazing, and I am so happy I was able to bring it back to life with Caleb and Brooke. Even without the cell service—which was probably one of the best parts, Marble, Colorado is a place everyone needs to see.

Thank you for reading!

I love you all!!

Stefanie K. Steck

A Brief History of
Marble and Crystal City Colorado

Marble, CO was founded in 1899 in an effort to mine from the Yule River in Gunnison County, CO. After the mining of the marble began, the town formed and served as a transportation hub for the marble industry. It earned its name from the marble.

In the 20th Century, it became one of the largest marble mining regions in the world. The marble mined there was used in hundreds of landmarks, monuments, and buildings throughout the United States, including the Lincoln Memorial and the Washington Monument. The marble from the quarry is still used today all around the world.

The population in 2018 was 144. It serves as the entrance into Crystal, where people hike or take tours to the Crystal Mill – one of the most photographed landmarks in the world.

Under the Marble Sky

Crystal City is now considered a Ghost Town, with only a few seasonal residents. It is local 6 miles east of Marble and 20 miles northeast of Crested Butte.

Crystal was originally a mining camp for the workers in Marble and had was given town status in July of 1881. It's peak was in 1881, where the population reached 500. It had a post office, pool hall, hotels, and saloons and even their own newspaper.

Crystal allowed several mines in the vicinity to become productive, including Black Queen, Lead King and Sheep Mountain Tunnel to produce silver, lead and zinc. However, due to difficulties in reaching the town, transporting the good became a large issue. Crested Butte was the nearest train station and the access areas to the town was mainly trails. They were able to use wagons to transport the goods; but when winter approached, the trails were covered, making receiving the goods extremely hard. Because of the difficultly in reaching the town, in 1889 the population dropped to 100.

In 1893 there was a silver panic, most of the residents feared this would cause Crystal to shut down entirely, however the town continued to support multiple mining operations. Two men, George C. Easten and B.S. Phillips promoted the use and built the powerhouse in the Crystal River – the Crystal Mill. This helped the mining industry for a few years, but unfortunately it didn't stop the decline of the city, taking the population to 8 in 1917.

Many years after the city was abandoned, the land was purchased by Emmet Shaw Gould from Aspen. Where he did not restore the mining industry, he saved the town from demolition, and it is now considered a Historic Landmark by the government of Gunnison County.

Acknowledgements

It takes a village to write a book, that much I've learned. After writing my first novel, I thought it would be a lot easier the second time around...right? Oh, how wrong I was! But thankfully, there are so many people who make it a little easier just by giving their feedback and all their love and support.

My sister, Brandy. My go-to person in my writing. She was always there to listen to everything I had to say and give me her honest thoughts and views. I love the tough love she offers, even if it makes me cry. I push through the tears and know she only wants to help, and I appreciate her for it every time I hit her with a new idea or beg her to beta read another chapter. Thanks, Big Sis—I sure do love you.

My best friend, Michelle. She is always willing to read something fast and offer advice, knowing how to turn a scene sweeter or have my book boyfriend say just the right thing. I hope

Under the Marble Sky

one day she gets to live out her dream and publish her own book. I would love to see TKC on the shelf one day.

Nicole and Kyle, simply for getting married and dragging my ass to Marble, inspiring this entire thing. Kyle may "hate" me—but I hope he knows how much I adore him!

My amazing new editor—Cindy Ray Hale. She helped me by giving the best comments and working so fast, making this the best novel it could be. Her kind words and easy emails made the daunting editing process so easy and honestly was the least stressful part of this entre book! Thank you, Cindy!

Finally, Jo. Again, Jo, without you—this crazy dream of mine would still be just a dream. None of this would have ever happened if you hadn't become my friend and mentor. One day, I'll be as good as you (maybe). Your constant love and support, through text and multiple in person visits make the entire thing worthwhile. I love our formatting parties and our laughs. Thank you, Jo!!

I am so grateful for each one of you, my readers, who help make this even more real. I hope this story brought you joy and that someday you will get to see Marble for yourself. I love you all!

Thank you, thank you;

With love,

Stefanie K. Steck

Be sure to follow me on Instagram @authorstefanieksteck for future books and content!

About the Author

Stefanie K. Steck is an aspiring romance writer, full time dental assistant, army wife and mom of three small humans and four fur babies (five if you count the hamster). In the little spare time she has, you can find her writing, reading, cuddling with her dogs or watching the entire Marvel Cinematic Universe in one sitting. She is the author of *All Because of Elowin,* and has finally found her voice and courage when it comes to her writing. *Under the Marble Sky* is her second novel.

Made in the USA
Middletown, DE
27 October 2022